BECOMING GEORGE SAND

BECOMING

ROSALIND BRACKENBURY

GEORGE SAND

a Novel

Anchor Canada

In memory of Elisabeth

LIBRARY AND ARCHIVES CANADA CATALOGUING IN PUBLICATION
Brackenbury, Rosalind
Becoming George Sand : a novel / Rosalind Brackenbury.
ISBN 978-0-385-66620-6
I. Title.
PR6052.R24B4 2010   823'.914   C2010-900660-7

Becoming George Sand is a work of fiction. Names, characters, places and incidents are
products of the author's imagination or are used fictitiously. Any resemblance to
actual events or locales or persons, living or dead, is entirely coincidental.

Printed and bound in the USA

Book design: CS Richardson

Published in Canada by Anchor Canada,
a division of Random House of Canada Limited

Visit Random House of Canada Limited's website:
www.randomhouse.ca

10 9 8 7 6 5 4 3 2 1

"Presque tous les romans sont des histoires d'amour."

GEORGE SAND

CONTENTS

SECRET

MARIA CROSSES THE STREET, where the cars are parked under their bonnets of snow, and only the swerving tracks of tires have left their ribbed marks. She's a little early, but in a couple of minutes the one o'clock gun from the castle will sound across the city, and wherever he is, still in his lab feeding his mice before shutting them up for the day, or hanging up his lab coat, reaching for his thick tweed overcoat, he'll hear it and think, she'll be there, she'll be waiting.

Buccleuch Street, Edinburgh, Scotland. A Friday in December. Friday afternoon. She's been longing for it all week. She peers in through the glass door, and pushes against it so that a bell rings her arrival like in an old-fashioned grocery shop, and she comes in with clumps of wet snow on her boots to melt on the doormat, and a sense of having reached the next, important stage of the day. She breathes out, a long sigh that nobody should hear.

At first glance it looks as if there's nobody in the shop, but she feels rather than hears a slight flurry out of sight and then sees the bookseller at the back, bent over and sorting books. There are boxes stacked, and the woman is unpacking them to put out on the shelves. She comes out, straightening herself, pushing back a strand of her hair. She has the slightly anxious look of a shy person who's afraid that what she says and does may not be appropriate. She also shows for an instant that she knows Maria, but she hides this knowledge, personal, even embarrassing, behind her professional manners. Maria is wearing the long dark blue coat she usually wears, still flecked with snow. Snow melts on her hair and her gloved hands—she's kept her gloves on, so that her skimming of pages where she stands, at a shelf of books that have been laid face up for easy examination, looks more like passing the time than any real curiosity. She looks up from the book she isn't reading, a collection of Maupassant stories, and smiles.

"Hi." She knows that the woman knows she's waiting.

"Good morning."

"Sorry if I startled you."

"Oh, no, that's fine. Just, I didn't really think anyone would come in today. Who would have thought it, more snow."

"Mmm, it was forecast, though."

Maria keeps her conversation to a polite but distracted murmur to indicate that she has come in here to find something she has not yet quite thought of. Bookshops are places where you can take your mind off waiting. Her hands hold the book as if it were a passport, one gloved finger dividing pages.

She says vaguely, "I wonder if you have any George Sand?"

The bookshop is a small independent one tucked away in an alley at the back of Buccleuch Place, not the larger, brighter, newly chained university bookshop where students mostly go to order the books they are going to be made to read. It specializes in French literature and books in translation. You can get yesterday's *Le Monde* here, and even *Libération*. Maria sometimes wonders how it can keep going, but then there are all the guidebooks too, and books about how to buy houses in France, how to cook like a French person, how to stay thin, and Peter Mayle.

"Oh, yes." The woman seems relieved to be asked about an actual book. "There's a course, isn't there, the French Romantics. I have some of the novels in stock, and the letters to Musset. That's all for now. But you know the big new letters to Flaubert will be out soon? It's being translated, I believe. Are you teaching Sand?"

"No, but I'm reading her. I'm thinking of writing about her. I'd like to order the Flaubert letters, but I want them in the original."

"Right, well, I can do that." The woman goes off to look on the computer behind her desk, runs her eye up and down the screen, her hand competent on the mouse. She has grey-brown hair, most of it scraped back, and a profile that belongs on a Greek coin, Maria thinks, very pure and classical. She knows from the woman's glance at her that she knows. There's an odd tension between them, as if both are wondering together, will he come?

Maria stands there, snow turning to damp stains on her coat and in her dark hair. The bookseller is placing her order.

"Excuse me, your name? I know you, of course, you've been in here before, but."

"Maria Jameson. Like the whisky."

Then the door swings open with the clang of the bell again and he comes in, cold air rushing in with him. On the street, a dark day, white gulls swooping white between the granite buildings, falling and rising in the gusts of snow. His coat flies open, he's blazing, in spite of the cold, and the red scarf at his neck flies out like a flag. His glance goes straight to Maria—who still stands with the unread book in her hands, any book will do, as a passport, an alibi, she's put down the Maupassant, picked up something on Derrida— and then quickly scans the bookshelves, the carpets, the woman bending as if to hide herself behind the computer. Then he looks at Maria again. The challenge of him: I'm here. She drops the book back into a pile, as he puts out a hand to touch her arm, meaning, let's go. She's moving towards him as if pulled by magnets, in spite of books and furniture, as if no mere object can stand in her way.

The bookseller says mildly, "There, that's done, you should have it in a week at the latest. Can you leave me a phone number? Or I can send you an e-mail?"

Maria scribbles her address, e-mail and phone number, no longer thinking about Flaubert's letters to George Sand and hers to him; those will have to wait. The bookseller retreats to her stack of cardboard boxes, to count books. She almost scuttles. Maria pays no more attention to her except to say a cursory, "Goodbye, thanks so much," because he is here, tall and eager and thin, with snow on his curly dark hair and his cold bare hands. She's flowing towards him, they have this brief time in the middle of the day, and it's all they have, the clock has begun to tick already. The woman in the bookshop is neither here nor there; she was an intermediary, a necessary stage on the way; later Maria will come back here alone and check on the other books she needs to order, but now she is going ahead of him out of the shop, into the street, into the blowing snow, between the iron-grey of walls and in the flurry of flakes flying sideways blown by the wind, forging her necessary way. The streets and sidewalks are icy beneath the latest fall of snow. But they stride together as if the day were warm, the air benign, the ground sure beneath their feet; they walk close, she looking up at him, laughing, he bending close to say something into her ear. They pass before the glass windows of the bookshop's front and are gone.

———

She opens the front door with her own key and they both go in, she leading the way. She picks up damp mail from the inside mat, places it on the hall table; even now she has the impulse to tidy things, even with him coming in close behind her like a tall shadow in his dark coat, even with the burning feeling she already has inside. The house is silent, with the dense silence of having been empty of its occupants for several hours. She feels it instantly, its moods and atmospheres. There's clutter in the hall, boots kicked off—Emily's old ones—too many coats hung on the back of the door, a sports bag nobody has claimed. There's still a faint smell of breakfast, old toast and coffee. The cat comes running, wiping herself around their legs. Edward left early this morning to go to the Department, and the children are at school till late afternoon, after which both of them are going to friends' houses for tea. Edward has a meeting and will then play squash, then bridge, with his friend Martin. She turns to smile back at the man coming in after her, yes, come in, it's safe, it's fine. They collide in the hall as she turns to shut the door, he holds her arm, it's all right, relax, we are here. The house is their space for now, and they have time. It's Friday, their best day, their longest, freest, the day to which all others bear no comparison. Friday, and she will soon have everything she wants, it will all begin to happen again.

They have driven here in her car, so that his can stay visible in the university car park, and hers, her five-year-old Renault, parked outside her own house, will not arouse any suspicion. Before he followed her into her house, he had to give a quick glance up and down the street, to be sure. Edinburgh may be a capital city, but it's still a small town, and people know him; he's been here for long enough and been involved in things for long enough—the church, the university, parents' groups, football matches, he's for Celtic and goes most Saturdays—for people to notice and remember him. He's also an unusually tall man, noticeable wherever he is. He comes into Maria's house cautiously, it's on a side of town and a street where he doesn't feel immediately at ease; something to do with class, with its associations, the New Town as opposed to the Old, nineteenth-century pretensions that still hang on in the size of the houses, the size of the rooms. He doesn't leave his coat in the hall—with its mosaic stone floor and the high ceiling of Victorian bourgeois Edinburgh houses, terraced houses yet too tall, overbearing he thinks, houses built with little notion of comfort but plenty of assumptions about superiority—but shrugs out of it as he goes, and carries it into the spare bedroom; there will be no outward signs, somebody coming in unexpectedly will not have the chance to wonder, whose coat is that? He hangs it on the back of the door in the bedroom, on top of a limp dressing gown that already hangs there. There's a high double bed made up for guests, the cover pulled tight.

She bends to turn up the heating. She switches on a light beside the bed, for the day is dark. She pulls the tall wooden shutters half shut, to exclude what light there is and give privacy—from what, the garden, the pale sky? The outside world. Something ticks in the house: the fridge, the electricity. Something else hums. She lives in a house full of electric gadgets which have their own lives, their own schedules, ticking and whirring when there is no one home, more permanent, she sometimes thinks, than any of the inhabitants. On the bedside table there's a large digital clock Edward bought, which gleams green and flashes numbers at her, and she turns its face to the wall. She wants neither time nor machinery to intrude.

Sean sits down on the bed at last and begins to pull off his shoes, large rather grubby trainers like the ones her son wears, which remind her of the age difference between them. He pulls his sweater off over his head, followed by his shirt and the off-white T-shirt that in summer he wears on its own. She, meanwhile, pulls off her boots—black, which she wears with her good black trousers, their uppers now stained with snow—and begins unbuttoning her own shirt. They do not undress each other, and she rather regrets this, as it always has erotic potential for her. Their undressing is almost businesslike in its swiftness and self-absorption, it's about getting naked rather than the performance of turning each other on. She watches him, though, as he unbuckles his leather belt and unzips his sagging jeans, which slide over his skinny hips, and reveal a white, flat stomach below a very faint tan line left from summer, and the beginnings of a pathway of black hair. He glances at her, grins. She's undoing her bra—and she wants him watching now, and he does, as her breasts fall forwards and the bra drops to the floor—a new bra, but white, not the black she prefers, as she has picked up that he likes a virginal look, or at least a practical one, in underwear. He sees her, and she sees him, just enough now, as his underpants slide off, and so do the rather prim white knickers she has on today, and both are kicked to one side; and then they are together, touching all the way down the length of their naked bodies, that first contact she loves, cool flesh warming fast, nipples rising to the chill air in the room—why does central heating never really warm these tall rooms?—and the weight of his cock rising against her, its thickening and lengthening as she holds it against her stomach. Such an extraordinary thing, that root of a man's cock under your fingers, the way it grows dense and solid; when she moves away, its tip is already gleaming. They fall to the bed, and hold each other again, but differently this time, because there's only one thing each of them wants, and that is to be inside and outside each other respectively, and for the miracle to begin again.

He is tall, taller than Edward, and his long pale legs go all the way to the end of the bed, and he pushes her head up against the wall as he rocks her, so she wants to push down, and her hand is on his buttocks, she pushes herself down to meet him so that their pubic bones meet, and she thinks of two flints rubbing together to make sparks, because they are both bony and it isn't entirely comfortable; and then he licks all around one of her nipples and begins to suck, pulling the reddened nipple up into a point, playing with it, sucking some more; she can't wait, it all begins to unfurl and open up, it, she, whatever she is, this body, this flesh, and as she begins to come, he follows, and there has never been anything quite like it, for her, anyway, and she is turning herself inside out, shedding skin, unravelling is how she feels it, becoming nothing, and then again, starting again, the mounting, mounting, and the long descent into what feels like annihilation, that makes her scream, only he has a hand on her mouth, shh, shh, darling; and the way he carries her then, where to, away, somewhere else, somewhere with no return, is what makes it impossible to be anywhere but here, now, and know that she is alive.

Darling, darling, the way he says it, the Irish softness of his voice, and yet she hardly knows him, not in the ordinary way you know people; she knows him completely, in this other way, the one nobody talks about, where you do this and you are together and love is in what you are, on the surfaces, in the depths. They rest, lying against each other, laughing with surprise, the way they always laugh with surprise, because it's astonishing, isn't it, the way this happens, the way they are together, this ease.

She'll never be able to give him up, because he shows her herself, the self she's never seen, because he opens her up to herself so that she'll never be the same. And he? He loves this, and fears it. She doesn't see what he fears, and if she does, if she sees it sometimes in the too-quick way he glances at himself in the mirror afterwards, the thoughtless hurry with which he ties his shoes, one foot raised on to the side table beside the bed, then the other, laces knotted and tugged tight, she doesn't register it, because there's nothing to be afraid of now, is there, life has opened itself up completely and shown itself, there are no corners, nothing left over, excluded, nothing to dread. Dread belongs to the future, and together they have wiped out the future, they have established themselves together, here, now, forever in this present.

Of course, the hours pass as if clocks are being wound faster and faster, and it's soon time for him to look at his watch, which he has taken off and laid beside hers on the bed table; and outside the light has nearly gone, and if they stay any longer they will be in danger of losing everything. Beneath them the sheet is sticky and cooling, and she feels herself soaked between the legs, and they get up to wash each other in the second bathroom, where there is a big old tub with huge taps, left from the last century, in which they can both fit while the rush of hot water heats the cold white depth of it, and there's nothing of hers and Edward's, just some old bath salts and soaps that her mother left here last time she came to stay, and an old sponge—whose?—to squeeze water over each other's shoulders and heads, in the steam that rises. They wash each other, serious and careful, cherishing flesh. The kindness of skin. The crevices, where tenderness grows. But by now they know the time, so they are slightly brisk too, like kind nannies with children who want to linger, and they are the nannies and their bodies the children, lazy, grumbling, making up another game to make the adults stay. At last, he's fastening his shoes, yes, the way he always does, as if he were about to run somewhere, and she's barefoot on the carpet, her fingers on his face, wanting her touch to remember this, his fatigued eyelids, the scratch of stubble, the wide soft contours of his mouth. Such a beautiful mouth. It will be with her, on her, now forever. She is all gratitude and calmness now, and it isn't she who will have to shrug on an outdoor coat and go out into the snowy cold of the street, and hail a cab to go back to the university car park; she can stay in her house, musing and amazed as women have been over the centuries, slow and a little forgetful, pottering and tidying and covering the traces of this time, so that her husband and children can come in innocent and unaware, to what is after all their home.

When he has gone—a kiss at the door, a running of his fingers across her face, a rumpling of her hair, a touch which remembers, which creates memory—she goes back into the bedroom, strips the bed. She bundles up the sheets and shoves them into the washing machine with some other clothes and their towel, and switches the machine on. She opens the shutters halfway so that the indigo sky shows between dark trees, she tugs back the curtains. She walks around, sniffing, and then sprays air freshener, though she hates the smell. She sprays perfume on herself, a sharp lemony Armani perfume that Edward likes. She goes down to the kitchen in the basement, switches the kettle on, and makes toast, two slices laid in the flat metal toaster on the AGA, so that the house smells warm and inhabited, and she sits on a stool in the kitchen eating a slice covered thickly with butter and honey, with a mug of tea in which a tea bag still leaks. Imagines them coming in—*Why am I eating toast? Well, I just felt like some, would you like some too?*

Did George Sand, she wonders, have to go in for all this subterfuge? How was it possible, in the nineteenth century, to handle all those comings and goings, all those men? There must surely have been a code, a way of going on; the servants, they would have noticed, what did she do about them? Or was it all conducted with such sangfroid, such aplomb—all those words which you could hardly even use in Scotland—that nobody could ever be sure? Chopin, Alfred de Musset, Michel de Bourges, Prosper Mérimée, Jules Sandeau; and the husbands, or near-husbands, Casimir Dudevant, Manceau. Marie Dorval? Not Pauline Viardot, whom she nevertheless adored. With Chopin, Musset and Casimir, she travelled. Mérimée was (she said) her worst mistake. With Sandeau, it was as two writers together, sharing a nom de plume to create a novel, with sex almost an aside. But he once climbed out of her window at dawn—having crept past the dogs and her sleeping husband—a happy, exhausted man. George Sand wanted men—and occasionally women—and she had them. She was someone who knew the secret that Maria is beginning to know. But how, for God's sake, did it translate into her everyday life, as mother, grandmother, writer, even wife? Of course, it wasn't just her. Other women, Louise Colet, who was Flaubert's lover, and had been Musset's too. The women who had been grand courtesans, and the ones who were grand revolutionaries. It was the time they lived in, it must have been; it was France, post-revolutionary, rationalist, pragmatic France moving into the era of romanticism, of the sublime, the picturesque; the passions of young Werther in Germany meeting Rousseau's noble savage, wild landscapes and wild passions being *de rigueur*. It may not have been easy, thinks Maria in the twenty-first century, but at least it was all possible.

Inside her still there beats the rhythm of his blood and hers, the throb and seep of his semen; she is still open, still aware. Her skin feels raw, porous. Edward will come into the house and look for her, and she'll be in the kitchen, perfumed, edgy, eating toast and honey at five o'clock in the afternoon. No, better if she were in her study, drinking a glass of wine. Reading George Sand, making notes. What can seem ordinary, now? She has no idea. She has arrived somewhere where she doesn't know the customs, can't read the signs, and there is no one, except a dead French writer, to give her a clue.

She never set out to be unfaithful to Edward, it's as if Sean has come up behind her, wrapped his long arms around her, closed his fingers across her eyes and held her still. The game of Grandmother's Footsteps: you can't move, you are captured, you should have heard the stealthy quiet approach, now it's too late. She knows this doesn't exonerate her; but somehow exonerating isn't yet the point. She has been offered something very beautiful that she never expected to have, and she is not about to start feeling guilty about it. You can love two people, Maria thinks. You can make love with two people, and because it is so different, there is no connection. It's having two different conversations; it's not about competition. In her bones, in her innermost mind, she knows now this is so. Thousands of people would disagree with her, try to prove her wrong. Let them. She feels, at this moment, that she has been allowed to understand something rare and essential which cannot be explained.

All her life there has been an inner sense of absence. Surely there is something on the inside of reality, something hidden, like a stone in a fruit, that must begin, grow outward and inform all the rest? She has felt the longing for it all her life. It. What she has never been able to name. A desire that has no object but only life itself, its kernel, its sweet nut.

When she touches Edward, his thick white skin, his blond smoothness, his so-English blandness, he sends her back to herself without mirroring her, just absorbs her. He is like blotting paper, unreflective, soaking her up. But he is also there, solid, she has never in all their years together imagined life without him. It's just that people are so unaware of the way they are. Edward is Edward, he is the way he is, and he can't touch her, not the way Sean can, and it's nothing to do with love or moral worth or character or any of the things that are so important; it's subtle as a leaf on a pond with a slight wind blowing it, it's surely something nobody can control.

Perhaps in another generation, in another century, this will once again be accepted and understood. In a hundred years, once again, nobody will think it strange.

It's only a year since she first met him at the university, where she teaches French in the Modern Languages Department, and where, she discovers, he is doing research for a PhD. Sean, tall like a striding stork, with a crest of wildly curling dark hair—as soon as she saw him she knew something would happen. There would be change.

She was in the same little bookshop behind Buccleuch Place, which a few years ago replaced the ancient dark second-hand one with the dust and cobwebs and vandalized paperbacks with their spines cracked that was here for as long as anyone could remember. The newer one is called Le Pont Traversé—a monument, someone has said, to francophilia. She was reading the first pages of a new novel, in the hope that this time, this author would bring her closer, give her a glimpse, of the hidden thing at the centre of life.

She skimmed the first pages. The clue would be in the space between sentences. If there was no space, no place for her to fall in and be led somewhere, she would close the book and put it back on the shelf. She was on page three when he came up behind her. He was heading past her, through the narrow space between bookshelves towards the back of the shop, as if looking for something. She glanced up. She knew that he had followed her here. He glanced down.

When she left the shop, the novel unbought (there was no space between sentences, no sense of a hidden clue), he followed her out. He looked at her sideways as he caught her stride and came up beside her, as if he had known her for ages. His hand out to introduce himself, his "Would you like to have a cup of coffee?" She knew that he had been watching her, that she was in his sights, and that what had not been in the book she'd been skimming might well be in the steps he took beside her, the gap between the two of them, the one that would narrow and shrink as they grew closer, but never entirely be filled. He gave back; she saw it at once. He set something moving that went back and forth between them, whether they were talking or not; and talk they did, urgently, amusedly, he in his Irish voice, she becoming more definitely Scottish than she ever was at home. Something had been started, a flicker of life, a small fire. She walked with him, almost without thinking, as he set going a fast banter of questions and asides, as if to keep them going, keep up the tempo, get them to where they wanted to be.

Was she newly back in Edinburgh, where had she come from, ah, England, and how was it, and was she happy to be home? And what was it she taught, French, well, he should have guessed it, seeing it was a French bookshop, and was she bilingual then, and how did she learn such good French, in Paris was it, well, great, that must have been, a great city, only he doesn't know it well. So.

Just up the street from the bookshop, they drank their coffee and smiled at each other across a small table in what had once been a hippie café with anti-war posters and sheets of paper pinned up for people to sign for trips through to Faslane and down to Greenham for protests against nuclear weapons, she remembered, and ads for health foods, and babysitting, and a book group for women only. Now it was painted in the colours of a Bonnard painting and nothing was pinned or stuck on the walls. The table was painted yellow and the chairs green. She noticed everything, the brown fleck in one of his hazel eyes, like a fault, the exact texture of the skin where he must recently have shaved. Everything very sharp and exact and just how she knew it must be, even down to the shape of her own gloves laid palm up on the table, the fingers curled.

"I used to come in here a lot, years ago. It was different then. A sort of feminist-stroke-anarchist place."

"Ah, things change. I remember it. I used to come here too, when I was a student. Did you go on the protests much? Were you a political girl?"

"I once went to a die-in at Faslane. We nearly froze to death. And of course, I went down to Greenham. But then I went to France, to the Sorbonne."

He was too big for his chair and sat on it as if he were in kindergarten, hunched over the table. The coffee was now caffe latte, rather than the bad old grey coffee she remembered, and they ordered croissants, not scones, and picked them apart and left crumbs behind them when they went. It was only going for a coffee, it was only half an hour out of both of their lives, but it was the start, they both knew it, and they were as harmless and happy as people setting out on a walk together, without knowing where it might lead. She was not surprised when he left a note for her in her pigeonhole, which she found next time she went to class. She put it in her pocket and all through the undergraduate class she was teaching, it was there, unopened, its secret still inside, the first clue.

She was teaching Marguerite Duras, and was answering a young man's question about the Chinese lover. How had he got away with seducing so young a girl? Were there parallels with *Lolita*, did she think? The note rustled, folded in her pocket, and she said smoothly that part of the answer lay in the whole social situation in Indochina at the time and the way a young European girl was seen. The young man frowned. Surely immorality was immorality, child abuse was child abuse, wherever it was found and no matter how beautifully it was described? Well. She wondered if she should give him Barthes to read: the body as text, disconnected from social values. But no, it would only confuse him further.

On her way out of the building, Maria unfolded her note and saw for the first time Sean's tiny scrawl. They would move on to e-mail, of course, and to text messaging, and handwriting would not play a part again in their affair. But it mattered, somehow, that he had written it hastily, nervously, in black Biro, and that she could tell from looking at it, the pressure of pen on paper, the shape of the letters, exactly how he felt. Not only in the words "I think you are beautiful," but in the downstroke of the *I*, the squiggle of the *you*, the way he said it, and made her repeat it to herself, beautiful, beautiful, as if in his own voice.

She'd had the books for several years already, had lugged them up here with the rest of their large library from the house in Cambridgeshire where they had lived their married life, she and Edward. A tall furniture van with big green letters on it had stood in the street outside their new Edinburgh house, and out of the back of it had come all their furniture, the boxes of cooking pots and clothes and toys and the equipment of a family's life, and of course, the books. When they were first married, all they had had was books. Edward had put up shelves made of blocks and planks, the way everybody they knew did, and their books had gone with them from place to place, always the first things to be unpacked and placed on view. So, her five leather-bound volumes of George Sand's *Histoire de Ma Vie*, found on a market stall in Paris when she had been on one of her trips to work on translations with Marguerite, had been brought out of the back of one more furniture van, and carried, with all the others in their containers, into the house. Where new shelves, bought at Ikea this time, had been installed to house them.

There was one volume missing; that was why they cost only twenty-five euros, she supposed. But she did not mind. It was like owning something of beauty that has an essential flaw. There would be enough in five volumes, she soon saw, to describe a life. Why George Sand? She could have found another writer in five volumes, she could have carried another writer, Zola or Balzac or even Jean Genet, home across the channel through Customs, and into her own life. But something spoke to her from the first volume, making her hold on to it and then ask for all the others, making her hand over her money, giving her the weight of all those words to carry through the market and show her friend Marguerite—"Look what I found! Such a bargain!" Why George Sand? Well, because of chance. Because of being there that day, at that stall, not another, and because of whatever it is that makes you stretch out your hands for one thing and not another, makes you open up your wallet and pay gladly, makes you convinced you have done the right thing. A vague feeling that you have found something you need, that will have meaning in your life, that may even last you years, carry you somewhere new.

It was only later, when she began reading, that she felt the urgency and persuasion of that voice. Your life matters, as mine did. You have choices to make. What will they be?

She remembers Marguerite saying, "You'll have to come to the country with us, Marie, Jean-François' family's house is just down the road from George Sand's." That would be for another time, she couldn't think when, when the children were old enough, when she could justify a trip down to the Creuse Valley. When life had moved on, the way it must, and she with it. Meanwhile, she would let that voice percolate through her own life, its vigour and its humour, its questioning of values, its humanity. Why George Sand? Well, because of who she was, Maria would have said, had anyone asked her at that time, which they did not. An answer presupposes a question. The question that she might dare to ask, at last, since the answer was there, waiting to be discovered.

George herself has been lurking at the edge of her consciousness for some time, of course. She was there when Maria as a student read Flaubert for the first time, she was there as writer of the series of Romantic novels, as Maria thought of them then, that had sold so well when serialized in the journals of the nineteenth century. You couldn't avoid knowing that Flaubert and she had written to each other for years, and that her letters to him had been kept, even though he apparently burned all Louise Colet's, along with her old slippers and the obligatory faded rose. (Was it because George had not been his lover, or because she was a far better writer than Louise, or because George would never have gone in for wearing a rose?) Louise Colet, who had slept with Musset, Vigny, Victor Cousin and Bouilhet, as well as Flaubert. Who had written poetry, novels and plays all her life, and lived the Romantic writer's life as thoroughly as anyone. Who had never gained the stature of George Sand, although God and Flaubert knew, she had tried.

You felt George coming at you from all corners of the nineteenth century, through her connections with all those others, from Dostoevsky to Turgenev, through Chopin and Liszt; you heard her revered, detested, feared, accused, admired. You knew she had somehow changed the face of literature, that she had been an early socialist, that her life was lived as a free, independent woman. But you didn't know, until you read her *Histoire de Ma Vie*, just what she would mean to you, in the intimate way of one writer's voice to another, in silence, over time, across the turning of pages. The conspiracy of words, across language, across generations. The phrases which would whisper in your ear and tell you how to live.

Sean, at one of their early meetings, when coffee is still the order of the day, says, "So, who is this woman you're reading? Sure, I've heard of her, but what's special about her?"

23

Leaning across the table, not daring to touch in public. He has this way of leaning on both arms, his head down, looking up at her in little flashes, there and then away. She longs to lay a hand on that wild hair.

"George Sand? She was a great writer, she influenced a lot of people, she also had a lot of lovers in her life."

"Ah."

"But that isn't the main thing about her."

"Only the one you're most interested in now?" He laughs at her, and ducks his head again; he has this don't-care-ish way with him, which provokes her. People will notice them, because of the way he is, people will hear.

"Not necessarily, no." But he catches her eye across the littered table, and she has to laugh. "But she was always looking for the perfect love. She didn't just collect men. Each time, she believed that it was the real thing, at last. She was a real romantic."

He said, "And that's what she wrote about?"

"That, and social issues. She was a socialist, she believed in justice."

"She sounds like quite a girl. Oh, wasn't there a film?" He pronounces it *fillum*. "About her and the composer? It rings a bell."

"There have been lots. It's rather off-putting. But then, nothing's new in this world, is it. The thing that intrigues me is really, what made her so brave? Whatever you think of her writing or her choice of men, she lived an authentic life.

Reading her is like a conversation. It's like you and me, sort of. Intimate." She wonders if he knows what she means.

"Are we being brave, then, are we being authentic, or are we just being eejits?"

"Both, probably."

"I should go. Hey. Can I kiss you in here, d'you think, or will the morality police descend?"

She goes in alone to the bookshop, another day, to ask about the other books; it's a Wednesday, not a rendezvous day. She says, "Nice of you to order the letters for me—do you think it will take long?" She feels a need to apologize to the woman, for some reason, for some rudeness, some inattention on her part. The woman is wearing a beautiful brooch, she notices; scarred amber, dark as honey and big as a blackbird's egg.

"I ordered the Flaubert letters. Can I get you something else?"

She has come in for the novels—*Consuelo, François le Champi, La Mare au Diable, Indiana, Lélia, La Petite Fadette, Cadio, Nanon*. Even though she's read at least half of them before. The bookseller finds a surprising number of the books on the shelves and places an order for the others. Is someone, unknown to her, teaching George Sand?

"You know, people were right when they accused her of potboiling. Some of them really aren't any good, and she does repeat herself. She's terribly patchy. *Indiana* is terrific, and so are *Lélia* and *Jacques*. *Consuelo* is probably the best. They're all about how impossible marriage is, not only for women, but for men too."

"Do you want me to order her *Histoire de Ma Vie?* It's just come out in a shortened version, in translation."

"No, no thanks, I have it. I bought the whole thing, in France. Six volumes, one missing. So there are some things I'm never going to know." She laughs.

The bookshop owner knows her name by now, because of all the ordering. Maria Jameson. Like the whisky. She uses her maiden name, Dr. Jameson. Dr. Huntley is Edward. But the days when she and the bookseller talk to each other are not the rendezvous days. When either she or Sean comes in first and they meet and stand, breathing cold like horses in a stable, fidgeting to be off, she notices how the bookseller goes immediately to the back of the shop and does some tactful rearranging of books.

The snow falling this winter so continuously makes the time extraordinary. Everything is softened, wrapped around. Darkness comes early, is sometimes even present at midday, as if the world has forgotten to come awake. The white of the snow turns the sky dark as a plum.

The bookseller gives Maria a sharp upward look. Whatever she was going to say remains unsaid; but something passes between them, so that Maria hesitates for a second, her eyes meeting the hazel-flecked ones of the bookseller, before moving away. Then she takes the heavy plastic bag with the George Sand novels in it, and heads to the university car park to find her car.

"What's your work about? What are the mice for?" She wants to know what he does when he is not with her. He has told her, sometimes he goes in the middle of the night, when he can't sleep, to see the mice. She imagines him tiptoeing through a house full of sleeping children, out into the cold. Maybe it isn't devotion to the mice that makes him go.

"They're telling me about the human immune system. I'm working on safety in food. Food allergies, how they develop, you know? Turns out, the only safe food is no food. Like sex, really." It's after they have been to bed together that he can say this.

Tonight, she is filled to the brim with him. Her mind wanders, her skin sings. His hands have redrawn her to herself, and she sees him as he is when he lies poised above her, looking down. She sees the point at which they meet, the dark thickets they share, his body branching from hers as if they come from the same root. She hears his voice, which talks and coaxes her into wanting him again, the consonants so soft you can skid along them, absorb the meaning, drown in the sound. She has never been with a man who talks in bed, who bewitches her with words and phrases, stories and snatches of song. It's a new kind of magic, which sometimes feels pleasingly childish, as if she should have found it long ago.

Focusing on reading is hard; when you have been making love, all other occupations seem irrelevant, she has noticed, it's as if it justifies your life so really you don't have to bother doing anything else. She stretches her arms over her head, to elongate her spine, turns her head from side to side to loosen the tendons of her neck—she must get back to yoga—and tries to bring her mind back to what she is reading. So George, who was born Aurore Dupin, went to Spain as a child, and then she went again at thirty-four with Chopin. The Majorca journey was an echo of the earlier journey. A long way to go in those days, all the way south to the Spanish border and then right across to Madrid. With Chopin, she must have been reminded all the time of the journey she made to find her father. Though the second journey took her through Barcelona, not Madrid. How interesting, that she had made most of that journey before, and at such an impressionable age. Only three years old, and having to face all that carnage. That would make you both terrified and brave.

Maria looks at her watch. Where is everybody? Having needed to be alone, to do what she thinks of as getting herself together after Sean left, she now wants them all to come home and make things normal. Abruptly, although she has stopped smoking, she craves a cigarette. The house ticks quietly around her, the washing machine finishes its cycle with the sheets, then there's the hum of the drier. Maria is in the small room she uses as her study. Her desk lamp throws light upon her page. Her laptop is pushed slightly to one side to make room for the heavy book. The house still smells of toast and honey, but nobody has come in to comment on it. The darkness thickens outside, she has pulled the curtains, poured herself a glass of Cabernet from a bottle that was open, and has felt it go stinging all through her body. But she reads. She lifts her head for a moment to imagine this: her heroine as a small child hearing, then seeing Napoleon pass in the street. Lifted in the air above Perret's shoulders, on the street near La Madeleine, to see the emperor pass, and her mother saying, look, Aurore, he looked at you, he saw you! The emperor Napoleon, with his grey cloak about his shoulders and his pale face. His stare. Nothing would be insignificant or small-scale about your life after that. The conquering emperor stares at the child as she hangs there, lifted into mid-air. The child stares back. Aurore Dupin, the child who will become George Sand. Who will go on those journeys, find those men to love, who will light up her century.

One volume is all about ancestors, and family. A second is entirely given to George's father's campaigns in Spain and Portugal with Napoleon. Only in volume three does George allow herself to appear, showing a proper respect for ancestry and her own small place in things. (Where does memory begin? A child with two others in donkey panniers, made of wicker. A chair upended, in which she is tied to keep her still as her mother sweeps the floor . . .) Volume five is the one that's missing, and will always be; her understanding will always be flawed and partial, Maria knows, she accepts the limitation, even though there's a modern volume, a compilation. She has decided, or a decision has grown in her, to write a book about George Sand. The woman who wrote these memoirs is someone larger and more interesting, she thinks, than the author of all those novels. She is someone more dignified than simply the woman who loved all those men; who ditched Musset in his sickbed in Venice and went off with the healthy Italian Dr. Pagello, who took up with Chopin and dragged him off to Majorca for a winter holiday, who married and then quickly divorced. The voice comes from these pages, modest about herself, magisterial on the events of her time. It speaks to Maria in nearly colloquial French. It has a calming effect. It takes its time, won't hurry, won't quickly deliver what she needs to know. But what she needs to know is there.

But what will they do? How will they live this? How can it go on? And will he call her tonight, will she hear his voice, which she craves, before sleep?

She should really try working somewhere else, the library perhaps. Being at home is proving too distracting; she's always waiting for her mobile phone to ring. Her own house has become a place for secrecy and passion, not work.

She has already read the volume which introduces Aurore Dupin's ancestors, and skipped through the one which is all about her father writing home from the Peninsular War. She's been longing to get to Aurore herself: the girl who will become George Sand. That's what looking down the wrong end of a telescope, and what the twenty-first-century cult of celebrity does for you: it makes you impatient to get to the point, which is the famous person, after all. George, she reminds herself, did not have this point of view. George filled volumes writing about those who came before her, her ancestors, in order to honour them, and to show that she herself was just a small part of the larger whole. She did not have a modern sense of her own importance. She didn't think: this is all leading up to me. She had no sense of herself as a precursor, a woman important in her own right. She was simply putting down as much as she could find of what was already known about her family, in which she was a small cog. This was the eighteenth-century way. The facts of her grandparents being the Maréchal de Saxe and the King of Poland on one side and a Parisian bird-seller on the other were neither here nor there to her. They were her antecedents, they were themselves, people, parents and grandparents. She was their offspring. She started, humbly, from here. Her father, a soldier of Napoleon in his long campaigns well before she was born, was bound to be a more important figure in history than she was herself. He deserved at least a volume to himself. There's no way she would cut to what a modern reader thinks of as the chase. Lives follow each other, with the slowness of past centuries, at the jog-trot of history.

But now Maria has reached George's own story, and being a twenty-first-century woman, a feminist and a child of the sixties, her interest sharpens. She reads George's account of her own first days, years—she has arrived at the journey with her mother to war-torn Spain and their terrifying return—with increased interest. (A carriage crunches its wheels along a road covered in bodies. The sound of broken bones.) This is where, for her, it begins. Because in this century, this is where lives begin, with the consciousness of the single individual. The protagonist. Or that better word, the *hero*. The "I."

The front door bangs open, a car accelerates outside on the street, and Emily comes in, she's been dropped at the door by Jenny's father; Maria hears her throw down her bag immediately and run down the hall towards her door. Her daughter, her face chilled with the winter air, her hair flying loose, her first longing always to find her mother and claim her, as soon as she's back. At once the house is inhabited, alive. The lights are on, and the vigorous cold outside is on Emily, her face, her padded jacket, waking Maria from the vision of starved French soldiers camping out in Spain and the soup they offered the hungry child, which was made from candles. Emily glows, and the curve of her cheek is smooth as an apple, her hair, blond as her father's, bunched at her neck. She has bitten her lips and stands there now, one tooth catching the pink of the lower one.

"Darling, how are you? I was wondering where you were!"

"Did you forget I was having supper at Jenny's? We had gnocchi!" She manages to pronounce it, with elaborate care. "Gnocchi! Do you know what it is? Doesn't it sound funny? It's made with potatoes, only it doesn't taste at all like potato! And then we had a sort of caramel pudding. It was really, really good. Hey, I can smell toast. Did you have just toast for supper? Where's Dad, and Aidan?"

"Dad's at his bridge night, and Aidan's at Jason's, I expect he'll be home soon."

"What are you doing? Reading?" She hangs over Maria's desk to see, blocks the desk-light, her hair filaments of fine wire. Her hands are solid, white with pink knuckles—Edward's hands. "What an old-looking book. Is it an antique? Mum, I have to wash my hair, okay, I'll see you later. Mmm."

Her kiss, with lips pursed and pressed to Maria's cheek; and she's gone, thumping upstairs to the next floor, where in a moment there's music and then the sound of running water, and Emily herself singing along with Paul McCartney—how strange, that they like all this sixties music—"*I wanna hold your ha-a-and, I wanna hold your hand* . . ." Whenever Emily comes into the house, she runs through it like a trailblazer, leaving her mark as if she fears not to be able to find her way back. "Here I am!" her presence shouts. She drops her things behind her, bag, trainers, coat, books. She lives in a world of shouted music, phone calls, odd-coloured nail varnish, and the obsessive scrutiny of text messages her friends send her.

Maria thinks, how quiet I have become, the mother, the one here to tidy up, make sure that they work, prepare other things for the morning. The one reading in a corner of the house, who forgets to have dinner, who can't express any more anything she really feels, because it has all, with the arrival of this man in her life, become taboo.

She's reading on in George's original French (she'll translate it later), smiling at the archaisms, astounded more often at the thoroughly modern turns of phrase. There's always a hyphen after *très*; I was *very-happy*, it was *very-late*; which gives the text a lighthearted feeling, whatever dire thing is being told.

A four-year-old is taken to a war-ravaged country and there she nearly starves and nearly dies of dehydration; all because her mother imagined that her father was being unfaithful to her, so far from home. She gnaws a raw onion. She dreams of fresh water. She closes her eyes as the cart trundles along and she hears the drumbeat inside of her own hunger. She sees an encampment of men. Soldiers. French soldiers. The soup made of candles. Candles! They would solidify in your stomach, wouldn't they, and block your gut completely. Why did they not die?

In her own protected century, any child subjected to this kind of treatment would be in therapy for years, would probably be taken into care. People, especially children, are not expected to go through such trials. Is Aurore's stoicism the forerunner of her adult resolve not to complain? Or do we all have such different expectations, these days, of what life contains? Sickness is sickness, thinks Maria, pain is pain. A child's physical misery is what it always was; but George's adult self, writing, has allowed her childhood self no leeway. Maria makes a note to check if anywhere in all these memoirs George has allowed herself to complain.

In her own life, she has had little to complain about. Complaining is not a Scottish habit, anyway. (Her mother brusquely reminding her always that there were those worse off than oneself, and that girning over trifles would do her no good.) Even now she really has nothing to complain about. But the complaint has lodged itself, small to start with, embedded like a thorn or splinter, reddening and then swelling all the flesh around it, until possibly there's going to have to be a major operation to dislodge it. She's fallen in love with a man she is not married to, a younger man with a wife and children, with whom she can't possibly have a life. They don't even discuss it. What she does with him, in the brief hours between their lives, when they meet in a narrow passage of time, a place of haste and concealment, makes her entirely happy. But the trouble is, she has attention for no one but him.

Him, that is, Sean. The father of four, the researcher in medicine, the master of the white mice, the boy from

Galway, the man with a conscience with which he does battle. He is in her life as a man stripped to his essentials, as he strips off his clothes when he enters her house. They are more intimate than either has ever been with anybody, in the absolute intimacy of sex. It seems to be what she has been travelling towards all her life. She adores it—him, herself, what they make together—and at the same time it has made the rest of her life unreal. All except reading George Sand. She doesn't believe that she has made the rest of *his* life unreal. She doesn't analyze this, not yet.

She has told him, "I'm going to do it, I'm writing a book about her, I've decided."

"Fair play to you, Maria. Was she really called George?"

"It's a nom de plume. She was really called Aurore Dupin."

"And she lived an authentic life."

"You remembered."

"And she had a lot of lovers as well as writing a lot of books."

"That's right."

"She must have had loads of energy, then."

He gives her his innocent, I'm-just-an-Irish-farm-boy look, and rolls her into his arms. Why should he know? She knows nothing about the physiology of white mice. Her Irish history is scrappy, more or less defined by Cromwell and the potato famine, with some Irish writers thrown in. He's been telling her, it's leaked from him at the margins of their conversation, all the ways in which history has welded his family's life, from the great-uncles escaping from starvation to New York, to the niece who's now working for the European Union in Brussels. He's the child of another country, and he wants her to know it.

"You're writing a book, so, and is it about the lovers, or what?"

"Partly. It's all of a piece, that's how it seems to me, the love affairs and the writing. She started writing when she was a child, she told stories out loud, she called it her writing. She wrote all the time, she simply never stopped. And honestly, I think her search for love was on account of her mother, who abandoned her when she was really young, to be brought up by her rather fierce grandmother—" But she stops, because his attention is elsewhere, she sees it, he's looking at her with his grin and his glitter of mischief; also because of the topic, why does one search for love?

"I'll write a book about you, if you don't watch out. I'll hymn you in deathless prose. Or poetry, even. I'll write poems about your elbows, and the soles of your feet, and nobody will know, and then they'll guess, and the secret will be out. Oh, and this place between your shoulder blades, that you can't reach and I have to scratch for you, I'll write about that."

Conversations ending in kisses and laughter. Life, when it comes down to it. Which would you rather, kisses and laughter, or writing a book?

―――

She should eat something more than just toast, and she craves another glass of wine. She stretches and looks at her watch again and feels suddenly cold and hungry. There's some leftover soup in the fridge that she can heat. She's glad not to have had to cook dinner; it's a relief these days when Edward's out in the evening and they don't have to sit together over dinner while he asks politely about her day, and all she can do is gabble about George Sand and hope he doesn't notice. Tonight is his bridge night. But enough time has elapsed now after Sean's departure; the house has had time to let Sean's physical presence go, and now it's ready, she thinks, for Edward and Aidan to come back. She wants, now, to see Edward. To reassure him, herself? The physical delight of her connection with Sean seems to exist even when he is not with her. But with Edward, there's what they have always had, a structure, in which they both live. She's had to wait till her forties to feel the strength of desire that she has for Sean. Being desired, responding, that was one thing. This longing to touch and taste, even consume, is quite another. But she's had to accept the conditions of an affair with a married man: not to call on the land line, not to worry when he's late, not to ask for anything more than what she is getting. In a way, she doesn't want any more. Her life with Edward and the children provides what it always provided; Sean is extra, he is life overflowing, he is what she has never felt she deserved, but now has in abundance. Their love affair seems to demand that some underpinnings to

life are excluded: plans, for instance, long-term prognosti-
cations. She lives, when she is with him, in an incandescent
present. The questions, how, what, how can we, only intrude
when she is alone.

"You're a wonder, you know that, Dr. Jameson? Purely a
wonder," he says as he nuzzles her, and then draws back
and looks at her as if he's examining her. His wide grin, his
crooked teeth, his thumbs in the sockets of her eyes, pulling
at the skin, so that she looks back squint-eyed, laughing. A
thumbprint, a back-of-the-hand knuckled caress: enough.
The extraordinary magic of what he does with his hands.

It's ten o'clock. She's been reading all evening, lounging in
her chair, one foot up on the rungs of a chair opposite, a
half-eaten apple at her elbow, a wineglass, her pen and pad
untouched on the desk. The story has her absorbed. Thank
God for it. They are arriving back at Nohant, after the grim
journey across the Spanish peninsula during Napoleon's
war. At the frontier they have been covered in stinking sul-
phur by the authorities, to cleanse them of disease. They
have crossed the Garonne in flood, the father holding his
sword above his head, the child carrying roses squashed to
her chest in the wagon that feels like a shipwrecked boat, the
mother in tears with her baby with its gummy eyes held
high. The little girl, Aurore, is safe, though dehydrated and
covered in lice. In the present, there's Em rushing in warm
and damp from her long bath to hug her mother and ask her

to come up later and say good night. She is wearing Maria's perfume Dune, she can smell it. The awaited phone call happened (just as she had stopped waiting for it, as soon as her mind moved on to something else, her mobile sang out the first few notes of Vivaldi's *Four Seasons,* "Winter"); that was in this life; and in that other, in the past century, the other country, on some far side of experience, Maurice Dupin, back from the wars, has dug up his dead child at midnight and carried him back into the house.

Sean says just, "I love you, more ways than you can imagine." And then he says it in Irish. It sounds muffled, on the phone. She can't say it back to him, not out loud. But it's enough. A pulse thumps deep inside her, and she crosses her legs to keep it in. His tongue, and her reception of it. The way they slide along each other on a film of sweat.

She wants to say to him, *You have turned me inside out.* To tell him she has no more secrets.

(A pear tree held a secret for centuries. A gardener knew where the baby was buried, but was not telling. He knew too that someone had come in the night and dug him up, taken him into the house, buried him again before morning. The baby brother born in Spain with the blind eyes like sea water with chalk in it had vanished. Where had he gone? A writer was told about it by her own mother, decades later, and had to insert it into her own life. It became part of her story, part of the myth, part of the mystery; what made this woman, this giant, George Sand.)

Maria knows she's also thinking about herself, her unremarkable childhood, her own life to date; nothing in it has happened that's this dramatic, this worth the telling, and she has wished that it would. You have to be made to live, in this century, she thinks. If you are western and middle-class at this time in history, you have to be dislodged from comfort, or dislodge yourself. If you want to live fully, you have to give something up quite deliberately, for nothing is going to do it to you, you are too safe.

Of course, what she is doing with Sean is not exactly safe; but she has no real sense of danger in it, either. It's like being pregnant; having a love affair, lolling in the sensual reminders of it even while the beloved isn't present, gives one such a sense of security that it seems that nothing bad can ever happen again. Maria flaunts her fulfilment as some women flaunt their huge bellies. But she also wears the mask of innocence. What, me, I look well? How extraordinary. I can't think why.

She hears the front door open and close with its soft *whuff*, and footsteps on stone. Edward comes in to her study unexpectedly, without knocking, since the door is ajar. She feels his discomfort, his decision to come close to her. He even clears his throat; impulsively she puts out an arm to him, beckons him in. He leans, kisses her head under the lamp, and she feels the cold from the outside come off him like rising mist.

"Hi. You surprised me. How was your evening? I've been so stuck into George Sand, I didn't even notice how cold it is in here. Why doesn't the heating work better? But you must be freezing! How was bridge? Did you have a good time?"

"Fine. Where's Em?"

"In her room. She was doing homework with Jenny, had dinner there, came in about an hour ago, she's washed her hair. She said they had gnocchi."

"Surely Aidan shouldn't be out at this time of night." He looks at his watch, strapped down upon golden hairs.

Always his sense of how things should be, always wanting order, she thinks, and expecting it too.

"Well, he's at Jason's, and they're only down on Broughton Street. I suppose I—I got carried away reading. Anyway, it's Friday."

She hears him hear her rattle on. He sits down on the chair her foot has been resting on, and looks at her.

"Oh, yeah, Friday. But I think I'll walk down and collect him."

She sees him thinking something else. After so many years of marriage, these trackways into each other's minds, like worn paths in a forest, amid undergrowth. Each knows where they lead—a thought which scares her.

"What?"

He says, "I was wondering if you'd come away with me. January. I was thinking of a trip to Majorca. Work, of course, but some time out too. Get away for a week or so after Christmas, what d'you think?"

"Do you have time? Aren't you teaching then?" She tries to find a middle way between too much and too little enthusiasm. Too little, and he will suspect her; too much, and she will sink back into the old familiar ease of it, the two of them planning a trip, going somewhere together, their old conspiracies.

"I've still got time from my sabbatical. The plants there, they're a microcosm of the whole of the Mediterranean. Of course, there won't be anything flowering in January, but there's a big seed-storage facility near a place called Soller, it's quite a new concept, I'd like to see it. And there's the wetlands park, greatest biodiversity in the Balearics."

"Majorca?"

"Did you know that seven per cent of the world's plant species are on the Mediterranean? The vegetation in Majorca is a microcosm of everything that grows around the Mediterranean. It's all there. And it's really well documented. They're doing great things in plant conservation, preserving endangered species. And it would be sunny."

She nearly tells him that George Sand and Chopin thought it was going to be sunny, too; but she doesn't. She just says, "Well, that would fit in with my George Sand project. Great idea."

"Okay, well, I'll have a look online, see what I can find in the way of flights."

Let everything fall where it will, she thinks. Yes, a trip together, why not. Time spent doing what interests us, and eating well, resting; who knows what may change. They travel well together, have been doing it for two decades; there will be few surprises there. And he, Sean, will just have to wait till she comes back. She will have to find a way to stay in touch, of course, or it would be unbearable. She imagines standing on a foreign street, her ear pressed to her mobile, his voice like a transfusion. The words that bounce off satellites, or whatever they do, circling the world, to come back to her ear. Or, like a lovesick teenager, staring at the tiny screen for the few dense abbreviated signs that have to appear, or life can't go on.

When you have begun to deceive somebody about one thing, everything else seems to fall into the same pattern. Even the way Edward is sitting here feels uncomfortable, and she wishes he would move. His foot on the chair rung, as if it were trying to hold something in place. The way he has clasped his hands. But she doesn't want to lie to him; it's just that she can't yet find any way of telling him the impossible truth. If asked, she would say that she loves him. Of course she does. Loving him is a habit that has not died, he has done nothing to make it disappear.

He's left the room and gone down to the kitchen to forage, and she hasn't moved, hasn't followed him down there to continue the conversation, and she knows he'll notice this, feel her absence like a draught at his back. Normally she'd go down there, still talking, asking about Majorca and the seven per cent of the world's plant species and the wetlands park. She'd ask, and he'd tell her, more than she wanted to know, probably, but it would be letting him know that she is with him. But she sits on, letting him go alone. If he wants to talk he can come back up here. She hears him slam a cupboard door, imagines him peering into the cold light of the fridge. The first sign of infidelity: letting your husband go and search for leftovers on his own. She turns back to the page; where was she?

Emily comes round the door, her girl's body long and soft in a loose T-shirt and sagging socks, a sweater over her nightclothes.

"Mum."

"What, sweetheart?"

"Nothing, really."

"Come on . . ."

"You said you'd come and say good night."

"I was coming. I was just talking to Dad. What's the matter, Em?"

"I don't know. I missed you tonight."

"I was here. Just reading. I thought you were listening to music. You could have come."

"Yeah, but. It didn't feel like you were here." She veers, these days, between bold teenage attempts at sophistication and babyish wheedling, as if somewhere between these two extremes she is deciding who to be.

"Come here." She reaches out. Emily slides closer, and she curls her arm around her girl's waist. "You can always come in, even if I'm working. I'm only reading, really. Come and disturb me."

"You won't go anywhere, will you?"

"No, I won't go anywhere. Oh, Dad and I might go for a short trip, Grannie Jameson might come for a few days and stay with you, that's about all."

"I don't know why, I was scared, you know, that you would."

"Oh, where would I go? Without you?"

"Well," says Emily. "People do. Parents do. You know, people at school." It's not the first time she has mentioned the number of people at her school whose parents are separated or divorced.

"I'm not going anywhere. I promise." Emily stands close to her, in her embrace. She smells herbal shampoo and feels her daughter's hand relax slightly in hers. The curve of Emily's hip against her own ribs, a new convexity.

"Just sometimes," Emily says, "it feels like there's nobody really here."

She moves away, and in the doorway she lingers, reluctant to go back upstairs alone, and Maria says to her, "I'll come up in a minute. Promise."

But then Edward comes back, swallowing the remains of whatever he has found to eat downstairs, and she sees Em's face lighten.

"Dad! I didn't know you were here."

She throws herself at him, he takes her hands and she leans back, all her weight held by him, her hair down her back, still damp and streaked blond and dark, her head nearly to his shoulder. When she was smaller, she would lean back like this and he would hold her weight as she walked up his body, her feet braced against his shins, then his thighs, then his stomach and chest, until she jutted out from him at a right angle, before somersaulting down out of his arms, a curlicue to his rigid stance, a blond question mark unpeeling from his firm statement, the two of them coming apart in her one swift movement. Now, she's too tall and heavy, and he smiles but shakes his head as she wants to begin her ascent. She blows out her cheeks—too bad—and falls back on an exaggerated sulk. It's too late for her to be this childish with him. Edward runs a hand across her head and through her damp hair, and Maria sees the gesture as a kind of farewell to Em's childhood, and her heart hurts for her daughter. Her own father had none of this physical ease with her.

Edward pulls Em to him in a brief hug, to cheer her up, and says, "I'm going down to find Aidan. Back soon, love."

Emily trails a long arm out towards him, pointing. "Come up and see me when you get back. Both of you! It's a command!"

You don't have to read George Sand, Maria knows, to believe that having more than one man in your life is not a sin.

But she lives in twenty-first-century Scotland, not nineteenth-century France, and things seem to have been turned backwards, so that freedoms won that long ago cannot be assumed any more. Did George ever think that her love affairs with men other than her husband might affect her children? In the nineteenth century people did not think this way about their children. The fact that George took hers to Majorca when she left with Chopin for the winter of 1837 suggests that it was the normal thing to do. (Although Louise Colet, in her *roman à clef Lui*, rather cattily described her character Antonia as debauching her children by behaving amorously in front of them.) In the twenty-first century, it seems to be necessary to lie to one's children as well as one's husband. What she is doing is simply not what married women, mothers, do. Not in this country, not in this town, not in this century, two hundred years after George's birth. When did the change happen? When did history turn over in the night and decree that adultery was a punishable offence again, punishable not by stoning or imprisonment, but by more subtle means? Being accused of cheating, of immaturity—the new sin—of being unfit to bring up one's children? She would like to ask Edward's opinion, but of course she can't do that. Is it Scotland, she wants to know, is it just that I was brought up here, and my mother lives just across town, and I was at school here, and John Knox's statue is still there on the High Street, and there are tears before nightfall if you don't watch out, and Calvinism seeps out of all the stones of this place? She tries to imagine a different place and time, where what she's doing might seem entirely normal. In the past, in the future; in California, perhaps, in the sixties, or in the south of France. Is it geography, is it history, that determines how we feel about what we do, and how others feel about it, and therefore, what happens next?

He hangs his trousers on a hanger and places them in the wardrobe, as he does every night. A meticulous man, he hangs his shirt up too; would never leave his socks lying on the floor as men are so often accused of doing. He goes into the bathroom to clean his teeth, wearing his pyjama bottoms, his white chest with its two prominent pink nipples on view, the little bushes of bright hair in his armpits, the slightly thickened waist. Maria sits in bed wearing a T-shirt and hugs her knees and calls to him to bring her a glass of water when he returns. She feels comfortable, at ease with him; the unthinking ease of long habit. He brings her the water and they both turn on their elbows to read their books. He is reading Philip Roth—a book which, she has heard, doesn't exactly condemn adultery. She's reading Jane Austen, to calm her down. But Jane doesn't go in for condemning people, either, even when they run off to Brighton in pursuit of soldiers, as the youngest Bennet girl does in *Pride and Prejudice*. Great writers do not go in for social condemnation, perhaps. Oh, but Tolstoy described Anna Karenina as an adulterous woman, and pushed her under a train. Flaubert was horribly sarcastic about Emma Bovary, and polished her off too. So perhaps that thesis will not hold. Again, she considers asking Edward what he thinks, but doesn't. The worst thing about infidelity seems to be that you have to censor conversation with your husband on all topics, so that Edward must find her unusually silent.

"How was your class today?" he asks her, closing his book.

Perhaps Roth has taken him to a place where he would rather not be.

"Oh—good. I think. I'm not sure that anyone really gets Deleuze, me included. But we try." She doesn't, of course, say anything about what happened after class, or about any of what she is thinking. Neither of them says anything more about Majorca; but the subject is there, it's between them like a present you know you are going to receive, but which you aren't sure you want. He raises a blond eyebrow at her as he turns to kiss her with closed lips, and then he reaches to turn out the light. She wonders if he knows. Then thinks, as long as he doesn't know, they are safe. All of them. Maria ends her day up close against her husband's solid warm back, in the bed she has slept in for nearly twenty years, and sleeps soundly without remembering any of her dreams. It's been a full day.

2

THE BITTER PATHS OF
MAJORCA

WHO WAS SHE? Standing on the deck of a battered old
ship, *El Mallorquin*, heading out of Barcelona back to
Palma de Majorca that autumn day: a woman probably in
her thirties, her complexion like a gypsy's, rapid as a young
man in her way of moving. She exclaimed as she stared
about her. Her glance was direct, her eyes black and bright.
The sailors saw a woman dressed the way no woman they
had ever seen would dress, in a long coat and trousers, with
a kind of bandana around her head. A flash of gold at her
breast. Her feet on the deck, small, in stout little boots. Her
head thrown back so that strands of black hair escaped
from her striped scarf, and her throat was bare. The men
averted their eyes and then looked again, secretly.

There was a boy who looked more or less normal, and a
younger child, wearing trousers and a bright blue jacket,
who rushed around the deck screaming, with nobody telling

her to be quiet. There was a tall thin young man with a pale face and light hair, who coughed. There was a very young-looking maid, hardly more than a child herself. They had all those trunks and bags, and left them scattered about the deck, in the way. The deckhands knew they would have to cast off soon and needed all the deck space to coil their lines and hoist the sails, but nobody moved to stow the luggage, and they certainly were not going to do it themselves. At last, the captain came and shouted out to a couple of sailors to stow them below decks, and then the men moved, touching the foreign stuff with caution. The travellers stood and gazed at the sea as if they had never seen it before and the woman waved her hands in the air, expressive hands like a dancer's; her eyes when she glanced at you were large and dark as a Spaniard's or a Moor's, and her hair, escaping from her scarf, was black and wavy. She was looking about her as if she had the right to stare at everything, she didn't keep her eyes down like a real woman, and even the child dancing away from her on the foredeck did not seem to cause her concern; she was like a child herself, rubbing her hands together, springing to look from port to starboard and back again, her face held to the sea wind, hair streaming. Perhaps she was a young man. But no, there was the shape of her bosom and the flush on her cheeks like the bloom on a fruit; again, they looked away.

The outside and the inside. A woman seen by a group of men, in passing. An eccentric, a foreigner. Dressed as a man, with a bold look about her. Their experience is of submissive women, their women, and of whores.

She's thinking about her mother, in fact, and the last days of her life this past summer of 1837, the terrible little room in the nursing home and then the room they found for her, and the way her mother grabbed her hand at the end, and the love she had always longed for flared up, a last spark, as the doctors said it was hopeless, liver cancer, one big tumour; and Sophie saying to her, "Paris, it's so beautiful, Aurore, you can't die in Paris!" Her last days. The black hair faded to grey on the pillow. The gone beauty. The brief exclamation that is life.

Nobody on the outside can tell what is on the inside. The exhaustion of those days, chasing across the country, leaving her children with people, quarrelling with Casimir, rushing back to Paris only just in time. Sophie wanted pâtisserie, croissants and coeurs d'Alsace. She wanted peaches, plums, grapes. She wanted to be taken to the Champs-Élysées. She wanted life, and everything that she had not had in life, poor little woman, poor child, poor mother who had not known what to do for her children, because she never knew it for herself.

Courage and optimism on the outside, even if you are afraid on the inside for your life, that's what her daughter knows. No matter what happens, you go on. You are a soldier in Napoleon's army. Your ancestors are the Maréchal de Saxe and the King of Poland. Everything in your life has challenged you to be brave. So you face out to sea and exclaim at how exciting everything is, you don't look back.

The steam engine between the main and the staysail blew steam into the air. The bo'sun caught the child in the blue jacket who seemed to be a girl, just as she was running up into the bow to climb on the lifelines, and dragged her back to her mother, if she was a mother, and said, "Señora, your child, hold her please." Then they cast off all lines, and moved out into the harbour to haul sails, running the engine too. The captain at the helm and in the bow a lookout boy who had come wild and barefoot to the dock in Barcelona, begging please to come on board to escape from the soldiers. Now, they could get on with their work. The boy at the bow shouted out, all lines were clear. Wind picked up and began filling the patched sails. The travellers stood at the railing and gazed back towards the shore. Perhaps they were exiled, perhaps they were criminals, being punished by being sent away from home. The bo'sun crossed himself. The helmsman lowered his eyes and drew his scarf across the lower part of his face.

El Mallorquin carried pigs from Majorca to Barcelona. It was going back empty to its home port, and they were not used to having foreigners on board, and this little family were the strangest people possible, like gypsies, like vagabonds, only with all this luggage that had to be carried and stowed and then brought out again in the morning, while they fussed and worried about its safety. The ship smelled, they complained; well, of course it did, it was a cargo ship for animals; the sailors could understand their complaint from the way they spoke to their captain, and certainly from the way he shrugged and raised his thick eyebrows and gestured them wordlessly to their cabins. Otherwise, what they said was incomprehensible. Someone said it might be French. But they didn't seem to have a word of Mallorquin between them, or even Spanish, and the helmsman said it was not Arabic they were speaking, and, no, he had never heard that language before.

Then there's Frédéric. A young man who has awoken such tenderness in her, it sometimes hurts. What is love? The total commitment to care for someone. The opening of a heart.

When she had first told him of her Majorca plan, and of how much good it would do Maurice, he'd said instantly, "It would do me good, let alone Maurice."

"What do you mean?"

"Well, what about me? Why don't you invite me?" He looked at her with what she thought of as "his look," almost an accusation. "You're always thinking of the children."

He has this habit of pouting: a spoiled child. But it is not his fault, he is an exile, far from home, he is a genius, he is more sensitive than other people. So she tells herself. When they first became lovers, the childish grasping, the mouth at her breast, the easy jealousy, then the turning away. She laughed at the boyish sulkiness, and the way she could charm him out of it: come on, cheer up, the world is waiting, Chop-Chop, Chopinet, my little grasshopper, Monsieur Velvet-fingers, my Frycek.

"I was thinking of Maurice, you know how low he's been lately." She didn't say, I was thinking of myself. She didn't say, I'm exhausted, I've been ill, my mother has only just died, I've been rushing across the country seeing to one thing after another, Casimir is being a perfect nuisance. She would never make such excuses. But her boy, her real child, she could justifiably put first.

"But how could you think of going without me?"

They had been lovers for less than a year. That evening at Marie d'Agoult's apartment when Liszt and he had played duets, and someone had sung Schubert's "Der Erlkönig" and Marie had served ices and tea, and she'd worn her white trousers and a frogged jacket in the colours of the Polish flag, just to please him; she'd felt his gaze seek hers across the piano top in the middle of a bold piece of improvisation; she hadn't known how he saw her, how he might feel, and then she'd dared to invite him to Nohant, and that had been the beginning. He'd been shy, reticent in a way that astounded and moved her. She hadn't dared ask about his ex-fiancée, Marie Wodzinska, but suspected something, that he wasn't at ease in lovemaking, and perhaps she had put him off by being too direct.

"My darling, I wasn't thinking of going without you, we

must go together, it will be a wonderful, wonderful trip. But you know, I do have to think of my children, and you, my sweet, can be one of the family too."

He was so sensitive, like someone about to be punished; he flushed and gazed at her, and she soothed him the way she knew how, the way she had soothed *le petit* Jules, her nineteen-year-old lover, Jules Sandeau, years ago. Boy-men, young geniuses, so delicate and tender, with such soft skin, both of them, and such nervousness, like young horses, she thought, ready to start up and gallop away.

But she had a real son, a real boy to think about too. Since he'd come back from staying with his father, Maurice had looked so pale, as if worn out by his own growth. He was a skinny fifteen-year-old, all wrists and shin bones, but it wasn't just the age he was. What the doctors said was rheumatism was worse. He needed a change of climate more than any of them. In her mind a plan had begun to form like the sketches she made for the plots of novels. She'd ask Mendizabel for help. Get letters of introduction, maybe from the Marlianis in Paris, and other Spaniards she knew. Find a boat, however you found boats. Find a house, among the palm trees. Live for months under a clear blue winter sky. Where she wouldn't have to put up with people calling all the time, the way they did in Paris, or coming to stay for weeks, the way they did at Nohant. In the daytime she'd teach the children their lessons. Maurice would get strong and brown and put on weight; she hated to see him so thin and pale, his chest like a chicken's, his head big on his fragile neck. Sol, wild Sol, her *chamois*, her tomboy, could run free in a way she couldn't in Paris without breaking the furniture indoors and making carriages clatter to a stop as she hurtled without looking into the street. It would be a new life.

The inside and the outside. Life rushes you along, and you have to be there, for others, for your mother, your children, the young men who trust you, the young geniuses who so need your help. You don't stop to think about what you need. Nobody has ever asked you what you need; it isn't even a concept. You are a child of your century, of the Revolution, of Napoleon. You pick yourself up and soldier on.

But God, how she needs it—peace and quiet, after this terrible year of her mother's death. She'll be free, to sleep, to work, to stride about unnoticed in her blouse and breeches, hatless, booted. She hasn't been sleeping; she has frequent stomach pains; her eyes ache and she has noticed the dark circles under them. It was the divorce from Casimir that started it, then the drawn-out lawsuit about the custody of the children, the trial in which she had risked losing her own beloved house as well as all her money, and the gossip that surrounded the whole thing, her behaviour, his behaviour, with people taking sides and accusing her of debauchery and the Lord knows what. Then Sophie, dying in Paris at the height of the summer heat. Sophie, admitting she loved her, years too late. And then, damn him, Michel, who always evaded her and made his stupid fat wife into an excuse. And the young men who came with Champagne and stayed up half the night, all of them, the Didiers and Mallefilles, with their demands and their jealousy and the way everyone, always, was short of money and came to her to be fed, helped, financed, listened to.

Frédéric said, "It would do me the world of good to get out of Paris, leave the fogs, this awful air, and this life, staying up all hours, salons, parties, concerts, you know the life I lead, how it exhausts me, people attach themselves to me and suck my blood, you know I can't say no to anybody, and your company does me so much good, *ma chérie*, I need you. I don't know how you can think of going without me, Aurora, it's a positive insult."

He insists on calling her *Aurora* always, won't use the masculine name of George. Doesn't like her in trousers. And as for those boots . . .

"Sweetheart, I wasn't. I wouldn't dream of it. We must all go together." Her hand is stretched out, always, for him to grasp. He brings it to his lips, warms it slightly with his breath; suddenly she wants him to bite her knuckles.

He was a virgin, she was almost sure. He touched her with a kind of awe, very delicate, as if she might break. She waited, holding her breath, that first time. Guided him in. Heard his exhalation, his gasp as he came. Lay there herself like a mother, like a *Pietà*. Wondered what in his experience this might match, and how she might speak to him of it, and how she could possibly fit herself around this childish painful need that ignored her completely.

She'd loved the music. It was extraordinary, what he could do at a piano, what he could make happen. That first evening, him leaning right into the instrument, it had been like hearing the world made, the pure essence of life. He was making it up as he went along, just as she did with her stories. He too opened his veins and poured himself into the narrative. She watched him, her kindred spirit, she opened herself to his improvisation, his invention, that evening, she fell in love. It was music she could never hear enough of, the pure play of the imagination. His fingers on the keyboard found snatches of song, birdsong, the sounds of far-off places; they caught the essence of the evening, this very evening, this moment, wherever they were; and the people who were there, the atmosphere, the wine and food, the clothes they wore, the vibrations between them, the spirit of friendship, the beginnings of passion, the touch of love.

His music came out of these glittering evenings, when they all ate and drank, talked and argued, at the Contessa's house, or at the Marlianis', wherever they were. He played late into the night, and the songs of the day, the jokes of the evening, even the jealousies between people were picked up and spun into his peculiar magic, played in another key. The piano drew them all together, it was their magnet. He was the magician who held the lives of all who heard him in his hands.

She asked him, "What do you hear in your head, as you play?"

"Everything. All the voices, past, present. I hear it all going on at once, like an orchestra."

It came through him and poured out, pure feeling, the way neither words nor lovemaking ever could. Life, its essences.

What basis this might be for a difficult journey together and months spent in a foreign place, she had not really considered. In spite of her decision, she felt the nag of doubt. Would he be able to travel? Would he mind the discomfort? Would he get bored? Well, she could look after him, she knew the world better than he did, she'd been to Italy with Musset, the Pyrenees with Casimir.

Leave it to me, she found herself saying to him about more and more of life, leave it to me. She saw his relief.

"We could ask Dr. Gaubert what he thinks. Leave it with me for the moment."

"Don't put me off, will you?"

"Of course not. How could I?"

Before they'd become lovers, she'd written a long letter to one of his closest Polish friends, Count Albert Grzymala. An older man, he would probably not be shocked at what she had to ask him. Thirty-two pages which Chopin was to know nothing about, to ask him whether he thought Marie Wodzinska could make Frédéric happy, if she was still in the offing, and in confidence, did he think that Frédéric held physical lovemaking in contempt? She was afraid that her Chopinet, her Frycek, was one of those people who could not really feel the passion of sex. Had some woman left him with a distaste for physical love? Was he excessively pious? Because she could consent to having a platonic relationship with him if his friend thought it advisable, but she couldn't really love someone who separated the body from the soul and did not understand that for her they were inextricably connected, and lovemaking the most serious, as she put it, of all human actions. But Frédéric as a new lover proved touchingly attentive, he'd spent most of the summer of that year at Nohant with her, he'd written and published a collection of études which he said he dared not dedicate to her, but longed to; he wanted secrecy, to protect her, not himself; he seemed to have forgotten all about Marie Wodzinska and her pale Polish chastity.

And now here they were, actually on the boat, really going to Majorca. She felt the damp salt breeze on her cheeks and turned with her ecstatic smile to him, she knotted his long fingers in hers, and together they stood at the ship's rail, facing west, while the men ran about the boat in their exotic rags and tatters, such strange-looking sailors, and the sails flattened and bucked and grew taut with wind, the strange little engine puffed steam and the sun was about to sink into the copper-green western sea, a red ball, bigger than she had ever seen it. Here it was: freedom. They had escaped. The adventure had really begun.

Beside him here at the ship's rail, she no longer doubted him, because she had decided to banish the doubt. He fixed her with his long intense look as she pressed his hand. She adored the way he moved, the way he held his shoulders, the aristocratic curve of his nose; she wanted to stand apart from him and simply admire him, and she wanted to come close, as close as possible, and feel the whole length of his body against hers, white skin against brown, cool against warm, his bony chest against the heat of her breasts, his long hands pushing back her hair and his husky voice with its accent telling her she was the most beautiful woman in the world. The children imitated the way he spoke, the Polish rolling of *r*'s and the occasionally pedantic French, and she scolded them and saw them run out of reach, their nursemaid running hopelessly after them; she laughed, she always laughed, because her children were so completely free and original, just like Rousseau's Émile, such children of their time.

She has also to forget the nights with Michel de Bourges. All those evenings when she'd galloped her black mare the twenty-one miles to Bourges to meet him, or he'd come to La Châtre and she'd ridden the road where one night her father had fallen from his horse and died, passing that same thirteenth plane tree on the curve and thinking of him each time, her papa Maurice, dead when she was four years old. They had often met there at an inn, she and Michel, so that she could be home by morning. Her body stinging, the memory of his hands and tongue in her flesh and of him inside her, his muttered words in her ear, his Varois accent, his Mediterranean eyes, the bones of his skull under her hands as she explored his ugliness, admired his phrenology. Michel was married, and wouldn't see her often because of "the Person," as she called her, Madame Michel, and because he was obsessed with republican politics and his legal career. Everard, she'd christened him when they first met, and in her letters which always had to prevaricate and hide the truth, sometimes Marcel, or even Marie, addressing him as a woman if she thought Casimir or the Person might be able to get hold of her letters and read them. Louis-Chrysostome Michel, her Everard, her brigand. In reality, a nearly middle-aged man, short, with little round glasses and receding hair.

She has told him that she no longer loves him. She can't love where she is not equally loved in return: it is her credo. But what do you do about the desires of the body for a passionate man?

Frédéric knows nothing of this, and will know nothing. She doesn't want to shock his modesty or change his opinion of her. So again, she takes herself in hand. She was only just thirty when she met Michel; now in her mid-thirties, she tells herself that she is too old for such adventures, galloping off at midnight—her half-brother Hippolyte taught her to ride like a hussar—to go disguised and breathless into country inns to meet a man who had already been in jail for his republican opinions and who believed that violent revolution was all that could cure society of its corruption. A man not afraid to show her what her body could experience; a first time, after the years of frustration with Casimir, who came to her drunk, more often than not, and left her unsatisfied and hurt. Yes, she will miss Michel. But she has set herself to love the young genius, Frédéric Chopin, so worthy of her love, so in need of her. The outside and the inside. You decide, and act. The inside remains hidden, not to be guessed at, not to be shown.

The night of the crossing to Palma de Majorca was warm, very dark, moonless but starry; it seemed to wrap them close around and make their passage secret. Behind them a white wake streamed through the phosphorescent sea. The boat's progress was slow, as if they hardly moved at all. They were under sail alone now, the creak of the boom ground in its socket, the mainsail flapping and then pulling as they turned south.

She was wide awake, and listening. What was that other sound? A man's voice, rising and falling in a long chant. She got up to go and look, and saw the man who sang; the Arab helmsman, his head wrapped, his body still, only his hands moving upon the wheel, singing to keep himself awake upon a sleeping ship. It was as if he'd lulled all the other sailors to sleep, or did not want to wake them, his voice rising thin and gentle as smoke in the air. A long shudder, rising, falling, regular as breath, as if the singer simply let his soul come up from his lungs and throat and wander unchecked, closer to breathing, or crying softly, or to the moans of lovemaking than to any music she had heard. A meditation? A prayer? A love song? She was eavesdropping on another life, one she could never know. The man did not turn, but swung the wheel gently with one hand, and the ship plowed on in the black glitter of water. She thought he did not hear or see her. She stood in the shadow of the mainsail and listened, and tears rose in her and came streaming down her cheeks so she had to lick them away. Tears for what, she didn't know: for Sophie, for everything that had happened this year, for the vulnerability of her little family on this journey, for the helplessness of love? The salt wind dried her tears so they itched on her cheek. She knuckled her eye sockets, pushed back her hair, made no sound. The music, like Frédéric's, seemed to pull from her all the desires of her life. There were no words in her head for it, none that would do. It was a foreign language. It caressed her and let her go.

At last she trod barefoot across the deck that shifted under her, leaving that whole world of nighttime sea and the few bright stars that swung across the sky and the white wake of the ship in darkness. Down the companionway, back to bed.

When she lay down she knew that Frédéric was awake too and listening in the dark, she could hear it from the sound of his breathing only feet away. He must feel it too. How could a man's voice be that gentle? Was there a race of men who were born and reared in such gentleness that they couldn't help singing of it all night long? In the daylight the sailors' chatter to one another had sounded incomprehensible. Now, there was this endless tender chant of a man's solitude. All night, the song of the wrapped and motionless helmsman as he stood at the wheel, one hand moving to steady their course under the stars he watched and reckoned by.

In the morning, her glance at Frédéric saw what the night had told him too. He never mentioned the song of the Moorish sailor, but when she heard the nocturne he wrote only weeks later, she knew. A minor interval injected in a melody where a major would be expected. The blue note.

Bright morning sun across the deck, then, and the sails tumbling down like clouds to be furled and stowed and the sea dashing in swirls of white against the ship, blue-green farther out, almost purple at the horizon; Solange racing about in her trousers and blouse, quite over her bout of seasickness of the night before, exclaiming at everything she saw. Maurice stood beside the helmsman as he took the boat in. Poor Amélie, the young French girl who was supposed to be looking after them, was being sick in the cabin. Frédéric stood with his long coat wrapped around him, and she glanced at him to share the intensity of her feeling—look, we have arrived on a foreign shore! He coughed, she noticed that he was wearing a silk scarf at his throat; was he suffering? She put out a hand to him, gripped his cold one. But it was such a moment, one in a lifetime! Look! Palm trees, sandy shores, distant mountains, the stretch of water between the boat and the dock that suddenly shrank so they were up close, docking in Palma, ropes flung, shouts, men everywhere; alongside the big solid ancient houses as if they had sailed up a street; the boat tied among the foreign boats, the huge cathedral right there before them and the trees that looked like zoo creatures from the Jardin des Plantes, said Solange, and will there be giraffes too?

One after another, they stepped ashore, handed down a gangplank by one of the crew. The sailors with their brown faces, their hands missing fingers, their broken teeth. The words of strange languages following them ashore. Sol said to the man who handed her safely to land, you look like a monkey, but luckily he did not understand.

Maria and Edward are in the station restaurant in Soller, Majorca. The railway wasn't built, Maria knows, until well after George Sand and Chopin left the island, and so neither was the station. In 1838 there was no way inland between these ragged hills. Now, the steam train tugs its coaches full of tourists all the way up from Palma, slicing through mountains, running through tunnels in rock and out again with a long blast of steam. The coaches are made of wood, finished with brass and leather. The view is astonishing. The people in the coaches crowd to the window, staring out. It's winter, and the sides of the mountains are in deep shadow, but above them the sky is a hard blue. There are only a few people on the train as it comes into the station at Soller and lets out its long whistle.

Maria and Edward have come up on the train and since they are hungry they have settled into the station restaurant, the white cloth spread for them on a small table but nothing to eat yet except bread in a basket. Edward is drawing in a small ring-bound book with pages of thick white paper and a grey cover with black ink doodles on it. He's drawing the room they are sitting in: the bare beautiful walls as he sees them, the tables with white cloths, the big iron stove that heats the room, the gently polished tiles, the vase of yellow flowers. The wine jug. A chair. Maria is writing in a note-book, covering two or three pages with bold spiky hand-writing, without stopping. A young man with close-cropped black hair and dark eyes comes quietly and brings a jug filled with wine. The room isn't warm enough for Maria to take off her dark blue wool winter coat. She pours a glass of wine, tastes it, goes on writing. They don't speak to each other; but there's a quality to the silence, tolerant, lacking in tension, because they're both busy, absorbed. They have their occupations and practise them side by side. But when the young man comes back with the menu, they both sit up, relieved, and begin to read it. They want hot soup to warm them, delicious fish, vegetables of all sorts, and the wine going down in the wine jug; distraction, satisfaction; they have done this many times before, and they might just go on doing it for the rest of their lives.

Maria, who knows that she is noticeable with the colouring she has of her Celtic ancestors, the white skin with some freckles, blue eyes, thick straight black hair which will probably turn grey quite suddenly one day, who writes in a vigorous scrawl, who bites back her cuticles, who walks fast, who wears a striped long T-shirt to bed, who has cold feet often and curls them against his calves to warm them. Edward who is longsighted and has suddenly started wearing little gold-rimmed glasses, whose hair is still fine as cornsilk, who lies on his back to read in bed, who bares his teeth like a lion's to brush them, who has a tendency to repeat himself, who has been her husband for as long as she can remember. They are the people they always have been, surely.

Edward says to her, "How are you getting on?"

Meaning, she supposes, her work on George Sand. It is now dignified by the name of work, not just reading, since Maria has announced that she's writing a book and has justified this trip by saying so. Maria has been given an Arts

Council grant to write about her heroine and has arranged time off from teaching for ten days. This means that Edward asks her how she is getting on because she has something to be getting on with, that he understands.

Maria says, "What? Oh, fine. I'm writing about the view from the train, which of course she wouldn't have seen. I'll get more when we go up to Valldemossa."

He says, "I'm drawing this room, for a start. Just to get back into the swing of it."

He always used to sketch; now his head moves up and down like a fine bird's, looking up, looking down at his paper, comparing what he sees with what he draws. Maybe it's a distraction he needs, just now. She finds it touching, the way he draws, with an old-fashioned attentiveness to detail. His sharpened pencil hesitant upon the page. It's so easy to take photographs instead.

The young Majorcan waiter brings soup. Maria crumbles her bread. This is not the whole story, oh, no, not at all; but work, travel can cover so much, as can eating in restaurants, ordering food, behaving as you always have behaved. There's something they aren't talking about, and if either of them begins talking about it, it may just flood the room and change the whole of their lives from this moment on. She feels both weak and curious at the thought. She smiles at him, decides to enjoy the soup, and her smile, unknown to her, reminds him of all the thousands of times he has seen her smile in that slightly challenging way above a lifted spoonful of soup. Hundreds and hundreds of spoonfuls of soup, hundreds of shared meals, smiles of agreement, smiles of complicity, smiles of tact.

She says, "How about you?"

He is working on his book about Mediterranean flora. The flora of this island and its geology are a microcosm of those of the entire Mediterranean, he has told her several times. He collects samples, and draws them, and when they go for walks, tells her about every tree. He has called the man who has organized the seed bank in the botanical gardens in Soller and talked to him about the plant he's interested in, which grows in the mountains of northern Majorca and would be about to become extinct if the seed bank had not stored its seeds. He tells Maria about this, and she listens more dutifully than usual, because it is safe ground. The plant—he shows her a photograph—is a member of the celery family of Umbelliferae and looks rather small and plain, with white flowers and dark green leaves. There are only a hundred individual plants left, as it has been eaten by goats and now can be found in only point-five of a square kilometre in the Sierra de Tramontana.

"What's its name?"

"*Ligusticum huteri.*"

"Doesn't it have an ordinary name too?"

"No."

She thinks how extraordinary and admirable it is to be so impassioned by the survival of this small, ordinary-looking plant that the goats have eaten. It makes her think of Sean and his white mice, and the way he visits them sometimes in the middle of the night. Men have this quality of being able to concentrate on something entirely outside themselves— or at least, the men she has loved do. It's a quality she both admires and is maddened by. What are you thinking about? A plant with a Latin name that may become extinct, is invisible in winter, and grows high up in one particular place in the mountains of northern Majorca, where it has mostly been eaten by goats.

She thinks meanwhile about George Sand and Chopin: George, whom she loves, and Chopin, with whom she is furious. But when Edward shows her his drawings, meticulous and beautiful, of plants she has scarcely noticed, she admires him again as she admired him when they first met. He loves the way things are, and that is a lovable attribute.

He has drawn an orchid that grows here in summer; it's copied from a photograph, as of course there are no orchids visible in winter. He tells her, there are orchids like this in the Burran, in the west of Ireland, and also in Cyprus and in Crete. It is the way that limestone warms them in its cracks and fissures that allows them to live, even in a cold place like Ireland, far from the Mediterranean. She wonders, through what fissured cracks in his deepest sensibility is he talking about Ireland, now.

Edward says, "I could use several more weeks here, though. I'll have to come back in the spring."

It's easier for them to be together away from home. They travel well together, have practised this for years; it's easy, as she imagined it would be. So much of life has become habit. There seems to be no reason, while they are sitting here, for not going on doing this. And yet, like two kites tugging at the hands that hold them, their secret dreams rise and pull and flap, and the question teases them—What if we were to let go?—and still the words haven't been said that would change all this forever.

She says, "What people say about him dying of rejection is completely untrue, you know. He refused to make love to her while they were here. It could have been his illness, but it was also all about his mother. Catholic guilt, reaching its tentacles all the way from Poland. But he spent seven summers at Nohant in her house, afterwards. Though after Majorca, they were no longer lovers." Now, she thinks, here; it will be here that we start to talk about it, because we have to. Because I have begun talking about people making or not making love. Because I can't any more use that contemporary ugliness "having sex."

"People prefer lies."

"But what's curious is, it's the lies that stick, rather than the truth. Why do they find the lies more interesting?"

"Oh, people want glamour and extremes. They want artists to live that out for them, a different sort of life from the one they have themselves, don't you think? But they don't want to live it themselves."

Now, Maria thinks, we could bring it all out into the open. But why? When they talk like this about a third thing, understanding each other, essentially absorbed in something else, they might just as well go on doing it for the rest of their lives. This is perhaps what love is: who was it who said it? Rilke. Love is protecting each other's solitude. Facing outward, towards the world, side by side.

Edward sighs, and begins on his fish, with evident pleasure and relief. He would probably miss her intelligence, her tact, her way of being able to leave things unsaid. She's still thinking about Sand and Chopin, not about them; she sees his relief. So it's safe enough for him to go back to thinking about the plants he has come here to study, all the Mediterranean flora which continue to surprise and fascinate him. Everything fits together, rock, water and soil and what grows from it, in Edward's mind, everything is this coherent, and she knows it pleases him to find this coherence all around him, within his reach. A small island, microcosm of the whole Mediterranean world, watered by streams and torrents that spring from an underground aquifer. A small lifetime, his own, that may, his theory goes, equally well be a microcosm of the lives of all people everywhere, of life itself, without his having to make too much effort about it. His sense of ecology lulls him, removes scruples, makes him admirably, annoyingly calm. If he's a part of the whole, he doesn't have to do more, that's how it goes. And if this attitude lets him sound complacent, it also allows him to protect both himself and her from anxiety. If he wasn't thinking about plants all the time, he might have to notice that she isn't faithful to him. As long as he keeps to rocks, watercourses, soil, nearly extinct plants, he won't have to pay attention to all the rest, including the messes made by the human heart. Her heart. Her body, really, its inconvenient desires. Being a scientist, he's excused from the moral dilemmas men have suffered for centuries, and can eat his fish in peace; therefore so can she. Whatever may come up, blossoming inexcusably, in the cracks.

She asks, "What are you thinking?"

They both have the habit of expecting a shortcut to be opened into each other's thoughts, and sometimes he minds, sometimes she does. It's like a gap in a garden fence between two houses; once used, it's hard to ignore it or close it and it seems pointless to try. But sometimes you might go round to the front door and knock.

He doesn't say, about the plant the goats eat, or about how the watercourses feed the wetlands with fresh water. "I was thinking of what it would be like being here without you, actually."

It's true, then, he's one step ahead of her, he isn't just thinking about plants. They have entered the dangerous realm of the human, after all.

"Permanently without me, or temporarily?"

"Permanently. I don't mean, with you dead or anything. I mean, without being married, without you in that sense."

"Thanks. Well. I mean, that I'm not dead."

She crumbles more bread, wants more wine. Now there is only coffee between them and the wreckage of the afternoon that seems inevitable. He has imagined sitting here without her, and this disturbs her sense of her own solidity. She would rather have imagined it first, sitting here without him. Or at least to have said it first. He must know, she thinks. Well, of course he knows; but he must be about to say something, so that words are put to it, and in that way it will become real, in a way it isn't quite, yet. He's imagined sailing on without her, master of his fate, mariner of his soul. Or whatever. Her stomach contracts. She isn't ready for this. She thinks, it is just as hard, even in the twenty-first century, as it has ever been. Not as hard as in the first half of the nineteenth, perhaps, but nearly. She thinks of Aurore Dupin, setting off to Paris to become George Sand; and of Casimir Dudevant, who probably hadn't envisaged life without her, letting her go. She, Maria, lives in a century in which all this is entirely possible, living alone, wearing trousers, ending marriages, having lovers, even lovers of both sexes, moving to other continents, living in attics, writing books. It's been done, many times and by many different women. Then why does her stomach contract and her mouth go dry? Why does it feel so hard?

When they leave the restaurant, halfway through that winter afternoon, they walk uphill, taking a road which narrows and becomes a track, which in turn narrows to a small path winding between orange groves and little kitchen gardens behind stone walls, up the steeper slopes of the mountain, where fires are burning, smoke rises, voices call out to each other across the valley, but they don't see anyone. They aren't talking, and something still hasn't been said, perhaps it never will be; each of them looks around as if alone, glances at the glow of oranges against dark foliage, sniffs up the cold and smoky air. Whatever they decide, whatever they say, there'll still be this, the permanent, reassuring outside world. When they come to the people who are building fires, three men and two women who are carting wood and tangled undergrowth to start up these winter blazes, and who shout to one another across distance, they say "*Buenas tardes!*" and "*Adios*" and are answered by people who straighten their backs to stare at them and wave. They have been seen, by some other human beings, at least. So everything still remains open, or at least, possible.

They turn to come back down the mountain track, by common accord. They are so used to going for walks together, it's one of the things that as married people they do well, walking at the same speed, carefully in step. Seeing those people in the purplish twilight with their bright fire allows her to take his arm in its tweed sleeve, and walk close. As long as nothing's said, she can go on doing this.

Perhaps, she thinks, we'll say to each other in ten years', twenty years' time, do you remember that afternoon in Majorca, outside Soller, when we nearly split up, nearly ended it all, when we really thought for a moment that we couldn't go on? Do you remember the fear of it, as we walked up that track? And how good it was to see those people making fires, and be seen? Safely, at mealtimes, in bed together, they might say that: gently underlining with their ironic evocation of that time, the present and future stability of what they had. She hopes so.

Coming back down, they see the little town as all yellow lights and dark alleyways before them. Oranges on trees glow in the twilight. There's a grain on everything, like dust. The shop doors are open and there are pots, pans and chairs in doorways, and the smells are of charcoal, woodsmoke, onions frying. Inside the houses, families are getting together. Maria feels a sudden need; and she's almost sure Edward is feeling it too. What have they missed? What is it their own countries, families, homes, never gave them? Why are they wandering out here, lost, outside their own language, full of longing?

Edward shakes off her hand from his arm and turns to her suddenly in the street, bars her way. "There's someone else, isn't there."

It isn't a question. The cooking smells, the warm, lit interiors: they are so far from everything familiar. His words sound like a bark to her.

Yes, she wants to say, but it doesn't mean this, it means that, and I've been meaning to tell you, and I wanted to, but somehow, and that's what we came away for, wasn't it, to talk about it, to get it out in the open, to understand, to forgive. But she doesn't say any of it. They won't be having that conversation, about how they nearly broke up with each other, in ten or twenty years. The breaking point is now, she can see it in his face. But why, why? It's not that I don't love you, she wants to say, it's just that I love him, or maybe it's over, I can't even tell, maybe I made it all up, it's a story, it's something I imagined, not to be taken seriously; it's us who are real, and this moment, this place, and ourselves in it, coming down from the mountain, isn't it, isn't that it? But she can't say it. She sees his face, pale in the growing darkness. There's a big bird croaking and croaking on the mountaintop and the smoky fires are bright as stars in the night, but have begun going out one by one since the first real star shone out in the sky. The last train is about to leave the station. They had better hurry, if they want to be on it.

⁓

Bare plane trees flanked the approach; the drive curved around, opened into a courtyard. In the grey light of winter there were gleams of sun. Water fell somewhere out of sight, intensifying cold and silence. Between the plane trees, up the grand curving avenue, they approached the great house. La Granja. George had the letters of introduction she'd brought from France, to give to the Majorcan nobility; they were expected.

In the courtyard, on the ground, a fire was burning. A silent man threw on wood, stirred up black embers, directed the leap of flame. The gnarled lumps of wood were the roots of olive trees. In the wood, ash made caverns as it burned, black holes; and the sparks rose in the still air. The man who was feeding the fire straightened at their approach. Heat quivered in the air. She held out her hands to the fire. The man held the horse's head. There was a pause, before anything was said. She was amazed, at the courtyard, the house, the fire, the silence, the welcome. It was the first time they had been made welcome by any of the Majorcan nobility. A woman came forward wearing long skirts, one over the other, and said something they couldn't understand, but her smile was easy to understand: it said, welcome. George moved towards her on an impulse, but Frédéric hung back. The children darted around the fire, shouting in French.

The house was yellow, and built like a cliff. It was pitted and studded with tiny stones, the walls pockmarked, there were strings of coloured things hanging, dried tomatoes, peppers, garlic. The wide arched courtyard was open to an inner courtyard. The windows, small and shuttered, made the vast walls seem bigger. The huge tree at the centre of the yard stretched above them. There was a faintness of shadow as the sun came out. In one of the outhouses another fire was burning and a woman stood next to it hitching up her skirts to warm her bare legs, while the flames jumped close to her, reddening her skin. Behind her were pots in unfired reddish clay. In the courtyard, too, a long table on trestles, with a jug of white flowers at one end, and a wide brown earthenware dish. The smiling woman handed them glasses with dark brown sweet wine in them and motioned to the bowl which held little smoking fritters. George bit, tasted. Frédéric smiled but shook his head, no. The fritters left sugar on her lips and oil upon her tongue and they burned her, hot from the fire, and the wine went down sweet and burning too. She smiled. She tried to speak a few words, but Spanish wasn't the same as Majorcan, it seemed. She remembered. The words of Spanish, the smells, something in the air? She turned to her companion, looking for explanations. There was no explanation, there was only the ghost of a memory, from far back. But with the wine, something like complete happiness spread through her, so simple and total that she wouldn't have thought it possible. It was like the moment in the chapel in Paris when she was a girl, when she felt herself received into the presence of God. How strange life was in the way it revealed itself to you, she thought, happiness when you least expected it, a lifting of loads you didn't know you carried.

Beyond the great gateway, in the house with the worn yellow steps to the upper storey, behind the cacti and geraniums, someone was expecting them. There was another table spread with fine cloths, perhaps, and heavy plates and jugs full of finer wine than this; but out here in the fitful winter sun, in the cold, she felt it already, the simple draught of happiness. She'd never forget it, and she'd never really know why. Later she would wonder if it was because nothing here was expected of her; she was a guest. Someone, some invisible person, had ordered all this, and within its structures she was safe. Someone was down the corridor, out of sight but present and awake, with his long sword at his side.

Bon día. The words were as strange in her mouth as the wine and food. There was a sense today of great spaces to be crossed. The empty spaces of a courtyard, the space of the silence and the calm near-motionlessness of these people: the woman smiling, warming herself, the man stirring the fire with the toe of a boot. Something self-contained here, something inviolable, that existed before her and would continue without her, that took no account of her, discounted her even as a person. A great spaciousness, within which you could simply exist.

In the house there were chairs in rows, made of dark wood, lined up against the walls, and dark portraits, and tiled floors in blue-and-gold patterns, and more spaces, dusty, faintly touched here and there with weak sunlight. There was a fireplace with more olive wood burning. There was a man at the end of a long room on an upper floor, smoking a cigar. It was all quite unlike the French bourgeois family houses she was used to; there was a grandeur here she had not experienced, and at the same time a bareness, an emptiness that changed the scale of the human beings who moved about within these walls. When she came to look out from the upper floor into the garden below, she saw orange trees and lemon trees with their fruit hanging heavy, blooming, touched with dust, in among the dark green leaves. A pomegranate tree naked of leaves, with its fruit like Christmas baubles. In the distance, the sea of the olive groves, stretching away, one man's kingdom, in waves of silver and green.

She thought, I have been here before; or somewhere very like it.

The man at the end of the room, smoking his cigar, stared at her. In the far rooms, doing needlework, must be his family, women, servants, children. He sat alone. His stare had a casual arrogance that was like acceptance. His round brown eyes beneath arched, delicate black eyebrows. Part of her wanted to stay here and live beneath that stare that welcomed her and yet held her at arm's length; that never questioned, ever, the order of things. He bowed his head slightly: Señora. He did not get up at once, and when he did, he bowed again over her hand. He inclined his head more slightly to Frédéric. The sweep of his arm moved them on the tide of his will. He would show them his estate, which was himself.

Later she will think, what was the appeal of a man so identified with his place, coherent with his destiny; that density of being? It drew her like a magnet. She would never be here again.

She held an orange in one hand, a lemon in the other. Each a little planet, held in the palm of the hand. The man had handed them to her, when they went outside. The skins felt dense, firm, a little oily. Yes, said their host in Spanish, take them, feel, they are good. The smell was of Christmas, in among the green leaves, in the cold, in the orange-smelling early dark. In the gardens, as they walked outside, there was the endless fall of cold water, discounting the passage of time, making yesterday like today, reducing everything to this: this simplicity, one orange, one lemon, held in balance. The dark-brown stare of a man she would never see again, who did not speak her language. Mediterranean eyes, warm and light-absorbing, grave.

The winter afternoon was short. Twilight darkened the orange trees, turned oranges blue. The earth turned dusty and blue as well, towards night. In the courtyard the horses stamped and the fire died down. A donkey screamed from behind the stables. The bare trees, the gleaming trunks, were still pale. The walls of the house would keep her here forever. And out here the garden and its firm fruits were locked up for the night, the guinea-fowl and roosters snoozed in the circular fowl-houses. The strange plants spiked their leaves against the sky. Above the high roof, one star.

The inside and the outside again: a sudden knowledge of connection. Nothing that could be explained.

Lemons, she would say later, as big as a man's head. In that secret Moorish garden, that paradise in which monks had once prayed and now a dark-eyed man smoked his cigars and ground their stumps on the subtle pavements, everything had been fertile beyond imagining. The Arabs had made those stone watercourses centuries ago to bring fresh water down from the mountains, and these had been maintained. There was water everywhere, in this dry land. She had put out her hand to take the fruit and the owner had so easily given it to her; there was no effort involved, no difficulty or unease. Just plenty, and generosity. Lemons, yes, and oranges, that big. She let her hands remember what they felt, uncritically.

Frédéric thought it was cold. Yes, it was all very well, these big houses with their rooms empty of furniture, their bare tiled floors, no glass even in the windows; but it was winter already and the chill from the uncarpeted floors had struck up through his bones. It was worse, he said, than her own house in the country, which was still draughty but at least there were some concessions made to comfort, you weren't left to shiver like an aspen poplar in completely unheated rooms. She should have thought of him, thought of his health. It was ugly, too. He didn't like the look, the feel, the smell of it, he had imagined something else, something far superior that these savages could never hope to attain. He couldn't think what she saw in it, and as for their host, with his absurd mangling of the few phrases he knew of French, his rolling eyes and habit of spitting into corners—and his way, surely she had noticed, of looking at her. He was impossible, worse than anything one could have imagined. It could hardly have been more uncomfortable when the monks had been there, before the present owner had taken over, taken all that land from the holy brothers. She shouldn't have brought him there, she should have thought about him before she accepted such an invitation. He'd caught cold, in those draughty rooms and the cold garden. His illness was probably going to get worse. She wondered then at the source of his anger: could he have felt jealous?

Later, when she mentioned it to him, "La Granja, do you remember?" he pretended to have forgotten the whole event. Memory, she thought then, is what we have to share with each other: it is the glue which allows us a common life. If someone doesn't remember, it's as if you have lived your lifetime alone.

There are other things that she's done recently that Maria can't imagine telling him about: things unconnected with Sean. There was the afternoon she spent once with her friend Cathy MacTavish, when they went into Cathy's empty house, Cathy's children at school, as hers were, neither of them at work, and took photographs of each other naked. Cathy drew curtains, lit lamps and candles. She poured red wine into big thick glasses, and the two of them took turns, draped themselves in fringed shawls to pose like Matisse odalisques, lay with a hand at their thighs like Manet's arrogant nudes, spread their legs like Picasso's. Cathy, the photographer, provided the equipment, a big old heavy Leica that had belonged to her father, and the wine. A digital camera seemed too lightweight for the enterprise, they decided. Maria brought the silk shawls, the dried flowers, the tiny scraps of satin underwear that she wore neither for her husband nor her lover, both of whom probably would have disapproved. She and Cathy, giggling, swigging the wine; the chill Edinburgh afternoon darkening outside into evening; a feeling they both had that if they did not seize this moment, this time, to celebrate their own bodies, give them permanent life, that life would slip away too fast unseen and unappreciated. Even though they were both married and Maria had a lover, there was something that could be felt and said only between women. It was that sense of a shared, undercover life: the admission of a fantasy, a desire that had no real place in their lives, but which for that afternoon was alive in them. A dream of fetishism, of artists and models, of the big camera lens focused on vulnerable flesh, of boudoirs and feathers and the languor of harems: all that in dark dour Edinburgh in November was hard to conjure to life.

Afterwards, when they sobered up, they hardly referred to it again; but Cathy had the prints made in a friend's darkroom, because the chemist would probably make a fuss about all this nudity if they simply took the film uptown to be developed in the normal way. The prints that came back were in sepia and black-and-white—they had decided against colour. They were matt-surfaced, postcard-sized, and very beautiful, Maria thought. Cathy had a fine sense of form, and the shadows that surrounded and emphasized each one's white flesh turned them into beauties. Their bodies glowed, set in a soft darkness of feathers, silk, fur, the room's shadows, the flickering light; looking, they fell a little in love with themselves. Each of them kept a set, tucked away in a drawer. To look at when we're old, said Cathy. To remember how gorgeous we were.

It was perhaps the sort of thing you had to do once in a lifetime, and around forty was the time to do it, because suddenly your flesh was changing, you were no longer quite what you were used to being. They both had a few grey hairs, and Cathy was putting on weight around the bum—look, I'm turning into the Hottentot Venus, or at least a Rubens—and so now was the moment, while the children were at school, the husbands at work, the world out there busy about its business, the sun sinking at four and another grim winter coming in, while the two of them were young enough to giggle and get drunk in the afternoon and old enough to fear mortality and its signs. Both of them said that they were sure their husbands would not have under-stood, although they might enjoy the photographs. "Maria, we're damn sexy, don't you think? Jings, what if they knew half of what we get up to!"

It was then that she nearly told Cathy about Sean. It would be so easy, another mouthful of wine, the silk shawl drawn about her, her friend with naked shoulders and her long hair down her back. *Cath, I have to tell you. Promise not to tell?* But she did not. She gave up the immediate pleasure of sharing her secret with her closest friend, because once a secret was said to anybody, it was no longer a secret, and would leak out somehow into the world. Maria knew that she wanted her secret almost as much as she wanted Sean. While it was not spoken, while no words were put to it, she was safe. The world still remained wide open.

So they hid the wine bottle in the rubbish, Cathy rinsed the glasses, they had their woolly winter clothes on again, trousers and sweaters and socks and clogs, and the silk shawls and scraps of lace were shoved away in Maria's bag, and the scene they had created was echoed only on hidden rolls of film, to be recreated into images that would only speak of it as the past. That time, that winter afternoon, halfway through their lives.

Then there was the time they dressed up as men and went down to the bar in Leith. They wore a mixture of their husbands' and sons' clothes: men's shirts, boys' shoes, black jeans and leather jackets and caps pulled down low. "Just for a laugh," said Cathy. "Come on, let's, and see if anyone notices we're female, or if we can really carry it off."

They parked Maria's car down a side street near the bottom of Leith Walk and made their way the rest of the way downhill, two slender young men whose stride might look a little too deliberate. In their narrow dark trousers, in their dirty trainers, with their leather jackets swinging and a little too much bust in evidence beneath their white shirts, they went unnoticed and unchallenged on the street. They reached the statue of Queen Victoria and headed towards the docks, towards one of the only bars which had not yet been gentrified, where men stood and slid pint mugs down the wet bar-top and the telly yelled about football, and the floor still had sawdust on it, and you couldn't hear yourself speak.

"Whit yer havin', pal?" Cathy growled to her, in an accent that sounded even to Maria a little too strong.

"Pint a heavy. Ah'll git it. Got a fag?"

They both smoked and coughed and ground their butt ends into the tin ashtray, and swigged their beer from straight glasses, and banged the glasses down on the table-top. Money slid from their strangely small hands.

"Where you two lads from, then?" the barman asked them. "Niver seen yer here before."

But they coughed and grinned, jerked thumbs to the back of the bar to indicate they were going to sit down. It was maybe the last of the Edinburgh pubs that had a separate room for women, which was why they had chosen it. A real spit-and-sawdust place, where big men in navy jackets with plastic across the shoulders and builders' boots, men off building sites and up from what was left of the old docks, came to drown the pain of the day; where no one would be happy to find a couple of women dressed as lads. They found a table, but sitting down felt too vulnerable, and they were already getting looks from the men at the bar. Smoke hung in clouds in the air, the ceiling was brown-stained from centuries of tobacco, the place was warm and damp and sweaty, and the men who shouldered their way to the bar might be harmless enough individually, but neither of the women wanted to tangle with them as a crowd. They swallowed as much of their warm beer as they could, raised eyebrows at each other, and left by the door past the men's toilet, in which someone was throwing up.

Out on the cobbled street, the yellow light and the roar from the bar, and black water licking at the quay. A moon slung low, and the air sudden and cold as knives. Farther down the quay, people thronged the wine bars; cars were parked that once would never have been seen down here. It was like being in a time warp.

"Jesus, Mary and Joseph," said Cathy, "I couldn't have stuck it much longer."

"Think they noticed?"

"I dinna ken, hen, and I dinna care. Come on, enough adventures for one night, let's gang on hame, while we have a hame to gang ter. Men! Who in hell do Scottish men think they are?"

Maria, whose post-graduate thesis had been about Roland Barthes, thought then about his idea of wearing a mask and pointing to it to show that you were wearing it. It seemed to make the idea of transgression work. Having it both ways, you could say.

So there are other things that she will never tell Edward, and none of them seem treasonable to the life she and he have together, only slightly weird and difficult to explain. You went out dressed as men? You took pictures of each other naked? What the hell for? It would all seem unnecessary, not threatening. It's outside some concept he has of the norm, but he would, if she told him, wave it away as weird, freaky, who would have thought what women get up to when they have nothing better to do. He would probably warn her off spending too much time with Cathy. Or he would think, hmm, hot pictures, who would have thought Cathy MacTavish had all that under her baggy jeans and sweaters? Nothing more. These exploits, which are, she knew, about exploring the boundaries and contradictions of that odd thing, human sexuality, the thing she is supposed to share fully with her husband, would only seem to him slightly peculiar, even incomprehensible. But making love with Sean, a man, twice a week in his, Edward's, own house, that would be something else. That would be real, because it involved a man, and it involved actual sex, which means penetration. That is always a different kettle of fish.

~~~~

The house in Establiments in the plain of Palma was called, appropriately enough, "So'n Vent." They were driven out from Palma, with all their luggage on a cart, and the children bouncing on the front with the carter, a stout old horse pulling them, Solange wanting to whip the horse to go faster, Maurice seizing her and holding her fast, her arms bound. The scream that came from Solange as her brother grabbed her made them all jump just as they approached the house.

"This is it? *La casa?*"

"*Sí*, Señora."

It was a shack, whitewashed, with no glass in the windows, a balcony hanging off it and a roof with slipping red tiles. Frédéric raised his eyebrows high and pursed his lips, as he always did when dismayed. Immediately, she began thinking of how to console him. There were always things you could do to make yourself more comfortable, and she would set about doing them as soon as they had moved in. The name meant house of the wind.

"I'm sure we can find some glass, and we must be able to buy some furniture, I'll go back into Palma as soon as we have settled in."

Solange said, "I don't like this house, it isn't a proper house, we don't have to stay here, do we—when can we go home?"

Maurice said, "Maman, don't worry, I will come with you."

"But look," she said, catching at Solange to hold her still. "See the palm tree? And the lemon tree? And look, there are even lemons growing on it."

In the last days of October and into November, it was fine and sunny. The upright piano she had found to rent in Palma, after a long search, had been delivered. Frédéric grumbled about its untuned dampness and tinny sound, but still, it was a piano. There were lemon trees and palm trees, as she'd promised them all, and everything was, as Frédéric said, just like the Jardin des Plantes in Paris only more so. And the sky! You could forget the house when you looked at that blue depth of sky. But by mid-November the rains had come; the little house had no chimney and no glass in the windows. The only heating was from a brazier that could be lit in the middle of the floor, and as soon as it started smoking, Frédéric started to cough, so Maurice poured water on it to put it out, and they all sat in the cold, smoky room that smelled already of the sour ashes of old fires, and felt the wind coming at them from all four corners. Amélie sat wrapped in a shawl, muttering that her mother would never have let her leave France if she had known.

"I'll go and find some glass. They must have some glass, and a glazier."

She scoured the countryside for panes of glass to put in the windows, miming a window with her hands, facing the natives' incomprehension. She dragged a man round to stare at the blank windows with an equal blankness. She puffed out her cheeks and demonstrated: wind! But nobody had any glass, and the man simply shrugged and walked away with the solitary defeated gait of the islanders, who rounded their shoulders against weather and put up with what came. She tore up old clothes into rags to stuff the cracks in the walls. She ripped up packing cases that their books had come in and nailed them over the windows so that they sat in the dark. There was a boy who had goats, she saw him pass on the hill opposite, so she went out after him and asked for fresh milk for the children and Frédéric. Demonstrated again: milking, milk. Pointed at the nearest goat, which stared back with hostile slitty eyes and then walked away, her bag of milk swaying. Tapped her palm, to indicate money. Money, I'll pay you. Milk! Every day. She began to feel demented, acting out these pantomimes before goats and staring foreigners. But the boy nodded and began the next day, delivering a can of warm milk. She wanted to embrace him; it was the first conversation that had worked. He stared at her with big dark serious eyes, pocketed the francs and walked away. But it was a start.

Then there was food. In warm weather you could exclaim with delight about being able to pick fruit off trees, but they needed more than this. She went searching, and found—goat. The nearby villagers had peppers and onions growing in their little plots, and she went and performed another little act: please sell me some of those. Money, ridiculous amounts of it, changed hands. You couldn't care, though: the family had to eat. Goat meat, goat milk, goat cheese. This was what they would eat for six months? Maurice followed a hen and found a nest of eggs and floated them one by one in water to test which were still viable.

"We could hatch one! Then it would lay more."

"You're a good little peasant, Bouli. But how long would we have to wait for her to grow up?"

Where were the pigs? All waiting to be exported to Spain?

She found dandelions and wild parsley, and made a salad, and listened to both children complaining that the milk tasted horrible.

"We want French milk. We don't like this, it tastes wrong."

"Well, there isn't any French milk. Find us a cow, and we'll have some French milk. But this is what we have, drink it, it's delicious."

Frédéric said, "I can't work without a decent piano, this is an insult. What on earth has happened to the one we ordered from France?"

"I'll find out. It's bound to be on its way, don't worry, Frycek, I'll go down to Palma again and send a letter, tomorrow."

Manuel Marliani had ordered one for them from Pleyel. It would take months perhaps, and cost seven hundred francs. Maurice sketched the little house and the trees around it; but he had to have proper lessons in the mornings to keep up with his studies. She started teaching him Thucydides; he paced the house chanting in Greek. Solange was sent to pick up leaves and fruit and do drawings of them, which she quickly tired of, so she wandered off and was found tormenting a stray cat which wouldn't play the game she wanted. In between, and when the day was over, George wrote. At night, into the small hours, a thick cloak around her shoulders and the wind whistling through the cracks, Frédéric coughing in the next room. A doctor came to call and charged forty-five francs for telling them it was nothing, and prescribing nothing except marshmallow, so the children giggled and called him Dr. Marshmallow. Another doctor gave them a note to take to a pharmacy in Palma, but when she went all the way there to get medicine, she found that there was nothing on the shelves. The rain fell and the house leaked; Frédéric coughed; and at last there came a letter from their landlord, the standoffish Señor Gomez, telling them that they were harbouring a person who was harbouring a disease which was intensely infectious and would be bound to pollute his house and infect his entire family, and would they please leave without delay.

"Solange, you are not to bring that cat in here, it probably has fleas, take it out at once! Amélie, come out of that corner you're hiding in and take care of her. You can both go out and look for quartz, and don't come back till you've found some."

"But, Madame, it is raining."

"A little rain never hurt anyone. When I was a child I was always playing out in the rain. Now go!"

She could feel her temper rising each time she was crossed. Now, they would have to pack up and find somewhere else to live, and she did not know how on earth they could do that, so she set off to speak to the French consul in Palma. Wearing a skirt, and her white cashmere shawl fastened with the golden dagger pin.

Frédéric—"our invalid," as she was to refer to him when she wrote about it later—was by now in no state to be moved. News travels fast in a country place, as she knew from the gossip around Nohant, and probably everyone was going to treat them like pariahs. Anyone kind enough or free-thinking enough to offer them shelter would risk being hounded in his turn.

"But of course, you must all stay here until you have found something else." Pierre-Hippolyte Fleury, the French consul, was delighted to be visited by the famous Madame Sand and her entourage, and politely said nothing about infection. At So'n Vent she had had to pay Señor Gomez back not only for the bedding that had to be burned, but the cost of replastering and whitewashing the walls, which he said was the Spanish law.

They had already seen the charterhouse at Valldemossa on a visit there in November. A couple was living there, the man a Spanish political refugee whose name was Ignacio Durán. She had got talking to him and his sad-faced beautiful wife, as they both spoke some French, and heard that they were planning to leave the country, so their rustic cell would be free. They were leaving their furniture, so it would even be furnished. For a thousand francs—"a modest sum," she wrote ironically—they had a completely furnished household, which would have cost them only about half that in France. So in mid-December they moved up to rocky Valldemossa in the northern mountains of Majorca, to the charterhouse perched on the side of a mountain which in winter the sun never touched, and where even at midday no light came in to the monks' cells. Ah, it would be wonderful, it was so romantic, it was the monastery in *Lélia* whose ruins she had described, it was the one she had imagined in *Spiridion*. Here she would be able to write. Abandoned monasteries were just what a writer needed for atmosphere. For a moment, she forgot Frédéric's illness and the cold. The roast fowl and Rhône wine at the French consul's house, and five nights in a comfortable feather bed had brought back her enthusiasm.

The day they moved in was fine and cold at the beginning of winter, and the mountains, as she remembered, were purple and pink in the late sun, the air clean enough to drink, the silence of the crags so intense that you could hear voices right across the valley, where two invisible people called out to each other; the intimacy of that exchange in the valley filled with mist.

"Maman, are you sure this is a good idea?" Maurice again, as the carts struggled up the mountain track, the mules straining, mud clogging the wheels.

"Oh, you'll see, when we get there it will be marvellous. You remember the old monks' cells? You remember the wonderful view? And the eagles, on the rocks? And the sunset?"

They were living in two rooms, she and the children in one, including Amélie, who was simply another homesick child with no desire to be of any use at all, Frédéric in the other. There was a table and chair for her writing, and in his there would be room for the piano. There was nowhere to cook, so they had to ask the neighbour, the woman who lived in the next-door cell, to cook for them. But at least there was a fireplace.

"Aurora, I need my own piano if we're going to stay here all winter."

He complained about it daily, and she said she had done what she could and would do more. She investigated and found that the piano had arrived—it was just before

Christmas—and was being held by Customs in Palma. She went by mule all the way back down to Palma to bribe the port authorities to release it. It cost three hundred francs, almost as much as the piano had cost in the first place. Then it had to be carted all the way up the narrow pitted roads to Valldemossa. She'd learned enough Spanish by now to argue with port officials, sailors, grocers, neighbours. She stood shouting at the carters not to damage the piano, as the mules strained and so did the ropes, and she and Maurice struggled in the mud and Frédéric hid indoors because he couldn't stand the sight. He'd be waiting for her when she came into the house.

"I need fresh milk. We need oil—this oil is rancid. We can't eat goat meat again. Will you please find me some meat that isn't goat?"

"Yes, of course, I'll go this afternoon."

"No," she said to anyone they met. "It isn't infectious, it's just a bad cold. Just catarrh."

And then, often, "Where are the children? I asked you to keep an eye on them." She wanted to know, coming back in. Here, running about on the precipitous crags, they could easily get lost, or fall and hurt themselves.

"They insisted on going out, I haven't seen them for hours. Really, Aurora, they are going to run completely wild if you don't look after them better."

She chased the children through forests, shouting their names to make them come indoors; a woman in trousers and stout boots, shouting in a foreign language, the villagers would hear her, think her crazy, but it was too bad.

"You have to come in now, you have lessons to do. Do you want to grow up illiterate, so that anybody can take advantage of you?"

She saw Maurice's resentment of Frédéric in his sulkiness. "He doesn't do anything at all to help, Maman, and I hate that music, it's so depressing."

Solange teased him, pretending to be a ghost haunting the cell. She moved his things around and told him there must be a poltergeist. But she watched his hands on the piano keys and asked him, would he teach her to play. He was too busy. Later. "He's always saying, later! Why won't he teach me now?"

At night, when everyone was asleep and the music from his room no longer distracted her, she lit the lamp, wrapped herself in her shawl again and wrote her new novel, until three or four in the morning, to earn the money to keep them all alive.

"It's cold, you never said it was going to be this cold. People here are so narrow-minded, there's nobody one even wants to talk to. I wish I'd never left Paris. You spend too much time with the children. This bread is inedible. I must have fresh milk, you must go and find me some fresh milk. The piano has been ruined in transit. The damp is so bad for it, it needs tuning. Where can we find a piano tuner in this damned country? These people are savages.

You don't love me any more, it's perfectly clear. It's all your fault that I'm here at all, Aurora, risking my death; if it wasn't for your lies about sunshine and warmth, I would be safe in Paris." Her beloved Frédéric complained incessantly.

And the Majorcans complained. The man was sick. He had an infectious disease. The woman was immoral, her books were immoral, the children ran wild, her requests for food were unreasonable, none of them ever went to church, their accents were impossible to understand. And what were they doing here? Why had they come from France all the way to Majorca? Were they on the run? Were they criminals?

The bitter paths of Majorca. He composed all day, she wrote all night.

"Aurora, I would rather sleep alone, if you don't mind; you disturb me when you come in the small hours, I can never get to sleep again."

"All right. I would hate to disturb you, you need your sleep." But she knew, by now, from the way he put her firmly away from him, from his turning away. She wept, and had pains in her stomach; but to him she would not complain.

He said, "I would hate to think that my mother might hear about us. She would suffer so. My family must never know."

"Isn't it rather late for that?"

"I was wrong to embark on that kind of relationship with you, it is not worthy of us, it will drag us both down. From now on we must live as friends."

But she would try to find a piano tuner for him, wouldn't she? And she would stop what she was doing to come and listen to this piece?

The music astonished her. Ballads and preludes, all the music he had contracted to send to Paris to pay for his part of the trip. Two extraordinary nocturnes, one after the other. He was serious, and in his music she rediscovered the seriousness of her love for him. Meanwhile she was trying to rewrite *Lélia* yet again and finish working on *Spiridion*. She too had her contract with Buloz at the *Revue des Deux Mondes* to honour. Work had to go on.

⟳

People are taking photographs. They have come there quite easily in huge buses, they are from England, Germany, France, Austria, the United States. Ignoring them all, a woman is potting geraniums, out in the little cell gardens, in worn earthenware pots, in the last of the winter afternoon sun, against a wall. Behind her there's the famous view, mountains, the black spread hand of a palm tree against the sunset, the bay of Palma far away, a strip of dark silk beneath the sky. Her hand in the earth cradling the roots of geraniums, perhaps about to take them in from the frost. Frost is cruel, it snaps plants in two, crushes flowers to damp spots, cuts through layers of clothing to the frail flesh of humans. The sun leaves the mountain. The steep sides of surrounding crags, the deep forests in shadow. Frédéric must have felt it like an attack, the cold. Here it's a drier cold, at least, than in the house in the valley. Here, George's children ran about in the woods and didn't feel it. She could have been in Nohant, or Paris, but instead, as so many romantic travellers do, she chose this discomfort and called it freedom.

Maria thinks, so she took on educating her children herself, writing a new novel to provide all the material needs of her little family, in short, responsibility for everything. Was she trying to be Napoleon Bonaparte, as well as the mother she never really had? What is it that makes us take on the nearly impossible? Why become Chopin's mother, for God's sake, looking after a man who will never look after her? For the music? For the nocturnes and the polonaises, for the sweet unforgettable notes that will last forever, long after her words are forgotten?

"Look," she says to Edward. "It's actually her handwriting." Here are the objects, her portrait, his death mask, her pen, his piano: the relics. They have come all the way up here in a hired car, to see the cell where George Sand and Chopin lived. Yesterday Edward was at the botanical garden at Soller, to talk to the seed man, today is for George and Frédéric.

The idyll. The place where two geniuses lived and loved. The guide is telling them, but Maria already knows. She knows how it must have been. Nobody could have written such a bad-tempered piece as *Winter in Majorca* unless they were having a perfectly terrible time. She's discovered the complaints that even this writer could not hold back.

"Jesus, it's cold," says Edward.

"Well, it's winter. Imagine what it would be like to live here for months. I wonder if winters were as cold then? It's hardly the place for someone with TB. But look, at least they had a fireplace, that was something."

Maria glances around her, a heaviness in the centre of her chest, as if she has swallowed something whole. The things, the death mask, her pen, his piano, her manuscripts in ink aged brown like blood. (What if her things and Edward's were to be left on view for posterity? Would anyone be able to guess any of what they were going through? What chance does truth have, so slight, so small, so hard to seize, when myths are invoked?) The photographs are taken here, people look through lenses, click incessantly, little lights flash in cameras, the guidebooks all say the same thing. Aurore Dupin is forgotten here, or rather, obliterated, a travesty is left behind. The Majorcan critic José María Cuadrado's words, and Robert Graves', are the ones in the guidebooks, not her own, because the Majorcans are still furious with her, even after all this time.

Maria turns and finds Edward has gone outside. The huge buses turn in the square, the drivers are bored but have to be here to earn their money from tourists. The sun is sinking, the chill grey of a January evening moves across the mountain, you can hardly breathe the air in its sudden sharpness, it's like drinking iced water. It's dark early, because the sun vanishes behind the mountain. There'll be, always has been, a long night. The cells where the monks lived were unheated, probably to further mortify the flesh; now, today, in this century, the corridors are like refrigerators. She hurries outside to join Edward, who is staring out over the valley, his shoulders hunched in his leather jacket, his scarf tightened around his neck. Only the sky in its green-apple purity at sunset gives any hint that the sun will rise again tomorrow, and the smoky fires in the valley tell of householders warming themselves at dusk. The guardian comes to lock up the relics for the night. Up the road there's a new development, the Urbanización George Sand.

"Have you seen enough?" Edward turns from the greying view, and the car is only feet away.

"Hmm. Yes. Let's get a drink, and some dinner." She shivers, and the habit of taking his arm and hugging his side is so strong that she does it again without thinking.

He detaches himself, moves a few inches away.

"Okay, we'll get dinner, we'll go back to the hotel, but we have to see this thing out, Maria, it's no good going on pretending. I want to know who he is, where you met, how long this has been going on, and what you plan to do about it. You can't go on pretending nothing's happened. I'm not stupid. I want to know."

"What?" she answers in a small voice.

Darkness fills the valley, the lights of fires are tiny down there, it's as if the whole world is showing them how small and insignificant they are. Why does it have to be here, why can't he wait till they're indoors, warm, fed, at least? Or does he want to make her feel this forsaken?

"What I said. Who, where, how often, the details." He shivers and yet still doesn't turn to go.

"Why does that matter?"

"If you don't know, Maria, Christ, if you can't imagine, you must be even more of a cretin than I thought. If you chose to risk our marriage, if you decided to chuck all this over just for some, what, sexual thrills you don't get from me, then you have to pay for it. I have to know, and you have to tell me."

She thinks, it's his sense of order I have offended; he needs categories, he needs to know what goes where, and I have broken this open and introduced chaos.

"Can we at least leave here and go somewhere warmer?"

"It was you who wanted to come here. Your research, as you call it, following that damn woman all around Europe. I don't give a damn about George Sand, or Chopin for that matter, and I'm frozen, and we should never have come on this bloody trip. I should have waited till spring, and come alone. But yes, we can go somewhere warmer, or we'll freeze to death and that'll be that."

She knows him well enough to hear in the tone of his voice, even with the harshness, just how miserable he is, and again she wants to take his arm, but doesn't dare.

"Come on then. Drive me somewhere warm. We'll talk." It's a huge effort for her to get these words out, and she even sees her breath puff out on the freezing air. But the habit of conciliation is this strong. She can say it. She can be kind to him. They are far from home. But what will happen next, unless he thaws a little, unless he lets go of some of that misery, she can't imagine.

The bitter paths of Majorca. Later, she understands that till he was cold enough, hungry enough, and felt far enough from home, he wasn't able to feel what he wanted to feel, which was angry with her, bitter, reproachful, hateful. Only standing there in the cold outside the cells at Valldemossa is he able to feel as bad as he wants to, and give vent to it. She's given him the pretext and the climate has confirmed it: he's been abandoned, cheated, frozen out, made to feel this isolated, driven to hate. And she, standing there beside him, feels terrified, because he has begun to destroy their life together. Now that they both know, it's inevitable. They have begun the real unravelling.

In the restaurant where they have dinner, on their way back to town and the hotel where the beds, luckily or unluckily, are twins, and where their habitual closeness can't be had casually, they drink wine in thick glasses and order bowls of Majorcan soup. He's embarrassed, looking at her. Suddenly what he said to her at Valldemossa seems extreme, absurd. It isn't in their register of behaviour. It came in from the outside like a sudden cold wind.

He says, "I'm sorry, I didn't mean to be that hard on you. I didn't mean it, that I don't care about George Sand. I'm sure your book's going to be great."

She feels the weight of his effort to be polite. He wants to mend this, surely.

"Thanks." She holds the wineglass, through which lamp-light winks. The soup comes, thick and hot and smelling of winter vegetables and garlic.

"I don't mean that I want to know everything. I probably don't. It would probably be too painful."

So they are suspended again above the abyss of what might have been. The raucous cry of the eagle on the mountaintop, the one George heard, and Chopin, has sounded but only its echo remains. What now? They turn almost tender with each other, wanting to heal wounds, make peace.

"I'm so sorry to have hurt you," says Maria; and again, she gives him that look, the over-the-soup-spoon look, that he noticed during lunch in Soller.

They have too much between them, surely, to be able to destroy it. But there are also the facts, the hard facts.

Infidelity is a fact. Sex with another, an act. You have to draw the lines, make things clear.

"You don't know him," says Maria. "At least, you may have met, once. But it doesn't matter, does it, who he is?" She thinks, am I about to betray him? Meaning the other one, Sean, the young man she loves, but in a different way from how she loves her husband. It seems inevitable. Men sniff up betrayal like hounds on a trail. It's everywhere, in storage somehow, waiting to be acted upon. She thinks of George, going back to Nohant with Chopin after their journey here, her "Chip," her "Chopinet," and the way she knew, as soon as he was installed in her house, that he was not going to tolerate any relationship she might have with another man. Did he know about Jules Sandeau? Musset? Aurélien de Sèze? Michel de Bourges? He didn't want her himself—not in "that way," the way that made him blush, and worry about his mother—but he didn't want anyone else to have her either. So she groaned and sometimes wept at the bottom of the garden at night, and then went back in, to write.

That was then, thinks Maria, and this is now, and has anything improved? Edward eats opposite her at yet another table, and gives her a cautious look, and mops his mouth with his napkin, and in the corner a fire burns, and the room grows warm around them and smells of the smoke of old fires. She loves him, she thinks, because he is here. It's the only reason. Perhaps it's enough. But for him, it isn't enough, for him she has to be not only here in front of him but his, exclusively. She is not to have anyone else in her thoughts, in her memory. With the same narrow-minded urgency that makes him focus on the nearly extinct plants of Majorca, the one with the Latin name that no one can find, he wants her exclusive love. Suddenly she remembers a photograph of him when young, eight years old, hair cropped in defiance of the sixties, a school cap on his head, being sent away to school. The young Edward, already baffled by loss.

"If it doesn't matter, then why aren't you telling me?"

"Because it will make things worse." Now, she simply wants not to hurt him.

"How can they possibly be worse?"

"It's worse to think about a real person than an imaginary one."

"But he's real, isn't he? You didn't imagine him?"

"No, he's real. But it's not the way you think. In a way, it isn't anything to do with you."

Steam rises between them. His spoon in mid-air.

"How can it not be to do with me? It's me you've been deceiving all this time—and you still haven't told me *how* long—so of course it's to do with me."

It's only because there's a table between them now, Maria thinks, and food, a tablecloth, cutlery, plates, a waiter coming back to ask what they would like next, that they can have the conversation this way. They are not any longer in front of an abyss, with eagles cawing and a cold mountain. You have to make things possible. You have to find a way through, that people can bear. She moves her heavy knife about on the tablecloth and looks at him, pleading with him, to see this, to understand. She wants to say, only it may be too definite, that she doesn't even know if her love affair will continue. The way the story will go isn't at all sure. Sitting here with him now, there is no doubt about which of them is the more real to her; it's as if Sean has become a tributary of the main river of her life, but one which she has to follow. She can bring him to mind, thin and white and vivid, with his shock of curly hair, his Irish voice, the way he has of smoothing the hair back from her face, studying her bones as he lies above her. There's the movement of them together, the flash in darkness, there and then gone as he gets up to leave. But this is all. Compared to him, Edward is multifaceted, with the everyday—moods, arguments, a million conversations. But she can't explain this. With Sean she is a narrow, intense version of herself, a version she loves; it's like meeting herself truly for the first time. He speaks love to her in the Irish language, with its softness, its vowels like water and its consonants like the lightest touch. She looks at Edward, who is looking back at her as if both of them are awaiting a prompter, someone to move them on into the next thing.

He's still struggling with the demands of facts, and she's off, he thinks, into fiction. He can never pin her down, and it infuriates him. Where, who, how long, these are easy factual things to say. Why can't she stick to the facts, so that they can see where they are?

Maria says only, "Well, for some time. A few months. Perhaps nearly a year. Only, not often. Not often at all." She thinks, compared to twenty years, day in, day out, with you. Anything beside this heavy, steady duration is light, insubstantial. A butterfly, fluttering past an elephant. Can't he see that?

"Oh. Is that supposed to be a consolation?"

"Yes."

"Well, it isn't. Where do you—did you—meet?"

"Here and there. At the university. In a bookshop."

"A bookshop?"

"Yes."

"You can't have sex in a bookshop."

He isn't usually this crude. Pain has sharpened him, changed his voice's register.

"No, I'm not talking about sex. We met in a bookshop."

"That wasn't what I asked you." Pedantic, now.

"Yes, it was."

He glares and tears bread in half. The waiter comes back. What would they like now? Fish, meat, a stew, specialty of the house, made with—how do you say it?—wild pig. They nod vaguely at the wild pig, to make the waiter go away, to make life go on. Do you remember, they may say to each other one distant day, when we had—how do you say it?—wild pig, for dinner? There's still a hope in each of them that comes with this thought, that this will not be the end. That they may laugh about it later, the way you laugh about dangers narrowly avoided. She still hopes so.

Maria says, after sipping her wine, "You will be much happier not knowing. Men always want to fight duels, make scenes, when they know. It's the other man, the one who's not you, that's all they can see, and it makes them wild. So I don't think I'll tell you any more." She thinks of George reading Louise Colet's mean-spirited book *Lui*, the novel she brought out in 1859 after Musset's death, in which she, George disguised as Antonia, describes how Musset could only have infrequent and painful erections. What good did it do, to know the details? Once you begin explaining, accusing, judging, you are lost.

"Oh, so, you know all about it? Men, huh? You're the expert, suddenly. You know how men think, what we feel. Well, let me tell you, my dear wife, you don't know anything at all."

He sounds like a hostile stranger. She thinks how George Sand managed the men in her life, one after the other; while Anaïs Nin, she suddenly remembers, kept a husband on each coast, one on the east, one on the west, and left them to meet up at her own funeral, decades later. There is still no blueprint; still nobody knows what to do. The only thing you can hope for is a little space, in which to try to be yourself.

A white plate arrives in front of him, filled to the brim with meat swimming in juice dark as chocolate, and he gasps a little. Maria's plate arrives next. The aromas are hot and complex. This is a dish which demands their full attention. The waiter, with his eyes like olives shining in oil, stands back and lifts his hands as if he's delivered the last word.

They begin to eat.

Back in the hotel room with the twin beds—the beds for tourists, so much more practical, nobody really wants a double bed these days, you can rent like this to anyone, the hotel manager knows—she sits down on one, he on the other. The conversation, or interrogation, has been stopped and may not begin again. On the other hand, you have to say something when you are sitting opposite each other on single beds; it isn't like being on a big double bed where you can just lie down and not speak, except out of habit, out of the ease of a long life together in one bed, out of a practised peace.

"I'm going to read, okay?" says Edward at last. He turns on his bedside lamp, reaches for his much-thumbed hardback *Illustrated Flora of Majorca*. In the pile beside his bed he has also the *Botanical Journal of the Linnean Society* and *Observations on Plant Taxa Endemic to the Balearic Islands*. He has made sure that he always has enough to read.

"Me too." Maria picks up *Un Hiver à Majorque,* the French edition because she wants the exact words and phrases.

They read until one of them snaps off a light, and the other follows. It's possible after all that habit, a certain kindness, a way of going on that skirts precipices, avoids abysses, will dictate what happens now. Reading may soothe them where nothing else will. Marriage, Maria thinks, is like this. Just when you think everything is crashing and falling around you and you will be left among the debris, alone, something happens. Something else is put in front of you—a plate of food, a book with a new proposition—and you take it with relief, as if from a *deus ex machina,* who arrives just at the right minute and removes the controls from your hand. Yes, if there were a big old saggy welcoming bed, they might well have rolled together half-asleep and begun the lazy, easy first movements of lovemaking, grown into over twenty years; and then who knew what would happen next. But the Majorcan Tourist Board has seen to it that there is not.

On the return journey the ship was full of pigs. It was the old tub the British had sold cheap, *El Mallorquin* again, that went back and forth in the 1830s from Barcelona to Majorca: it arrived in Majorca empty of non-human passengers and returned with two hundred pigs on board and a few human passengers thrown in. The stench was bad enough, but the groans of the seasick pigs at night were heart-rending and kept them all awake.

"Maman, the pigs are sick!" Solange said, tugging at her dress. "Maman, Maman, the pigs are sick!"

"Yes, I know, *chérie*. Poor pigs. But we will soon arrive."

Then, there was the question of Frédéric's illness. George had tried to keep it as quiet as possible, but he looked ill, the cough sounded terrible, and people talked.

"Señora, he cannot sleep in the best bed in the cabin," said the captain, "because we will have to burn it, and I would prefer to burn a less good bed. You understand?"

"No, I do not understand. Go back to your pigs, and leave us in peace!" She was in no mood to compromise, or be polite. "If you can't give us a good bed, we're not staying on your damn ship. Will you please take us back to port?" But there was no question of that, so they spent a day and night listening to the pigs squealing, and both Amélie and Solange vomited, one beginning where the other left off.

After this, they stayed in Barcelona for another two weeks, waiting for a French boat, *Le Phénicien*, to take them back to Marseille. Compared with any Spaniard, the French captain was a veritable angel, George protested with unusual patriotism; and of course, he was not an illiterate, not like the Majorcan sailors. Oppression made people behave like pigs.

"They are like pigs," Solange said, with her usual self-satisfaction. "The pigs are like people and the people are like pigs."

George flirted with the angelic French captain and he took the mattress off his own bed to give to Frédéric. When she came to pay, the Frenchman said she was offering too much; whereas the Majorcan had tried to make her pay double for transporting an invalid. How good it was going to be to get back to their own country! Oh, what a relief to be able to speak French again and be understood.

So, with the kind, solicitous and gentlemanly French captain of *Le Phénicien*—such a gentleman, such an angel, she said over and over till he almost believed it himself— they came back to Marseille, where they had to stay for ten days, until the stink of the streets, with the garbage spilling everywhere, was unbearable.

"Ah, this city, it is too uncivilized!"

They tried to find a house in Aix, or Avignon, but there was nothing to be had. Frédéric had to be made stronger before they could travel home to Nohant. On arrival in Marseille, he weighed only ninety-five pounds.

Nohant would be green, cool, just as it had always been. (That first time, coming home with her parents and the sick baby, her cool room, her grandmother's cool hands, the boy who threw stones up at the window and said that he was her brother . . .) Chopin would say again how it reminded him of the tree-lined avenues of his birthplace in Poland, and collapse into its comfort.

But the love affair was over; he told her he couldn't possibly share her bed again, even when he was better, and besides, the act of love was a bestial one, and he liked to think their relationship was above all that. She would go out into the dark, then, and smoke beside the river, listening to its flow in the night beyond the willows, and sometimes she would slip off her clothes and swim. Then she would go in to write, till dawn. In the daytime, she gave him all the attention he needed, brought him grapes, figs, the newspaper come from Paris, and smiled to hide her frustration.

So when Edward insists, "How long?" Maria finally admits, "A year."

"A year! You've been lying to me for a year!"

"Not lying. Just, not telling."

"It's the same thing."

"No, it isn't, not exactly. There are things you don't tell me, and I don't say you're lying."

"If I were having an affair, if I'd been having an affair for a year, you would."

"Maybe, maybe not."

"Maria, what is the matter with you? Have you lost all sense of reality?"

"No," she says, and knows suddenly that their marriage is not going to last beyond the airport in Palma and the flight home. That will be the end of it. It's like watching someone cast a line, hook a fish, pull it struggling to the surface. Some things can't survive being pulled to the surface, and they die. She says, "I know it's hard for you to understand, but we just fell in love with each other, that was all."

"No, it wasn't all, you had sex with him, didn't you? You still haven't told me, where, how many times?"

They're driving towards it now, hard and fast in their hired car, on the last afternoon, coming into the airport area, their plane maybe already on the ground, a flight crew preparing for them, takeoff only a matter of hours. Straight down the new road, no mountain roads and passes now, into the suburb of Palma where the airport is, towards their agreed end. She notices that it's the sex, not a mention of love, that has infuriated him, as if falling in love may be got over, but sex, never. It's like an obsession with actual virginity, a focus on the factual, a kind of fundamentalism that amazes her. What she feels for Sean, after all, is inexplicable: there are no words, none of the current expressions will do.

"No, and I'm not going to, it isn't the point. I didn't marry him, I didn't spend twenty years with him, I didn't buy and live in a house with him, I don't have teenage children with him."

"But in doing what you did, you undermined all those things. None of those things count now. They've all been wiped out. They don't exist." His hands high on the wheel, eyes on the road, jaw tense, his blond hair blowing up slightly in the breeze from the half-open window; a handsome man, her husband, telling her that she has with one movement—that fluid movement of hers that he has never seen—wiped out the whole of their life together.

"What, by sleeping with another man?"

"Sleeping!" he snorts. "Having sex. Committing adultery. Fornicating. That's what you've been doing. Sleep probably didn't come into it."

Those afternoons, after her classes, before the children came home, before Sean went back to the university, to work late at his research into the human immune system, the white mice and sometimes rats being tested for their reaction to what might kill humans; those snowy afternoons lightening into spring, and his car parked on her street, the curtains drawn against snow and darkness, then against the light of summer; a year, passed behind those curtains that fluttered when they opened the windows, pushed back the shutters, and when they lay watching the streetlights come on behind them, made them feel as if they were in a cocoon, evolving, becoming something else. The softness of wings unfurling and the grip of the strange creature they had given birth to, that still hung on its branch, evolving. You could say, people did, that it was just sex. But what about sex that involves the whole of you, that transforms you, turns you inside out so that you feel new-born, licked into life? The trouble is, sex makes something happen; and it makes some of life not matter any more. There is more to it than people ever admit. And the ones who know this are not saying.

Maria says nothing, because there's nothing she can say. Everything she might say will make matters worse. In our house, in our spare bedroom, before the children came home, twice a week, while you were at work; she can't say it, it will make him drive off the road. Or, one time Emily came home early and it's possible she may have seen us. There are some things, many things probably, that it's better not to know. But she thinks sadly, briefly, of the flora of Majorca, as carefully drawn by Edward, which are a microcosm of the whole Mediterranean world, and that now, if he means what he says, she won't be living with them any more. She will miss the story of the mountain plant with the small white flowers that the goats like to eat, and she wonders if he will miss George Sand.

There are all the hundreds of details which will change: habits, conversations, glances in passing; irritations, jokes, disagreements, all the minutiae that add up to the huge reality of living together. Hundreds of uneventful evenings, thousands of meals. She can't take it in, will perhaps never be able to; or may only after years spent apart. She and Edward have made something together, almost in spite of themselves, which he says must be demolished. She sees a wrecking ball swing towards a solid building, and the dust fly. What she has done seems so small beside the enormity of what he proposes. What she has done is a small green plant splitting the concrete; it is not a wrecking ball. The shocking difference of their individual visions of life has come into the open. It's as if they have gone back to the beginning again, annihilating everything they have done together. To a place where there is suddenly no future, where real life does not count.

3

REAL LIFE

BENEATH THE TREES, French nineteenth-century trees, the giant pine and the chestnut and the spreading lime, people sat about. Someone passed the cups. A child giggled and scratched herself in the sun. In the chairs in the shade, adults were talking. A woman was doing embroidery, her head bent, her slight fingers nimble with the needle, so that no one could tell what she was thinking. The afternoon stretched, there were long hours between meals. Pale violets grew in clumps beneath the lime tree in among last year's leaves. The house at Nohant was closed against the sun, but suddenly a boy jumped out of one of the windows and landed in the grass. Someone was drawing a portrait. It was Eugène Delacroix, come for a month from Paris. Upstairs, he had a studio with everything he needed, but out here there was more air. The sitter, come from the village, moved in her chair and the portrait was disturbed, a line lost, never to be regained. The artist wiped his forehead with a hand-kerchief, began again.

Letters came by the morning's mail and were read and tossed aside, leaving no trace on the surface, like stones dropped into the river, although they would be kept for a hundred years. Words, in the heat of afternoon, were few and far between; it was such an effort to speak. In the distance, change could be gathering: revolution, or war. What mattered was that the plums were picked and brought in for jam-making, that this evening's dinner was prepared, that a horse was re-shod, a wall repaired, the borders weeded, the flowers arranged, the vegetables watered at sunset, the new dog made at home, the children kept from idleness, a new tutor found for Maurice, who would otherwise go on jumping out of windows.

George raised her head and frowned. She heard music coming from the shuttered rooms of the house. He never would come out of doors in the afternoons, and was always pale as a turnip. The phrase repeated, slower, in another key. She felt a sharp discomfort, thought of two people coming together in a room where the only light was a burning fire and flesh touched flesh; chased the thought away. Solange, who had been yawning and scratching, jumped up suddenly and went into the house. George wanted to call out, don't disturb him! But stopped herself. Let things fall where they must. Then she heard the twinned notes of a duet, the music climbing, his melody, her boisterous refrain. The afternoon shifted, shadows began to lengthen. Somebody carried a tray back into the house. Then the chairs were all vacant, an emptied circle beneath the trees. This summer, and all the other summers, life going on.

She found a donkey for him to ride, so that he could go on picnics with them all and not get exhausted. The donkey, named Margot, followed her round, nipping at her pockets where she kept crusts of bread, and turned to kick when she did not feed her. On the donkey's back, Frédéric with his long legs dangling, a straw hat on his head, Solange, his favourite, marching at his side.

One year, he brought a machine for making ice cream.

One year they arrived in a calèche, the next it was possible to go as far as Orléans by train.

In the early morning, an owl regularly dropped its small parcel of bones upon the doorstep, where it was the first thing she saw, opening the door at dawn.

When they returned from Majorca, she'd spent ten days with him in Marseille, trying to decide whether or not to go on to Italy, as Frédéric had been prescribed a month of absolute rest. Dr. François Cauvière, a friend of the Marlianis who had shipped the Pleyel piano to Majorca, took them in for a few days to his own house and then found them lodgings in the Hôtel de la Darse, owned by Manuel Marliani's brother. But she owed money: the fortune she had been left had all been used up by Casimir, Nohant was hers but the money to keep it up was lacking. She must write to earn it. She wrote to Buloz at the *Revue des Deux Mondes* asking him to advance her some more money, since the manuscript of *Lélia*, posted in Barcelona, was stuck in the labyrinth of the Marseille post office and could not be found, even if she shouted. She would retrieve it and send it to Charlotte Marliani in Paris, and then Buloz could pay her the seventy-five hundred francs in the contract. But the Marseille post office took a week to find the manuscript, although she went there every day. Buloz sent five hundred francs and reminded her she owed him forty-five hundred from an advance he had made her four years earlier. Probst, the music dealer, sent Chopin five hundred francs instead of the promised fifteen hundred for the twenty-four preludes he had posted from Majorca. So there was little either of them could do except stay put, fume about their respective publishers, and complain about the smells of Marseille.

She went to answer the knock at the door several times a day. "No, Monsieur Chopin cannot see you, he is resting. I myself am ill, so is he. I warn you to keep away." Next time, she swore repeatedly, she would announce that they were both dead.

The literary mob was at her heels, having discovered their whereabouts, and the musical mob was at his. But he was getting better.

By April he was putting on weight. "I think I'll take a glass of Champagne. And why don't we hire a carriage and go out for a drive by the sea?"

"You'll soon be as fat as a pig, my darling."

"Ugh, don't talk to me about pigs."

But they still slept apart, and touched only in passing, like young students too shy to go any further, and she guessed that this was how it would be from now on, and that also he would not tolerate another lover in her life. She thought briefly of Michel, to whom she had not written in months. Would he still be there on her return to Nohant? Probably he'd fallen in love with someone else by now; and anyway, she felt old, past it, she told herself, and with her Chopinet so fragile, only just coming back to life, how could she inflict on him that particular pain?

Maria stops writing as if listening for a voice that has grown faint. She's drawn in, fascinated, on the trail of something; but what? Ah, she has heard the telephone, that modern version of the unexpected knock upon the château's door and the person standing waiting on the threshold.

It could be him. She can't risk leaving it to the answering machine. (Imagining Edward, "Who was that? Someone wanting you, sounded Irish to me.") Though of course Sean would not leave a message. (Why doesn't he ring her on her mobile?) She thinks once again that as long as no truths are told, no crimes confessed, no words put to anything, life is smooth and easy and completely manageable. Now, Edward is constantly suspicious, and when he leaves the house and comes back to it again, he casts a malevolent glance around him like someone in a bad thriller. They haven't talked about what they will do, and Maria is relieved, but worries that the day will come. Meanwhile, meeting Sean here has become impossible. They have hunched over expensive coffee in a café on the far side of town where no one, they think, will see them, and tried to make plans. Hotels seem too sordid, someone will see them going in or out, this is a small community after all, and Edinburgh isn't Paris, where a room can be rented by the hour. There are her students, his colleagues in the School of Medicine, her friends, Edward's friends, the risks are everywhere.

He can't, he says, get away for a night in a hotel out of town. They have nobody to lend them a room.

"It's far worse than the nineteenth century!" she exclaims to him over the frothy coffee and pastries, things she never usually eats. He's eating as if he were famished. Two Danish down and one to go.

"Why the nineteenth century?" he wants to know.

His face is very pale, she can see the black points of stubble pointing through his skin, and his eyes are blue-shadowed. He looks as if he has not been getting much sleep. A muscle jumps in his jaw.

"Oh, just that I'm spending so much time in it, with George Sand. She had lovers, and nobody seems to have cared. Well, she had a château in the country, I suppose that helped."

"And it wasn't Scotland."

"No, it wasn't."

"Or Ireland. If we'd been in nineteenth-century Ireland, we'd probably have been flogged by now, by some venal old priest. Excommunicated, at the very least."

"Ugh. We're better off here. But I still can't think of anything. There is Anne, though. Maybe I could ask Anne."

Anne Fleming, who lives alone, teaches the eighteenth century and has a flat high up near the castle, on the right side of town. Maria has thought a couple of times of confiding in her, since she once wrote a book about *Claire d'Albe,* the daring French novel which came out in 1799, presenting adulterous love as a positive act of self-definition and liberation. Did George Sand, she wonders, read *Claire d'Albe?* But you never can tell what people who write academic studies of books about adultery actually think of the real thing. Also, Anne scares her slightly as a thoroughgoing feminist, who might have feelings about lending her flat for an assignation with a man. "Or, there's Muriel. She lives alone."

"I'd rather you didn't."

Maria thinks, not for the first time, that men need secrecy as they need cars, and clothes, to contain them. "Well, what can you suggest? You come up with something." If she sounds angry, she thinks, it's because she's cold and frustrated and she doesn't see why life has to be so unfair.

"I'll try. Look, Maria, I have to go. They're expecting me back. It's Matthew's birthday, you know. I love you,

I do." And then he says it in Irish, in a phrase he has taught her, and she melts inside in a way she doesn't want to, not today.

She leaves the café with her book under her arm and a swatch of her second-year students' papers in her bag, feeling suddenly more alone than she ever has before. What would George do, why was it easier for George? There was always a room, there must have been, a room in Paris or in the country, a borrowed space, an agreed-upon, allowed time. Probably her lovers just made more of an effort, rather than leaving it all up to her. No, Chopin wouldn't have had a clue about finding a room for them, would he. She tries to imagine him, asking for a room in a Paris hotel, and fails. George would have done it; she was the one who knew the ways of the world and organized everything, and she, Maria, would have to be like that too. But then, Chopin didn't have a wife and four children; just a mother and a Catholic conscience, not so different probably from Sean's. Some things hardly change.

The next time they meet, it's to turn his car and drive south-east out of the city instead of north over the Bridges. They skirt Arthur's Seat to go down through Portobello and Musselburgh and head for Gullane and the beaches along-side the Forth. It's a grey day, rain only just holding off, but at least it's a little warmer. Clouds are deep and dark over the Forth bridges behind them, and lie over the city of hills and spires they are leaving behind, but at least they don't today have the gun-metal tinge of snow in them. Arthur's Seat reaches its black crags out of worn grass into a wreath of cloud. But to the south, it's brighter. Sean drives, one hand on the wheel, the other on her knee.

"I was worried, not to hear from you more. Was it okay?"

"I'm so sorry, I couldn't plug in my mobile, I forgot the adaptor, and I couldn't really ask Edward how to get one in Spanish, or do it without him noticing. We called the children on his." On such things life depends, now. A British gadget that won't fit a Spanish plug. And so, no contact between them for ten days.

"But he knows, right?"

"Yes, I told him. I had to, it was like the Inquisition. But not the details." Sean gives her a sideways glance.

"What did he say?"

"He was furious. He said I'd wrecked our marriage. That in doing what I'd done, I'd undone twenty years of marriage."

"Ah, God love you. That was just him being angry and upset, wasn't it?"

"Well, he's stayed angry and upset. He's got all the moral high ground. I haven't a leg to stand on. I can't justify it at all."

"Except that you fancy me something rotten."

"Yes, but that makes it worse."

"D'you think he'll get over it?"

He turns off the main road to a smaller one that runs between the low-lying hills and the sea, thick bushes of holly and sea buckthorn on both sides. There is a gleam of sudden sun that makes the land for a moment brighter than the sky, a peculiarly Scottish effect.

"No, I don't. It's why I can't take you home now. The whole place is wired like a damn airport. Sirens would go off if you so much as stepped in at the door."

Sean parks, far away from the few other cars, brakes and turns off the engine. He turns to her and his lips cover hers and his warm breath enters her, his hands pull her to him, and there's nobody about in the car park, but still she's nervous, and it's not the same.

They link arms, like siblings rather than lovers, as they walk down the narrow sandy track towards the sea, its grey choppy edges coughing up driftwood and plastic, its comings and goings drawing wet patterns on the sand. Homeless, Maria thinks. They walk along the water's edge, their boots darkening with the wet, and then turn up inland behind a big sandhill, where a path leads between the bents and marram grass. He draws his coat open, shrugs out of it and lays it down in a hollow, under cover of a copse of bent little pine trees, and she lies down with him here, but it's too cold to undress and the small touch of him shrinks in the wind, his buttocks goose-pimpled, and she's lying on a thorn, and all the warmth between them isn't enough.

On the way back, they joke about it, but there's a sadness, all the same. Marriage, thinks Maria, always has a place to be; illicit love, rarely. It feels as if they have been thrown out into the weather, to try to survive.

⁓

The dream was a recurring one, through her childhood, but George did not expect it to echo through the nights of her marriage to Casimir and wake her sweating again when she was back at Nohant with Frédéric.

Her grandmother, before the Revolution, had made journeys from Paris to Nohant as a young woman, crossing through the forests of Orléans. It was always a hazardous journey, on the rutted tracks where brigands might leap out from behind trees and attack. But one image, one thing her grandmother had seen, stayed with her. In the dreams of a nineteenth-century child, an eighteenth-century corpse, that of a woman brigand, dangled from a tree where she had been hanged. She had long black hair. Aurore's mother, Sophie, had long black hair. Was there some unconscious motive in the grandmother's telling this story to the child? Maybe, George thought, she was not really a brigand at all—could there be woman brigands?—but simply a poor woman, desperate with starvation, who had stolen to feed her children. The woman hung and dangled throughout George's childhood, sometimes behind the door, sometimes suspended from a tree in the garden, at other times simply hanging in the dark before her when she opened her eyes in bed. In spite of growing up, in spite of the Revolution, in spite of the Age of Reason and the improvement of roads and the Napoleonic code, she would not go away. History had strung her there for all to see, but particularly for her, the child who was Aurore. The grandmother travelled these roads with trunks and boxes, gloves and hats, smelling-salts and bodyguards. She did it still when Aurore was a child, moving between her house in Paris and the château de Nohant. She remembered these journeys, the deep forests, the silences, the shriek of birds at the roadside; even if there were no rotting bodies, the fear remained. They would just turn the next corner, and there would be the horror, the hanged woman, just waiting.

During the years of her marriage to Casimir, she used to wake with the same desperate feeling, again and again. Something was wrong. A great injustice had been done. The woman who was the victim of it was there again, visible, a warning to all. Now, back in her safe place with her beloved young friend, here it was again.

⁓

Marriage, Maria thinks (agreeing with Casimir Dudevant on this topic, though she isn't aware of the connection), is fine as long as you can also have a lover in your life. She has enjoyed daily life with Edward most of the time and still sees no reason for it to come to an end. Ever since they met, when she was still a student, there has been an easy sense of compatibility, rather than anything more passionate. She herself chose it, Maria knows now, it was not thrust upon her: she wanted to marry a man she did not feel passion for, she opted for something easier. Like George, she would not want to imprison him, or make him be anyone other than he is. If she could choose—which apparently she no longer can—she would choose to go on exactly as before, Edward living with her, Sean visiting. But the dangling woman, the hanged brigand, the outlaw, is in her dreams these days just as she was in George's: there are some things which remain, from century to century, some images of which it's hard to rid ourselves, no matter how we try.

It comes quite soon, the moment she has dreaded without admitting to herself that it is even possible. Sean sits at the wheel of the car, his, that's parked in yesterday's inch of packed snow; it's the following week, and the forecast is yet more snow, the sky blooms with it. He bends his head when he speaks, and Maria has to strain to hear him. He always speaks softly, she's loved the softness of his voice, not the quietness of timidity but a caressing way with consonants that still echoes his Irish ancestry. He's caressing each word now as if he's saying goodbye to it. He's telling her something she can't bear to hear.

He says, "We have to change."

"What do you mean?" She has dreamed this, it has been here always.

"What I mean is, we can't go on."

It seems to be the hardest thing she's ever had to hear. Yet he says it softly, even lovingly. The snow begins to blow thickly on to the windshield. The wheels will soon be up to their hubcaps in snow. The sky is dark and low, flakes thicken and whirl against darkness, always more snow coming, that quietness; it's already at an end, this particular afternoon, and they haven't driven to her house, they haven't warmed themselves and undressed quickly, and come laughing together. She knows now she's going to have to give up everything. It's already done, she hears it in his voice. It's too late to retreat.

She thinks, the world isn't as I thought it was, not at all. It's colder, emptier, harder. There's no protection.

He's trying to soften something. But beside the remorseless softness of the new snow, he's bone-hard; a profile raised against her. His hand on her knee is a goodbye. Nothing has ever been this difficult. Edward moving out was a matter of furniture, arrangements. But now she's in a country she's only guessed at, a Siberia of the heart. It's been there all the time; here, in her own country, near to home, because it can't be travelled to any more than it can be escaped from by travelling. It's now. It's this minute. It's what she has to have next. This terrible quietness, with no reprieve.

He's saying, "So I won't see you, not for a while at least."

It's as if curtains of snow come down and block off the entire world, and then a small circle is inscribed in the whiteness for her to peer through. In reality, the windscreen is covered, he'll have to get out and brush snow away before the wipers can even function. She can't speak. She can't defend herself. There are moments like this, like snowstorms, like strong winds, and you have to bend before them. It isn't about Edward, it isn't about not being able to find a room, her whole house is open to him now that Edward has just left. He's been talking about his wife, his family—four young children, the youngest only a baby—and she knows, she always knew it would come to this.

He says, "You do understand?"

Yes, she understands, not the words so much, or his plans or intentions, but the order of things. This is what life is like. You can't argue with it.

He talks about his marriage, his wife. "You know, she's struggling with it, I don't think she knows about us, exactly, but she knows there is something. Life is hard enough, Maria, with four kids, you know, the way we are. And I don't want to lose what we have. I couldn't bear it, to lose my family."

She understands now that while she has been carefully demolishing her own marriage from the inside, working outwards, she has been strengthening his. It's what she has been for. It's what she has known, in spite of herself, to do.

What if she should tell him, Edward has moved out, he has left me? Would that scare him more?

"We should go, or we'll be snowed in."

He looks at the sky with relief. It's full of snow, yes, full of another load of winter. "I'll give you a lift home."

"If you've time." There's this curious politeness you seem to go in for, with someone who has just removed you from his life. There's something wrong here, she is being done-to, not doing, she has been removed from the controls of her own existence.

"I'll just clear the snow."

"I'll do it, I've got leather gloves." She feels as if she's suffocating, and it's something to do. She holds the tears in until later, when she is alone.

Her leather gloves, soaked and blackened with snow. He, sitting inside at the wheel to start the engine, and she outside, seeing him through the bleared half-circle of glass that glazes with ice as fast as she clears it. In the silence, the engine turns over, the car starts. She gets in again and sits beside him. She is always sitting beside a man who has just made a decision and is relieved by it. His hand reaches out to touch her knee again, not the gears: what does he expect? Something small and long ago in her struggles, far down, with the pain. Only weeks ago, in Majorca with Edward, she thought she was choosing something, that she was able to; now she's been chosen, to be someone else. She's the older woman who has to walk away with dignity, holding her pain, keeping it out of sight. Because he's right, of course. Children have to come first. There's no protest she can make: nothing she can say in her own defence. Only a sound that will rise in her soon and must escape.

"Let me out at the corner, I'll walk."

The ways through the city that they have carved together, shortcuts, turns, the quickest ways to cover distance in the time they have allotted, the ways from the outside, in. She wants now to take back some small degree of independence and walk to her own front door. She wants him not to see her, not to know. Anyway, she sees, her street is still blocked with snow, for trucks have not come yet to spread gravel, or salt, and no wheels have come to flatten it. She lives in an empty palace, in a countryside of snow. The landmarks of the city, ordinary buildings, have disappeared. Cats cross the street delicately stepping deep into the white softness. Everything's soft, blunted, different. The sharp path of her own life, like a way not yet dug, is about to grate like the iron cut of a spade. She sees her neighbour, Eric, cross the street and step through snow to his own back door. But he has not seen her, he's intent on getting home, with a disintegrating box of groceries under his arm, and he doesn't recognize the car, which is roofed with a thatch of snow anyway, and is crawling along like something out of a spy film.

Sean gives her his soft kiss, goodbye. She feels it, with shame; there's less bone and muscle beneath their flesh than before, the grip has slackened, the urgency has gone. Softness and hardness, redefined. She opens her mouth to speak, she has to say something, she can't remain silent.

"I can't, not just like this."

"Please, Maria. I have to, I'm sorry."

Like Edward, I have to, it's the way things are in my universe, this is how it goes.

She won't beg. She won't be ashamed in front of him, in her need. She struggles out of the car, lands in a deep drift at the curb, snow seeps in over her boots to wet her feet, she picks her way. The icy road. The front steps lost in snow. A car door slams behind her, the engine roars, she hears him turn the car and go. Her key fumbles in the snowy lock that her gloved hand has brushed clear. The trees in the Botanics behind their iron fence shift and let slide their weights. Oh God, damn this bloody snow, damn it all. Keep going, one foot after the other, don't fall over. The pain is enormous, but it's blunted and blocked by snow, it won't thaw and run. Maria thinks, you have to prefer reality to illusion: you have to choose it. It is the only way to stay sane.

She fumbles with the key, opens the door and goes in. Damp rumpled letters have been shoved through the letterbox and lie on the mat, but nothing that can be important. Entering alone, for the first time truly alone, no myth or story or fantasy to console her. Prefer reality, choose it: the heartbeat, the mantra of loss. She'll close the doors and windows, shutter her house against the invading whiteness, switch on lamps, light fires, patrol her way, do the archaic things, notice herself alone and suddenly older in the mirrors that face her now. That's the nineteenth-century way, of course. A small, protesting part of her, born in this new century in which she now lives, suggests that there are now mobile phones, text messages, e-mail, there can be virtual meetings online, connections have been invented so that nothing has to stop dead, no one is allowed to go completely out of sight. The time she lives in is, after all, on her side.

When the children come home, Aidan goes straight to his room and she thinks, I have lost him already. At some point in this winter of her obsession with Sean, her son has seen that her attention is gone from him, and has removed himself accordingly. He doesn't comment, doesn't ask. He's in there playing rap music and practising juggling. When she goes to knock, she sees his exasperation. He's had to open the door to her, and it means he had to stop flipping the little soft leather balls up in the air. It's as if he's juggling to keep himself in balance, as if without the little balls he'll collapse. And the music, the ugliness of it. The insistent beat of rap, the ugly shouted words. At least his sister plays the music of the sixties. He throws her a glance. She doesn't want to ask what he knows. What has Edward told him?

Maria sees his angular boyish body arc away from her and she sits down on the bed, while he juggles on, chucking up the soft balls he practises with. He drops one, then two, then all of them. His hair falls across his eyes as he bends to retrieve them. He glares at her.

"Aidan."

"What? Can't you leave me alone? I'm trying to juggle, can't you see?"

"Okay, can we talk later?"

"If we have to." She gestures towards him, but he jerks away from her, and she sees his misery.

"Come down when you've finished, all right?"

Downstairs, Emily comes to her, longing, eager, speechless, angry. She flings her bookbag to the floor, kicks off her shoes, one foot at a time prising down their backs. "Mum."

"What, Em?"

"I don't know where anyone is."

It's as if since they moved here, she has never come to grips with the size and height of their house. It's too big for her, she keeps on saying. And leaves her possessions scattered about as if to take up as much room as possible.

"Well, I'm here."

"Yeah, you're here *now*."

"Darling, I'm not going anywhere."

"Well, why isn't Dad here?" She kicks at the carpet with her socked feet, a pink toe poking out through a hole.

"He's found somewhere else to live." Is this how it is done, telling children their family has dissolved, their lives are changed? It has all happened so fast, she can hardly believe it. It's as if he has had a bag packed all along. "Em. Come here."

"Why? Are you getting a divorce?"

"Maybe. But you know—"

"Yeah, I know, people get them all the time." She swipes at the air with a long arm, as if swatting mosquitoes, an Emily gesture, a reproach to the world. "But do you have to?"

"Well, yes, it seems we do. I'm sorry, I'm so sorry."

"Who was that bloke who was here?"

"What bloke? Who do you mean?"

"There was a man here. I saw you. One day when I came home early from school."

"Oh, Em, he was just a friend."

"Oh, a *friend*." Her voice rises with scorn.

She's thirteen. Maria thinks, I never had to deal with this at thirteen, seeing my mother with a man, knowing my father has moved away. My mother would have died rather than inflicted this on me. My mother whom I have not contacted for weeks on end, simply because I'm afraid she will guess from some inflection in my voice, some look in my eye; the way she said she could tell I was no longer a virgin, because mothers know these things. But George, now, she had her men friends to stay and expected her children to take it in their stride. So, who is right? And is it all a matter of the ebb and flow of history, after all?

———

"Edward," she says to him on the phone. She has his mobile number, and hears him answer, but she can't know where he is, what he is doing; she has given up that right.

"Oh, it's you."

"Yes. D'you have to sound so icy?"

"I can't help how I sound. I'm busy, Maria. What is it?"

"I told the children. I didn't mean to, without you there, but I did."

"Oh. How did they take it?"

"Well, how d'you think? They're upset. And angry. You have to come and talk to them too."

She hears his silence, as he takes this in, as she makes it real to him: he has left, is leaving, not just her, but his children. She wonders what masochism in him has allowed him to do this, and if it can last. Edward loves his children, she knows it, and nothing can change that, surely.

"Lots of kids have to deal with it these days, separation, divorce. They'll get used to it. At least we're both in the same town." His voice grates with misery; but he won't let her in, if he can help it. She hears him clear his throat, then silence.

When, she wonders, did he turn into this hostile stranger? He can't even bear to talk to her. It's only weeks since they came back from their trip to Majorca, and it's as if he has cut her surgically from him. A nerve throbs in her head, and her hand is shaking as it holds the phone. She doesn't want to plead with him, but for them, she must.

"Could you come round and talk to them today? It would be only fair. Edward—" She has been going to say, do we have to do this, can't we go back, isn't there another way? But his voice has placed her out of reach; she can't say it. Replay, she thinks, rewind, oh, if only we could go back to that place, where was it, on the mountain, where we came down past the little fires, and people called out to us, and there were cooking smells, and start again—but she can't say this to him, not into the silence he has imposed on her, so she doesn't even try.

"He's gone, hasn't he." Aidan stands in the doorway, his long arms dangling nearly to his knees, his pants hanging low beneath his skinny hips, his trainers unlaced. His long neck jutting from his sweatshirt, suddenly a young man's thickening neck, not a boy's. "He won't even tell us."

"He's going to tell you. He's coming round tonight. Oh, love, I'm sorry."

"Coming round? Where from? It sounds as if he doesn't even live here!"

"Well, he's found another place. A flat. Just for the moment."

Aidan shouts, "But he lives here! He can't just find another flat! What happened? What did you do to him? I don't believe this! Fucking hell!"

"Aidan!"

She holds out a hand to him. In his own time, at his own pace, like a young horse stepping cautiously towards her, will he come, is there a faint hope, that he is after all still hers?

"But it was your fault, right?" he says from his distance across the too-big room. "You did something to make him go. Or he wouldn't have gone."

Emily comes in, scenting something important; she shivers as if somebody has touched her, moves close. Her rivers of hair, her layers of sweatshirts, the trailing laces of her trainers, the smell of her, warmth, shampoo, yeasty girl-sweat from some exertion at school.

"Well, yes." She speaks to Aidan. When did her son become her judge?

Emily hangs close to her, undecided.

"What did you do?" Aidan stares at her, his level grey gaze, his lifted head, his lips full and dusted at their edges with a faint fuzz of hair among spots, nostrils distended, his whole self in evolution.

She wants him close now, and is afraid he may never be again. He shakes his head in its tied bandana as if to clear his ears. She sees her children sharply, as they are forced into defining themselves.

"I had a man friend," she says evenly.

"You mean, a lover? Is that what you mean?" His voice, since he has been at school here, has a marked Scottish lilt, and the word, the surprising word, comes out with a certain flourish.

"Yes."

"Who is he?"

She wants to say, if it is any of your business.

"It's over now."

"Oh. Well, as if that changes anything." His voice has broken, too, that growl to it that is still a slight shock to her.

"Well, it does change something. The situation is different."

"But you still did what you did. I can't fucking believe it. It's insane."

This time, she doesn't challenge him. He's at a distance, pulling away from her, his glance at her narrowed with disgust.

"Does Dad know it's over?" Emily asks.

Maria thinks, I never, ever wanted this conversation with them. This is something I simply do not know how to do.

"I don't know."

"Because if he did, and you were sorry, if you said so, then he could come home again, couldn't he?" Em clings to the belief in forgiveness: all you have to do is apologize and then you can come out of your room.

"No, love, I don't think he could."

"Oh, but that's not fair!"

Her girl who cares about fairness, who knows still that nothing is too bad to forgive, whom she herself has taught. Aidan's look of scorn, his arms folded across his chest. He has leapt out of his long sulk, his lone waiting in his room for life to happen, and this is what he has found.

"Mum, I'll talk to him! He has to forgive you! If you say you won't do it again!" Em persists.

"Darling, I really don't think he is going to."

"You mean like, saying sorry is enough?" Aidan tells her, "That's nuts! This isn't dolls' tea parties and girly-girly games, Em, this is serious."

Emily rushes at her brother and he holds her wrists, forcing her away from him.

"Give it up, will you, Em? You don't know what you're talking about. You're just a kid."

"I'm not! I'm not! You're just a—just a—a freaky monster!"

"Stop, both of you. Can we stop talking about this now? Your dad's coming in an hour. We'll explain it all to you then." We, she thinks. Her children have stopped struggling with each other, and face her together.

"Explain it, huh," says Aidan.

Em decides to copy him, after all. "Explain it, huh," she says in the same tone of voice.

They glance at each other, allied against her now.

She can't hold it back now, she's crying, for them, for herself, for the loss of Sean, for the obduracy of Edward, for the existence of things in the world that can't be forgiven, and for the hope of the young that everything always can be. Something that was entirely private, hers alone, is now out in the world to be judged, and they are judging her.

Nothing can be put back, unsaid, restored to its warm obscurity. She hears her children rampaging overhead as if they too were moving out, and waits for Edward to ring the bell.

He has said he'll come back with a van for the furniture that he couldn't fit into his car, one of these days, if that is okay with her. There'll be yet more space, then, between objects, more empty floor. When she saw him the first time, loading things into the back of his car almost cheerfully, she felt as if she were being marooned. What do you need for life on a desert island? A can opener, your favourite music? What else? Tools? A vision of the future. A belief in the possibility of escape. That's what people are asked in interviews—would you try to escape? Some people get out their pocket knives and start making rafts immediately; others just sit there, waiting for something to happen. Most of the first people are men, most of the second, women. But is that because men have the pocket knives in the first place, and have spent the whole of their lives practising making rafts?

She has watched Edward sail away, raft shipshape, a shirt for a sail, against the sunset. She isn't an escaper, she sits down beneath the branches of the only tree and will not cut it down for raft-making, because she wants its shade. She'll endure, that's what she'll do; she's good at it. It's the alternative to escaping. And the nature of things is such that if you endure long enough, something will change, because change is what happens in life, it's the way it works. (But is enduring all you can do, these days? Is it really all beyond her control? The voice, which reminded her about mobile phones and virtual reality, nags at her again.)

She sits down at last in one of the armchairs left to her, and shunts it closer to the radiator. It's cold in here, and the door that has been left wide open lets in draughts from the hall. Then she notices. There's a packet, something in a padded bag, on a table that's been left in an odd place, as if he has changed his mind about taking it. The table looks strangely provisional, but the packet is addressed to her. Edward must have picked it up days ago and left it for her, to stop it being spoiled by snow. It's damp on the outside, but bubble-wrapped, so the book inside will be safe. She tears it open. Ah, yes, the book she ordered all those weeks ago: George Sand's letters to Flaubert, and his to her. A correspondence. A two-way flow. It will last her the winter. Thank God for that.

The doorbell rings. Edward still has his key to the house, but maybe he's ringing to show he has really gone, or out of politeness to her, she can't tell. She goes to open the door, the book still in her hand as if it might afford some protection.

"Hello."

"Hello. Are the kids home?"

"Yes. They're expecting you. Edward, they know. Why, I mean. About me." It sounds and feels to her as if she's admitting something, the existence of a shame that was not there before. She has been made to admit it. She is the person everyone will blame.

"You told them? Why?"

"Well, they asked. Aidan asked."

"And you told him you had an affair?"

"Well, he asked. There wasn't another reason for you to leave, was there?"

"But do you think that was wise, or even sensible?"

"I've no idea. I've no idea what is wise or sensible any more."

"Well, I mean, you're their mother."

"Exactly. They wouldn't care otherwise, would they. If I was just Mrs. MacWhatsit down the street? It wouldn't matter, would it, if she had an affair?"

"Mrs. Who? What are you talking about?"

"Well, nobody, I mean, just anybody, a woman who wasn't me. It wouldn't matter then, would it?"

"Maria. Look, can I come in? It's freezing out here."

She steps aside, and the noise the door makes—*whuff, whoosh*—as he pushes it to behind him, and the way the mackintoshes begin to fall off their hook as they always do is so familiar to them both that they stop, stare at each other, and for a second she sees him, that he wants it all to go back to normal, only it can't. Can it? She looks at him for that second, and his face closes, says no, no; and then the children come downstairs from their rooms and it all has to be gone through, talked about, made plain, reduced to its barest outlines, the story of what is happening to them now.

She does call him, of course. Sean, that is. His number's in her mobile phone, impossible to ignore, and she's sitting at her desk and the phone's within reach; she touches the number, sees the light flare to life, hears a ring. But the automatic voice comes on, his name the only two words pronounced in the accent she longs to hear. Dr. Sean Farrell is not available, please leave a message, send a fax, wait for other options, press star for more. The list of numb possibilities one has to listen to so often these days. Then she looks at her e-mail. Fifteen messages, and none of them from him. She goes through deleting, skimming, then presses "write." She writes five words to him. "Please meet me at Cramond." Then adds, "2 p.m. tomorrow." Presses "send." Your message has been sent. Now there is simply waiting till tomorrow. She thinks about Emily and her belief, now apparently lost, that if you are sorry for something and apologize, you should be forgiven. That world of fairness in which she has not lived for so long. But the truth is, she is not, probably will never be, sorry. Sorry to have hurt her husband, yes. Sorry to have caused, however unwillingly, this state of affairs the four of them, her family, now live in, yes; but sorry to have done what she did, no.

Cramond, where the Firth of Forth begins to widen out into its huge estuary, is where they used to meet before they met, really met, at her house in the lunch hours of school and university term. Away from anywhere they might be recognized, they thought; although in reality there was no such place, for anyone might be out walking a dog or two, sketching, wheeling a baby in a buggy, simply looking out to sea. To begin with, he used to bring the family dog for cover; two people striding briskly with a red setter wheeling and dipping around them, his ears flowing back and his banner of a tail, could look blameless, however close they walked, however often one surreptitiously squeezed the other's hand. It was after the initial meeting in the bookshop, and before the nakedness and glory of the bedroom. He in a thick charcoal tweed coat, jeans and trainers, a scarf wound around his neck, sometimes a woolly hat. She in her walking boots and quilted jacket, a red beret pulled about her ears. Their hands, gloved, ungloved. The currents between them. And the grey Firth, stretching to their right as they walked out, towards the point where the fast brown seething tributary branches at Cramond, and on their left as they returned. The hills of Fife, low, grey, suddenly lit from between clouds. The great iron humps of the railway bridge, the smooth curve of the road bridge. And always gulls, blowing like torn paper over the water, hurtling away and back. They used to walk, and talk, the talk urgent and necessary, a stage in itself. Being Irish, being Scottish, coming back here for her, emigrating here for him; and the history, the politics of the time, the fear of America, the disgust with England, the shame of governments, the lost ideals of their youth, their desire for a better world. The red dog ran ahead and looped back, called to heel, and gasped up at them, his long tongue, his urgent brown gaze, and she felt the domed skull under the red fur, the long pointing muzzle and the black cold nose under her hand, as she could not so caress his owner; and the dog, loved and gratified, chased sitting seagulls up the beach, up into the air. He barked, he ran nose-down at the water's edge, he was a flame against all the grey, and to Maria, he was their guardian. Nobody, if you walked such a lithe and beautiful dog, could wonder what you were doing, or with whom. "Whatever you say, say nothing, say nothing to you-know-who," Sean liked to quote from the old song, the sentiment and warning of his ancestors, "For if you know who knows you know what, you know what they'll do." The silences, the talk, the dog-walking of those early days: and then, back in their separate cars which they had parked away from each other at the road end, they would drive back down through Granton and into town, their cheeks stung with cold, their lips chapped and stretched with the kiss they'd exchanged—a quick look around, nobody in sight—as the dog panted in the back of his battered station wagon, its tongue dripping, and he turned her gently out of the wind.

Cramond, a signal and a plea.

She is there the next day, parking her car at the road end as she always has, but the day is so dreich, there are only two other cars in sight, neither of them his. She sits, looking in her mirror at the empty expanse, the road, the sky. Two o'clock. Two ten. Two fifteen. She turns on the radio, hears a strident voice talking about traffic jams somewhere on the ring road, turns it off. Then she sees his car appear, and she watches it come, watches him park it directly behind hers, watches for his face in the windscreen, will he be smiling or not, will he be angry as Edward is angry, what will he be to her next? She opens her door. The air is rawly cold, and wind blows off the Firth, and the snow which has been melting in grey patches is still in clumps at the roadside, and the whole landscape is in tones of grey, brown, white. There is no leaping red dog to blaze a way into the heart of it, this time. He comes towards her, his coat collar turned up, his face pale as ever, the crests of his hair tucked under a cap.

"Hello, you."

"Sean. You came." It's as if the words have to be sparse, minimal; she has to hold as many as possible back.

"Yes, I came. Not in the usual sense, but still, I came." He's laughing at her, holding her at arms' length, looking at her, he's still the same person after all, he hasn't changed in any noticeable way in the last few shattering days; it's as if nothing has happened to him.

"How are you?"

"I should say, I'm very well. Considering." He laughs again, mystifyingly, and then says, "How are you?"

"I— Well. I had to see you. I couldn't just leave it, say goodbye that way, I felt as if I was dying, if you want to know."

"Shall we walk? I didn't bring Leo, as I have to go to the dentist later and I didn't think he'd behave in there too well."

So, she's been fitted in before the dentist, and presumably, after lunch. She imagines him staring into a bathroom mirror as he cleans his teeth, bares them to make sure there's no lunch on them, and satisfied, leaves the house. She knows his house, she's seen it from the outside. She has no idea about the bathroom. He knows a lot more about her than she does about him; she wonders briefly if this is always true between women and men.

They set off down the steep slope, with patches of ice still, and lumps of snow, the grass flat and slippery and dun-coloured underfoot. They slither and slip, he catches her arm, they're running and sliding suddenly, dangerously, and together they arrive at the path that runs along the stony beach. They gasp, catch their breath. Out in the Forth, a tanker sits moored. There's the oil well moving up and down out there between them and the coast of Fife. Nobody on the beach but a single man picking up driftwood and stowing it in a black plastic bag.

"Was it hard for you to come?"

"Nope. I told you, I've a dentist appointment. But really, I'm glad to see you, I wanted to."

His face, turned towards her as he says this, is suddenly simple and open, it tells the truth. His mouth, closing on the words, his direct glance, his whole face broad and peaceful.

"How are things at home?" Not that she really wants to know.

"Same. Everyone's fine. Matt's got a bit of a cold. It's Annie's birthday in a couple of days. Maria, I wanted to see you. I expect I always will."

There's nothing she can say. She looks at him, waiting.

"But I can't see you in the old way, I told you that. It's not easy, far from it, but it's something I have to do. Not do, rather."

"So what will we do?"

"I don't know. Go back to walking the dog?"

"No, no." She's speechless with the unfairness of it— *unfair*, the childish word, her daughter's word, the word you give up using as soon as you're an adult. Unfair, because something has taken him beyond her reach, and he's agreeing with it, it has all been his idea.

She knows, deep inside, under the layers and layers of behaviour and ideas and concepts and propositions that her life over the last forty years has laid on her—in there, where she lives, small, crouching, protected—that a great injustice has been done. Because of it, life has become unrecognizable. She wants to know now if it is the same for him. He bends, picks up a flat round pebble and with the long-armed arc of a practised thrower, out of his Irish boyhood beside loughs, out of a past that never included her, skims it out across the water. It sinks, white into grey. The birds rise and scream, and dive upon something on the shore, a dead fish, a picnic remnant. Suddenly Maria feels the place as her enemy, it is too cold, too drained of colour, too pocked with snow and ice, wintry, dour, alien. She wants now to go home. But then he opens his coat to her and draws her inside, as if into a tent, and holds her against him, her head tucked in under her chin, his familiar peppery scent, the roughness of his sweater and scarf, his hand in the middle of her back, pulling her in to him, hard. They stay there for a moment, at the edge of the water, in that stony, icy time and place, and for that moment, a little warmth is conjured back, as she feels beneath her cheek the slow strong steady thud of his heart. She thinks, it isn't about sex, not now: it's about knowing somebody in the bone-deep way you know yourself, and to give it up is heartbreak.

⁓

"Would you like your chocolate in your room, *chéri?* Then you can be quiet until it's time for dinner."

The bell rang for dinner at five. She joined him, after teaching the children in the afternoon, having got up at midday herself. After dinner, they played games, played the piano, Solange accompanying him sometimes in duets. He made them laugh by imitating Liszt, pulling his hair down over his ears and loosening his cravat to look like a bohemian. He played wildly, boisterously, then moved them suddenly to tears with a change of key. He was her child, her friend, her inspiration.

"We don't bore you, do we, my love, with our country ways?"

"No, I have never been less bored in my life. And you know, Aurora, you have saved my life, I owe it all to you." Aurora, he called her still; never George.

When she was ill, and she increasingly felt the pain in her liver and stomach when she was tired, he nursed her, bringing her flowers from the garden, reading to her, stroking back her hair. She had nursed him back to health, now he could take care of her, he said.

That summer, he had completed the Sonata in B-flat minor, an impromptu in F-sharp Minor and two nocturnes. These were followed by a waltz, a scherzo, a second ballade, this one in F-major, two polonaises, two études, three mazurkas. In her house he worked solidly as he did nowhere else. The hard bargain was working: her sacrifice was what he had needed.

But she felt it, his desire to return to Paris. He was most himself when playing at society dinners, in grand houses, or at intimate salons, where people would beg him to improvise and he'd burst into the wildness the music demanded, even if it wore him out. Writing it all down on paper and posting it was not at all the same thing. She knew she must let him go; he was not hers to keep. She got up, lit another little cigar and went to her desk to sit in clouds of smoke and write to Charlotte Marliani, asking her to find two apartments for them in Paris, separate, but not far apart, so that she could still make sure he had enough to eat. It didn't matter how much it cost, she would furnish places for them both.

~~~~~

Maria lies out on her long couch with a tartan rug over her legs, and reads. She wants never to stop reading, now. She reads the Flaubert letters, then goes back to the Musset letters, wishes once again that George had not burned all her letters from Chopin, then dips back into the *Histoire de Ma Vie*. She makes notes on pads and scatters them about the floor. She has a glass of wine at her elbow and a half-eaten sandwich in her lap, and the tortoiseshell cat, Gigi, comes and sits on her feet, purrs and nudges her with a wet little mouth.

Emily, before she goes uptown to see the latest Harry Potter film with Harriet and Kirsty, comes to her with her urgent inquiry. "Mum, are you all right?"

"Fine, thanks, love." You have to practise saying it, to have it come true. "Have a good time. Have you got your key, or shall I leave the door on the snib? Come back straight away afterwards, won't you, it's a school night, don't forget. Is Harriet's mum bringing you all home?"

"Yes. Are you sure you're okay? Right, then, I'm away. I've got my key." Emily bends to hug her, her warm face briefly against hers. She has made her own decisions; she is still her mother's girl.

Aidan when he goes leaves the house with a brief shout and a slam of the door and feet going slap-slap down the stone steps and away. It will take longer for him to come back to her; he is busy finding out what the appropriate responses from a man might be, and is taking his father as a model. Disapproval, a look of moral superiority and a habit of being mostly absent and not saying when he is going out, or where. She wishes he could have met Sean. Could have. The sadness of tenses. Maria puts a postcard to mark her place in the book and hears Emily being picked up, voices on the street, a car door's slam. They are going to the multiplex on the other side of town.

"You okay, hen?" They call each other by this Edinburgh endearment when they want to be equals, women together.

A couple of hours later, and already when she comes in, Emily seems to have grown older, perhaps from being with her friend. Change happens when you are not looking; it shows in the space between conversations. Her daughter, asking if she is okay.

"Yeah, I'm okay, hen. You?"

"I miss Dad."

"I know. He'll be here on Saturday, to take you out."

"I don't want him to take me out. I want him to be here. You know, like before. Why can't he?"

"Because he's still angry with me."

"Couldn't you make him be not angry?"

"Well, it's a hard thing to do, Em. I wish I could."

"You know, in the film, in all the books, they use magic when things are too hard otherwise. Spells, that work. You just learn them. I really like that."

"Well, if I had a spell, I'd use it, that's for sure. But you know, it's not real, all that, it's made up."

"Yeah, I know, of course I do." Scornful Em, asking, haven't you noticed, I'm grown-up? "But sometimes you can kind of believe in things you know aren't real. Just for a wee while? Like, I mean, you can kind of use them?"

The winter's deep and long, the long northern withdrawal of light which has always felt hard to her. Majorca and the weeks there in January feel like another life. Maria is alone late in the evenings with George Sand, and the cat. The cat loves her sitting still so long, she kneads and purrs and drips saliva. Maria reads George's pleas to Flaubert—she's in her sixties, he in his forties, but they both sound like old people, joking about the facts of age—come and stay, surely your mother will be all right alone for a few days, it would do you good, you stay too much at home. And she reads his answers, I'd love to, but I can't, my mother needs me, I have to work, you work so fast and are so prolific, I sometimes manage only a sentence a day.

Gustave Flaubert, the friend of her old age. Not the

Flaubert of the exploits in North Africa, the prostitutes, boys, orgies. The Flaubert of rewritten sentences, of dark country evenings, aches and pains. Flaubert who takes care of his mother. Flaubert who dreads travelling even for a few hours. When he first read George, he mocked the fluency of her prose; when they met at last, he adored her. It's a relief to Maria to have moved on into the relative calm of George's later life. The terrain of passion has given way to the terrain of friendship. Illusions drop away.

She sees that these two people, although they love each other, are not going to spend even a day together, because of everything that's in the way. But they write. They have their letters, and their lives pour into their letters, and that is what makes the letters so compelling, that's why she feels after reading them that she's spent her evenings in the company of warm, witty, generous, intelligent people. The letters are everything. The people who wrote them are gone, and in their lives they failed each other, put each other off, prevaricated, even lied—Flaubert who invented absurd excuses to avoid leaving home, George who always wanted everyone to come and stay with her. But the letters are magnificent, they can warm you and fascinate you two centuries later, and make you feel life is worth living even when your lover and your husband have both left you and the dire cold of a northern winter keeps you indoors, and your children are often out with friends, whose own houses just possibly they prefer to their own. There's a Dad in some of these houses, Maria knows, and things happen like computer games and ping-pong matches and someone comes in heartily in the evening from work, bringing with him a glow of success of some sort, or at least a fish supper to be shared.

In her own house there is just herself to welcome them, and they let her know this is not enough. But George and Flaubert are here for her, like two people having a discussion in the next room. She can hear them through the wall. Wisdom comes, she hears, when everything else is lost; and it doesn't leave you alone.

Cath, her old friend, shyly rings the doorbell, stands on the steps in her padded jacket and jeans, huffing on her hands until Maria answers.

"I thought, maybe, you could do with going out somewhere? Should we try the new wine bar round the corner?"

Perched on high uncomfortable stools, they sip Grenache and watch suited young men come in with girlfriends also in business suits, their necks wrapped tenderly in cashmere against the cold, their good coats hung on a wooden hatstand in a corner. The waiters wear long aprons as if they were in France, and the wine list is long and international.

"Do you miss him?" Cath asks her.

"Yes and no. I miss—something. Not exactly Edward, because he's being so nasty, no one could miss him. But I miss things as they were. You know? It feels like waking up each morning to find someone's moved all the furniture around." She looks around her at the brand-new furnishings, wicker and standard lamps, an attempt at sitting-room coziness. "Wasn't this the old dry cleaner's? Or was that next door, where the spa is?"

"I think it was here. Look, the door's at that same angle. But that might not be such a bad idea."

"What?"

"Moving the furniture. They do say, if you move your furniture around, something has a chance to move around in your life. It was in a book about feng shui."

"Well." Maria drinks her wine, which tastes thin; she should have chosen a shiraz. Her daughter wants her to cast spells, her old friend wants her to use feng shui. "I get the feeling too much has been moving around in my life already. Moving out, mostly." She has told Cath about Sean, since it is over. "But I did get rid of the bed, the one we'd always had, and got myself a new one."

"Good move. Well, maybe you should get some more new stuff."

"You mean, go shopping to cheer myself up? Isn't that what the American president said after they'd taken the Twin Towers out—go shopping?"

Cathy says, "I didn't mean it like that. But if you like, I'll come round and give you a hand, if you like, move some stuff around, maybe paint a wall?"

"Oh, Cath." She looks at her friend, who doesn't fit in this wine bar any more gracefully than she does, among the young and glossy, the suited, the highly employed, "Thanks. I'm sorry to be so negative. Thanks for thinking of it. And here's to bringing in the new—whatever it turns out to be."

"Cheers." They raise glasses to each other, as they have before.

"Seems like an age since we did those photographs," Cathy says.

"And since we went to that pub. I wonder if it even exists any more, a place like that."

"But tell me, how's the book going? How's George Sand?"

"I'm reading her letters to Flaubert, and his to her. They are wonderful. They keep me company. I sometimes feel they're showing me what to do."

Cathy looks uncomfortable. "Well, so long as someone is, but don't spend too much time alone, pal, it's not good."

Edward is leaving them alone, and she guesses it's because he feels hurt, unwanted, and a host of other things. But how can feelings keep you from your children, she wants to know, how can he be letting this happen, to them, to her? He has taken a flat across town, just off the High Street, and moved his few necessary belongings, and begun quietly, firmly, on another life. Is he waiting for her, as Emily thinks, to apologize? Is he planning to ask her what she wants to happen next? Is he seeing lawyers, thinking of divorce; even seeing another woman? She has no idea. It is peculiar, to say the least, to have lived with someone for twenty years and have him walk away this easily, like someone stepping cleanly out of a suit of discarded clothes. And all because she had a brief affair with another man.

Why, she wants to ask him, why does it have to be like this?

One day, as the days have begun lengthening, she crosses the street to go to the Department, and sees him walking towards her from the opposite direction, from the Meadows. He is striding, his coat open as it's slightly warmer, the low sun is still on his side of the street; he looks youthful, purposeful, a scarf flung back over his shoulder. She thinks he looks slimmer. And he has some new clothes. She sees him before he has seen her.

"Edward!"

He comes towards her. He's a handsome blond stranger. He's also the father of her children.

"Edward! It's been ages."

"Hello, Maria." He lays a hand on her sleeve, as if afraid she may escape. "Funny, I was thinking about you. I've just been in Majorca again."

"You were?" She wants to ask, what, what were you thinking?

"Yes, I was thinking we should get together, have a talk. It's been about a month, hasn't it?"

Yes, thirty-one days, as it happens, since you walked out.

"Okay. Whenever you like. How was Majorca?"

"Good. I got a lot done. So, when d'you want to meet? Perhaps when the kids aren't home?"

He obviously doesn't want to chat.

"Or," she says carefully, "perhaps somewhere else?"

"You could come to my flat. We could have tea."

"No, I don't think so. Somewhere else, preferably."

"Okay. Neutral territory. No man's land."

"Well, or just a pub, perhaps." She has noted the reference to war.

"Right. Are you on your way to work?"

"Yes, are you?"

"Yeah, I'm late, actually. So, see you soon. I'll give you a ring. Still got your mobile?"

"Yes," she says, "of course. We'll give each other a ring. Soon, okay?"

It's strange, she thinks on her way to her class, unbuttoning her coat, unwinding her scarf, pulling her hair back, feeling in her bag for her notes: strange, that there seems to be no halfway house between the extremes of intimacy and this stilted, formal behaviour. One day you are standing in your underwear next to someone, both of you brushing your teeth and spitting into the same basin, the next you are behaving as if you have hardly met. She wonders, suddenly, with curiosity, if Edward is having an affair. If once the intimacy, the nakedness, the tooth-brushing, whatever it is, is established with another person, it is drained from the first person. If nobody can help this, it is just a law like a law of physics, just something that happens. She goes in to meet her class.

They are waiting for her, sitting at the too-small desks the Department provides, and they all look up and smile as she enters, they like her, they enjoy this even though, she suspects, most of them don't really give a damn about French literature, still less the structuralists, who still seem to be obligatory. With her, they can discuss all the big topics, love, infidelity, death, all seen through the lens of these books, some of them written centuries ago, others coming straight to them across the Channel from France, where perhaps people snatch them up on publication, rip the covers off and devour them, sending these ideas straight into the bloodstream of their lives.

Today, she notices shiny hair, taut skin, bright eyes. A room full of people much younger than herself. The spring sun showing their white skins, the unblemished youth of them. She wants to tell them, books do change lives. What you read today will form you tomorrow. It isn't just a text, after all, it's a lifeline.

One of them begins, the usual protest, "I didnae have time to read the pages for today, Dr. Jameson. Life got in the way, sort of. Know what I mean?"

The others laugh. The boy whose name is Ruaridh, one of the few Scots in the class, buries his head in his arms on the desk, clutches his spiked hair.

Dr. Jameson, who is herself, says, "Well, sometimes it gets in the way, sometimes it doesn't. You may not need it now, Ruaridh, you may never need it, but who knows when you'll suddenly remember and be glad you read it. Now, who wants to start?"

4

CORAMBÉ

THE MORNING AFTER FRÉDÉRIC'S CONCERT, she thought, I have been arguing for years with my deepest desires. I need both: muse and lover. I thought they were the same person, always, and they are not. How we do live and learn. She got up and opened the shutters on to the day. Outside, the slope of the hill up to Montmartre and its vineyards and gardens, beyond the roofs. The sky over Paris, pearly cloud and sharp light. The roofs dark and shining with early rain that she had not even heard, but could smell now, even from up here. The freshness of April above the city.

After last night and his triumph, she knew that it was over, really over this time, although they would go on being friends, among other friends, although the tenderness would not fade, because his need of her was done. She went barefoot in her wrapper into the next room, her green room with the lilies from the market giving out their nighttime scent. This was what it was like getting older, finding wisdom: sadness mixed with the knowledge of rightness, of understanding. One day Maurice would leave her, and Solange too. They would all of them leave, and she would be alone. She stirred bitter chocolate into a pot of hot milk. Frédéric, my darling boy, she said, you have given your concert, you are launched, nothing can hold you back now.

She had woken earlier that morning to the vivid memory of a dream. She was at Nohant, and Hippolyte, her half-brother, was leading her away from the house to go and see the pigs. She felt the familiar sense of dread, but could not of course let him know what she felt.

The pig-man's name was Plaisir. The day Hippolyte had first taken her to see him, in reality she went with him slightly unwilling, but curious all the same. She was only a child, and he nearly an adolescent, her big brother, so maybe he would keep her safe. She'd never liked pigs, as they seemed mean and stupid; there was the old-man pig, the "*cadi*" as they called him, who had vicious eyes and would run you up a tree as soon as look at you. But Plaisir had the whip-hand over him, jumped on his back like a circus-rider, he bossed this band of marauders that snuffled and dug and rooted their way along the edge of the forest, stared with their horrible little eyes and plotted to attack children. Aurore looked at them, drew back, thought of the bird in the cage in Spain, which had shrieked at her and obviously wanted her to die. Plaisir was a wild man, a *loup-garou*, half-man, half-wolf, earth-coloured, root-eating, pig-hardened, and the fascination of him was that he understood these pigs, these evil-doers. He was of the earth, like them; while they snorted and excavated and laid waste great tracts of ground, he was in there among them with his triangular iron implement, digging and scrabbling under-ground like them, or crawling through undergrowth after snakes and small animals. While the pale winter sun lit the frost on the pig earthworks, and Aurore and Hippolyte stood and watched, and saw that life down here was all about this excavating, this fumbling and snouting about underground.

"I don't like them," she said to Hippolyte, taking his hand.

"But, Aurore, they are really people! They've only been turned into pigs."

In her dream, she was not sure what they were. People could be half-animal. Animals could take human form. Why not?

In the dream, something terrible was going to happen, and she did not know how to avert it. What could this possi-bly have to do with Frédéric Chopin and his wildly success-ful concert at the Conservatoire the night before? She moved about her room, still not dressed, smoking a cigarette she had rolled herself.

Plaisir could bring down a bird with one stone. He stoned

the magpies and crows which hung about pigs especially in winter, feeding off the worms they turned up or the germinating seeds. He wore the same earth-coloured shirt always, and his hands and face were earth-textured, and he spoke few words. His name was the same as pleasure.

Corambé, his opposite, was the god of the forest, a perfect being. He shimmered between the trees, more beautiful than Jesus, more human than the gods of the Greeks. It was for Corambé that she waited.

The pig-man was only for the moment condemned to a pig-man's life, to free the soul of another, she imagined, to expiate his sin. The old boar, the *cadi*, was an evil spirit, who would in the end be won over and tamed by Corambé's marvellous gentleness; the birds on the bushes were sylphs, who came to console Plaisir for his grim labour. If the pigs were people, Corambé would set them free.

As Plaisir in the deep forest sang the old "*chant des porchers,*" the unwritten song of the Berrichon pig-keepers from centuries back, she too sang her own made-up song, with its thousand verses, none of which needed to be written down. The song, the story of Corambé: the rhythm of her inner life. This was her world, the world of a country child; between myth and reality, finding her own way.

In her dream she had run from the snouting pigs towards Corambé, who disappeared among the trees. There was no Corambé. There was only the pig-man. There was only Plaisir.

———

Childhood, where it all begins. The flash between the leaves, something passing, half-seen, beautiful. Also, the terror.

When she came to build her altar to Corambé, she chose the wild far garden at Nohant where the young trees grew among thick undergrowth and where nobody went. Three elms grew there from the same trunk, the surrounding scrub stifled in their shadow so that a little green room was made, just the right size. The earth covered with moss, the branches laced tight as a roof against the sky. She was quite alone there and quite safe, even if only yards away people were walking up and down the garden paths. She found pebbles, snail shells, moss, dressed an altar at the foot of the largest elm and placed above it a crown of flowers. The strung shells were a chandelier hung from the lowest branch. She cut away some of the branches to make the place more exactly circular, she plaited ivy, she hung crowns and wreaths of leaves, with birds' nests, and shells for lamps.

She made sure she was alone before entering the temple, which was quite a painful and scratchy business, as she took care to come in from a different angle so as not to leave any traces of broken foliage or a path. When everything was ready, she sat on the moss and began to think up sacrifices she would make to her god. To kill animals or even insects for his pleasure seemed barbaric and not suited to his gentleness. So she would do the exact opposite: that was, to bring life and freedom to his altar by liberating birds and beasts upon it. She hunted for butterflies, lizards, frogs and birds, set traps, hung cages. Liset, the boy from the farm, brought her wild birds he had trapped in the fields and woods, so every day she could set free upon her altar a swallow, a robin or a thrush. The smaller offerings, bugs and beetles, hardly counted. She put them in a box, placed the box on the altar and opened it, murmuring to the god of freedom and safety.

At that time there was also Monsieur Dumai, the poor crazy man who used to come from La Châtre, impeccably dressed and polite, who would wander through the garden into the house until he met someone, who had once even wandered into Aurore's grandmother's room and watched her while she read.

If anyone asked Monsieur Dumai what he wanted, he would reply, "*la tendresse.*" Tenderness. I am looking for tenderness.

"And have you found it yet?"

"No, not yet. And yet, I have looked everywhere."

"Have you looked in the garden?"

As if struck by a sudden hope, he went outside and began looking behind bushes, striding up and down the paths, and only answered, when anyone asked him the question, "*la tendresse.*"

One day, she heard that he had drowned in a well; perhaps while looking for tenderness still in its depths.

~⌐

Note on Corambé: muse, god, animus. Spirit, trickster. Sexless, perfected. Invisible. To be awaited, expected, lured out. Other. Other self. Human, superhuman. Hero. Shadow. Self.

The problem is to incorporate him. Received ideas from the twentieth century: that the muse, for women writers, is also female. But who then is the one we meet at the edge of sleep, wait for in the clearing, build shrines for, temples, houses; for whom the bed is made, in the rushes, in the hay barns, in clean sheets? Who inhabits us and invades us, mocks us, haunts us? Who will neither quite arrive, nor quite go away?

Twin, brother, playmate. Twin who died at birth. Other half. (Frail brother with unseeing eyes, gifted with inner visions, stifled on a breath before his life really began?)

Husband. Lover, but less in the flesh than in the spirit. Foreigner, stranger; without language, or speaking in tongues.

Ambivalent. Ambiguous. Bisexual. Whose gender is no limitation, but depth and breadth. God? Local, pagan, accessible, to be found in particular places: trees, rocks, beside the river, the lake. Reflection in water. Seen in dreams.

Unreliable, yet utterly to be trusted. Muse.

An earth-coloured man who kept pigs, whose name was Pleasure. A crazy man who wandered looking for tenderness. Who is this child, Maria thinks, if not herself, if not her childhood twin? She remembers the dens she herself built, the shrines, in the tangle of trees and bushes at the end of her parents' garden when they lived in Comely Bank. The grate in the pavement on Broughton Street with steam coming out of it, which she knew was the entrance to Hell, where you would go if you swore. Memories come back insistent as dream, as hard to place, but as vivid. Who was the old shoe-mender who lived down the street in a filthy hovel with no bathroom, with his wife in carpet slippers, and scrapbooks full of faded newspaper cuttings about Oswald Mosley? An old Edinburgh came back to her, a city of ghosts and ha'nts, of lamplighters and cut-throats, of streets hidden beneath streets, of hanged men, of the Deacon Brodie and Jekyll and Hyde, the stories she grew up with, that terrified her and made it hard to go up to bed once the light was gone from outside, and someone might come and turn off the lamp on the stairs? Her child-hood city: all black stone and deep fissures cut through rock, streets like canyons, walls like cliffs; a man who was bent nearly double, who wore an ancient kilt and sporran and smelled rank and sour, who muttered as he walked and cast a crooked shadow on the wall. The dead stags with their blurred eyes that hung from metal hooks outside the butcher's shop on the corner, the bloodied pheasants and rabbits laid out in the window, the limp limbs and mouths and beaks open in a frozen last grimace. Men who cursed and ranted on street corners. An old woman bunched in several wool skirts who sat up by the Tron and showed her knickers and sang on one eerie long note like a bird whistle. Don't look, walk on by. All the murmured, muttered, whispered things that adults knew and would only half divulge: warnings, predictions, tears before nightfall, the Lord helps those who help themselves, faith without works is dead, cross the street when you see the sweep, never walk under a ladder, keep your penny in your glove, don't speak to the crazy man, walk fast when you pass this tenement, or that. A world in which Hogmanay was celebrated, but barely Christmas; Halloween, but not All Saints.

She thinks of Aurore and Hippolyte (conjuring the devil from below the floor boards, poring over Deschartres' books of magic, *Le Petit Albert* and *Le Grand Albert*, pulled down from the high shelf, on summer afternoons when he was away; watching for ghosts and werewolves), and she's there, in that time and place where the dual nature of reality showed, as it once had so clearly in this city of her birth.

These days, Edinburgh is very different from its old dark dirty self. The Parliament building crouches at the bottom of the Royal Mile, dwarfing Holyrood, posing in front of the grey-green swell of King Arthur's Seat. The twentieth century has given way to the twenty-first, as the eighteenth did to the nineteenth, as the superstitions and country beliefs of Aurore's childhood did to the rationalism of her adult world. The old cafés and sweetie shops have gone, the shoe-menders and the tailors, the strange old shops with moth-eaten kilts and stags in the window; the butcher's on the corner with his stiffened hares and hanging deer. A huge change has taken place, and she is still a child of the twentieth century, of her girlhood here, the days when she swung up on to the step of the maroon-and-white buses as they turned the corner of her street in Comely Bank, ten pence in her palm for the trip to Mary Erskine, with her giggling white-socked friends. But what about her beliefs? What about her assumptions?

Has she, Maria wonders, ended up high and dry, with the two men in her life leaving her quite clearly for their different reasons, her children looking to her for explanations, because she is simply out of kilter with the times in which she lives? A romantic, believing in sexual love, in freedom, in promises kept and apologies accepted; a woman committed to love; an anachronism? A person who has allowed transgression into her life, who has deliberately given it a place? A homing Scot who hasn't found the home she left years ago, a woman whose beliefs and instincts have turned out to be wrong, a leftover from the last century, a bit of a freak?

Corambé, she thinks. Aurore waited for him, as she waited for love. The muse, the lover who is inside us all. The pig-man, pleasure, or the god?

Muses, thought George, sun making patterns on the floor in her brown bedroom in the apartment on rue Pigalle. She had lain down again on her thick mattress on the floor, feeling suddenly exhausted; watched the patch of light move towards her. She should get up, it must be after midday, but for minutes more she lay thinking about the night before, and her dream.

The suddenly mature and distant figure of Frédéric Chopin on the concert platform, bowing gently from the waist to take what was due to him. He whom she'd seen coughing and terrified, emaciated and covered in sweat, who had clung to her, needing the strength of her love. Aurélien, Stéphane, *le petit* Jules. Her light-skinned boyish muses, like fauns, like young horses, who came to lay their heads in her lap. De Musset, Frédéric. In all of them, the echo and sign of Corambé, the god who was not the pig-man, whose name was not Plaisir. Her son's tutors, Didier and Mallefille. Hardly more than boys themselves, and she always older, always in control, the mistress of Nohant who could keep them or let them go. The napes of their necks under their hair, the hollows of their flat stomachs strung between tender hip bones. She saw it now. She used to have herself bled regularly when she had her periods, because of the sharpness of desire that rose up in her, in the years of Michel, when he was not there but with his stupid wife. Michel, closer to the pig-man than Corambé. He had known her, he had drawn her to herself, her body under his hands, only two days after they first met, and with that straight look of his, from the eyes behind glasses, black eyes from the midi; he had taken her before she knew it, made her his. But he had not been—had he?—her muse?

In the dream, Corambé was gone. There was only the pig-man. She had come through her fear of him. In her middle age, just as she had let go of Frédéric Chopin, as she had seen him launched, away from her now, the sign had come to her finally: this, the earth, your own nature, is your salvation.

~

Maria wakes in her big cold bedroom in her Edinburgh house and reaches for the notebook beside her bed. She tries to stay in her dream, in which she's in a green place, a forest with light coming through trees, and a river nearby. She's waiting. There's a clearing, with a kind of hut in it, and she knows that something or someone is going to appear, and possibly enter the hut, which she herself is afraid to go into. The hut grows, becomes a cottage with low roof and wooden walls, almost overgrown with foliage. The person she's waiting for will make her both fear and love. But the dream is all waiting, and she still has a sharp sense of the nearness of him, the what-if, the only-just.

Muse, she writes at last. Of course, dreams are about yourself, not really about other people, she's read enough

Jung and later dream theorists and even been to dream workshops run by women in this city. You are dreaming about waiting for a part of yourself. The masculine part. The part—she smiles—that makes rafts, decides things, sails away.

She makes her coffee and waits for it to bubble up in its sudden little spurt in her Italian coffee pot. She pours it into a cup she brought back from Majorca, rather thick-lipped with a clumsy handle, but with flowers and painted birds running around it. It reminds her of sunlight and clear air.

She tastes her coffee and thinks about her book. Her book is what is keeping her company now, and she loves it, the way she can conjure it to mind anytime she wants, with nobody to interrupt her and nothing else in her way. Every time she misses Sean with the sharp hunger for him that has not faded, a stab in the gut, an ache in the vagina, she goes back to her book. When she thinks of Edward and all they have been to each other, that decades-long companionship, she goes back to it again. It's like being a child again, playing an imaginary game that goes on day after day, in spite of school and adults, and bedtimes and mealtimes, that runs on like a river, unstoppable, only sometimes caught up here and there in small eddies and side streams, just to run on again thick and smooth and easy. It's actually easier, without Edward there; the children seem at last to have accepted her as one of them, a flawed person who has been punished as children are punished; who has been absolved of the adult world.

And, though she hasn't quite admitted this to herself, it is also easier to write when she isn't waiting to hear from Sean.

It isn't a biography, or not a conventional one. She has written biography, or biographical essays, when she was doing her degree: on Céline, on Camus, on Gracq: cut-and-dried men who have given her no trouble. Her PhD thesis was on Roland Barthes and his *A Lover's Discourse,* a popular subject at the time. It now seems wryly amusing that this was so. But this book, the one she struggles with now, seems to her like an elephantine pregnancy that weighs her down and may never be brought to term. Pregnant by George Sand? Stuck in the mire of a life so long, so full, that it overlaps her own, a wide river to her narrow stream, and she can't get the measure of it? Barthes at least had the tact to die young.

Her book will not be anything that her contemporaries would even recognize, let alone approve of. Or, maybe a couple of them would, the stranger, more intelligent ones. The ones who can recognize something new when they see it; this is what she thinks on good days. She thinks of Sartre writing about Flaubert, making his own life similar to the great writer's by linking their childhoods: a way of hitch-hiking into a shared fame? But Sartre as a child was unfashionably doted on. Perhaps it isn't so much misery that a writer needs, but events. A life in which things happen.

What was it with George? Why Aurore Dupin and not Hippolyte Chatiron, for example? They had both wanted to write; she had done it, he had not. (How do you do it,

Aurore, how do you find your form? Just let it run on, Hippolyte, it will find its own form in time, all you have to do is get it down.) But she went on and he took to the bottle. It can't be all about class, can it, and opportunity? It can't be just education, and having books around you. Something— and she raises her coffee cup to sip the last dregs, before going back to her desk, with its laptop and printer—makes you want more than anything in the world to tell stories, to make the world new in them, to make them matter more than anything else. Something runs stories through you, as a river runs between its banks.

And something has to happen, to make you the person you are capable of being. You will need, if you are going to be George Sand, to go to Spain and see dead bodies, you must nearly die yourself, you will have to find magic in the deep woods of rural France, you must lose your father and then your mother, and in the silence left by absence, the clearing where the trees have been felled, you will run from the pig-man to meet your muse, and call him Corambé.

This same day, she thinks suddenly of Marguerite, and writes an e-mail on impulse to her novelist friend who lives with her husband, also a writer, in the Creuse Valley, not far from Nohant. Marguerite, with whom she spent all that time in Paris working on translations when they were both young, who has always said, you must come to our country place, where Jean-François' family has lived for generations; you would love it.

She gets an answer immediately.

"George Sand is almost our next-door neighbour! Come whenever you like. Let us know and we'll meet you. *Tendresses,* M."

"Yes, I'm going to France, they've invited me. I don't know for how long, probably a couple of weeks? I want to do some research there, you know, the George Sand book. I thought, late July, August. Can you take the kids, maybe organize something, a holiday?"

She's tentative with him still. She hears him at the other end, mentally or actually consulting a calendar. Edward has started calling her, to ask rather too anxiously if she is really all right. Has he heard about her ending things with Sean? She doesn't know. She guesses that he misses her. They have, after all, spent twenty years in each other's company, and it must have made some difference to him, surely. She never tells him that sometimes, when she wakes in the night, she finds her pillow soaked with tears, although she hasn't remembered crying, and doesn't know who she is crying for.

They have begun talking to each other, at last. Perhaps everything works out, if you give it enough time? At least he doesn't sound quite so much like an enemy.

"Yes, I suppose you can all stay here, why not. But I'd really rather you didn't. Couldn't you take them somewhere, the Highlands, the west coast? They need a holiday too." She doesn't say, taking Aidan out of Edinburgh would be a good idea, he's spending too much time with people who probably smoke dope.

This is the next conversation, and she notices how hastily he agrees, no, of course he won't stay in what is now her house. He might take them away somewhere, if they want to come. Perhaps down south with their cousins, perhaps the west coast. Or somewhere up north. A cottage, a campsite. He'll see. There's a strange, heady, almost frightening freedom about this; as if they can all of them do anything, and no one will care, or even pay much attention, so free-floating has life become.

He calls her back. He's arranged a camping trip to the Highlands, a place near Aviemore, where there will be plenty for them to do. They can climb the lower slopes of the Cairngorms and do some fly-fishing.

"The Highlands?" groans Aidan. "Can't he take us abroad? He's always going off abroad. Can't we go to Florida?"

But then Aidan gives in, says he could do with getting out of town. Edinburgh in the summer is so boring. Of course Em's up for it, she wants him to teach her how to fish. He'll come round later, and they can talk plans. Something is thawing, something is melting. Aidan wanting to leave town, Em wanting to learn to fish? Do they have to find ways to say they want to be with their father? But people change. Thank God for it, people do change. She breathes out, and notices that the long evenings are getting warmer, the shadows flung across her narrow strip of garden stripe the grass until after dinner, the season has changed, and change has come with it: slight, almost imperceptible, a warmth renewed between them, a respect.

He never mentions Sean, and neither does she. Sean never phones her; they have not met since the day at Cramond. Life, she can't help noticing, does have its own progressions, as the seasons of the year do. Just when you think nothing is going to happen, something small shifts, a finger of light, the inflection of a word, a hand touching yours, a difference in the air of a morning; birdsong, absent-minded humming, a child who looks at you without anxiety, a man who forgets to be stern. It must all be connected. How did she not notice this when she was younger? Awed, she begins to let time pass.

She buys her plane ticket to Paris, and will get the TGV down to Tours, and then on to Poitiers, where her friends will meet her. Spring turns to summer, and sudden inexplicable heat, which brings people out-of-doors to strip off and sunbathe in the Princes Street Gardens and the Botanics as if they were on a beach. It's summer, in a country where summer sometimes refuses to appear.

Maria walks along beside the Water of Leith, having let herself out through her own back door on to the path that runs beside the stream. She sees that the water is high, bubbling brown and fast beneath overhanging branches, hawthorn and elder. All the snow has melted, and fed this water. An old pink sofa lies upon the far bank like a beached boat, gently rotting into the stream. The river used to be full of them, discarded pieces of furniture, bike wheels, garbage bins, even supermarket trolleys. The old sofa is a last relic, a last piece of junk. All this time, the river running past her back door, and she has hardly even noticed it. Two boys lean from the bridge that crosses to the Colonies, a line dangled into the water. This is the old Edinburgh, hidden beneath the glitter and roar of traffic, the insistent rise of the new buildings, the walkways, the tourist sites, the changed skyline. She walks in the direction of Leith, under the bridges, the first time for ages, and occasionally bends to skim a stick into the flow. You can't change the course of a river. It can shrink, run underground, be buried over, but here it still is, just as it ever was—that sofa, how did that get there?—and when she looks back, the boys have gone. A man in new jogging shoes comes barrelling past her on the path, fists clenched, breathing hard. She opens her jacket, strolls in the frail sunlight of today, summer, coming, everything moving on.

5

THE HOUSE ON THE CREUSE

FORTY POUNDS OF PLUM JAM, made on September 1, 1844, by Madame George Sand with her own hands, there in the well-lit kitchen with the orchard at its window, at the table like a butcher's block, the fruit piling up, sliced golden and open, in the big dented copper pan, and the sugar melting, sinking like snow, and the smells spreading through the house. Forty pounds of plum jam, and then back to writing. Turgenev came to stay. Dostoevsky wrote that she had made a difference to European literature. But, the jam. Guests departing, the house quieter, cooler, and all this to be seen to before she returned to Paris for the winter months. Frédéric's room to be repainted, that smell that annoyed him investigated—could it be the drains?—and Solange must be sent back to school because she was too turbulent. Then there were letters to be written, newspapers to be read, the jam to be put to set. Only then—

Late at night, every night, with coffee and little cigars to keep her going, while the others slept, she wrote; till three, till four, till it was nearly light, using the silent hours, casting her hook into the silent depths, her river. In the early evening in summer, going down to swim. All night, hearing it run.

Maria sits under the big lime tree with her notebook and a glass of cold water with dust motes settling on its surface. The day is hot, it's high summer, and the air seems to hum faintly all around her, though there's no specific noise. Far away across the big yard where the carts would have stood loaded with hay a century ago, she sees Jean-François go back and forth with tools and a wheelbarrow. He's repairing a wall that lost its coping and top courses of stone in the last storm. She can see him go up the ladder, his legs in work pants, shirtsleeves rolled to the elbow. Dust rises. Back and forth he goes in the heat of late morning. Soon Marguerite will call from the kitchen door, time for lunch, and they'll assemble from their different corners of the domain, their different occupations, to sit in the cool kitchen and eat salads and cooked vegetables from the kitchen garden, little cheeses from the neighbouring farms, and stewed plums from last year's crop; a cold bottle of wine from the cellar the monks built long before the Revolution brought this house into

Jean-François' family's hands. Everything going on the way it always has, decade after decade, century after century, since the great upheaval happened, and land that had belonged to the Church was suddenly given to Jean-François' republican ancestors. Light falls in condensed pools between the leaves of the lime tree and it sends its little spiralling seeds pirouetting to the ground, or on to her page. She shouldn't have imagined she could really work out here, it's too distracting, but the green filtered light under the huge tree drew her, and the white table in its shade, freckled with seeds, and the way, when she leans back, the sun comes suddenly blinding between the cracked arches of the branches. She's been working indoors for days, in the converted pigsty they call the Porcherie, which has a rag rug on the tiled floor, a bed, a table, a Godin stove, a jug of gerbera daisies put there for her, and a small high window through which the sun comes in early and wakes her with a glance so direct upon her face on the pillow that she blinks, dazzled.

But now there's someone coming towards her across the wide expanse of sunlit grass that separates her from the dusty stone of the yard. Damn! She's forgotten that a cousin from Paris is due today for lunch. The silent ruminations and tastings of their threesome, the inconsequential remarks of three people who have been immersed in their separate thoughts and occupations all morning, will be broken. Jean-François, choosing the right-shaped stones for his wall,

Marguerite upstairs in her study writing, she herself making her notes on George Sand. Now they'll have to be polite.

The man is wearing a jacket and tie and only his unbuttoned jacket agrees with the idea that the day is hot. He's walked from the big house on the other side of the park, another part of Jean-François' family's domain. He comes towards her a little unwieldy, a little unused to it, making his way through the uncut grass. Any sound he makes is suddenly drowned by the whirr of crickets. Of course, that was what the hum was, only now it's suddenly louder, as if the man has disturbed some balance of nature and the crickets are annoyed. Maria gets up from her table to shake hands, as you have to in France.

"*Bonjour*, Madame. *Je m'appelle* Xavier, I am Jean-François' cousin. And you, you must be the writer who is writing a book about George Sand."

"Yes. I've been here nearly a week already. It's a beautiful place." She speaks French to him, feeling like someone else, a person she is not, or is not yet.

"And your book, how is it going?"

"Oh, quite well." How she hates being asked this, in any language. The book is a series of messy notebooks, a sketch, a dream, a conversation, a poem, an argument, all of these, and yet not quite any of them, and she certainly doesn't have words to tell anyone this, in French or in English.

"You have been to Nohant? Where she lived? It's quite near here."

"We're going on Friday. Marguerite and I."

"George Sand, she had all those lovers, at least ten men, she made no secret of it."

Ah, here we go. Maria says nothing. It's the first thing you hear from most men on the subject.

"You know, Chopin died of it, after the journey to Majorca."

Maria wants to protest that Chopin did not need "it" to die of, that the process was well underway before they even left France. But she says evenly, "She went on that journey with two children, a novel to write and very little help. That's what gets forgotten. And Chopin had TB from childhood."

"Ah, but he died after their return, you can't deny that, Madame, she broke with him and he died, I understand."

"In fact, they lived together as friends for seven years, until two years before his death. Did you know he came to stay at Nohant every summer for seven years? She even had a room decorated for him." Maria, standing, has the sun in her eyes and suddenly the shout of the crickets, the glare from the yard, the heat of the day, the argument, are too much. She wants her silence back.

"Ah, you are English, Madame," says the visitor from Paris. Inconsequentially, but as if he's read her thought.

"Scottish, actually."

"Scottish. It's not the same thing?"

"No."

"Well, maybe we should go and find the others? Or must you go on with your—uh—work, Madame?"

He must know I was just daydreaming, Maria thinks but remembers that this man is part of Jean-François' family and that the one thing you have to be in France is polite, and not let your feelings show.

"There's Jean-François, coming down off the wall. And Marguerite—oh, there she is."

Marguerite, taking off her long apron, coming down the steps, the wide worn stone steps beside the hollyhocks that line up their dark heads against the wall, Marguerite with her long plait of hair over her shoulder, coming quickly across the yard to save her, to make things move on, to say what happens next.

Over lunch, the Parisian cousin comes back to the subject of Maria's book as if he can't bear to leave it untouched.

"You know, there are very many books already, about George Sand."

"Yes, I know."

"And you still want to write another one?"

Maria looks at her plate, on which a piece of Camembert sits oozing in a bulge from under its papery white crust. There is no point in explaining, really, but she can't just say nothing, with everyone looking at her expecting a reply. She remembers that in French universities you have to do something called Defending Your Thesis. It's not aggression, it's just a way of carrying on, foreign to her, cautious person that she is, but entirely normal in France. Conversations here proceed by attack and defence. She takes a mouthful of her wine and swallows. But Jean-François comes to her defence.

"Maria's book will be different, because she is different. Most of the books have been written by French writers, and only a few by Anglo-Saxons. And anyway, she is Scottish. She will be able to throw new light on the subject."

"Ah," says the Parisian cousin, and folds his napkin to dab his lips with it. "Of course. This wine is delicious, Jean-François." He's lost interest in a female foreign writer who can't stand up for herself.

"It's our own."

"Which year?"

"Two thousand and three, I think. Yes, two thousand and three."

"A good year."

"One could keep it a little longer, perhaps."

And so it goes.

After lunch, everybody goes to have a brief siesta, although the Parisian cousin protests that in Paris, these days, everyone is far too busy to do this. He stretches out on the divan, pretending to read an article in yesterday's *Le Monde*, and Maria escapes by the kitchen door out into the hot bright afternoon.

To the river. To George's river, this river, the Creuse, which flows here and also past Nohant. To the place where the canoe is tethered to an overhanging tree, in among water-rat holes in the soft giving mud.

She finds the green canoe in its usual place, nose to bank, turning on the shallow water, and unties it, rocks it out into deeper water, throws the painter inside and climbs in after it, one bare foot after the other, in her swimsuit, leaving her clothes rolled in a bundle on the bank, tucked under some leaves. She takes the paddle and strikes away upstream, steering between flat rocks, pointing the canoe's nose a clear way forward between the grey willows and the poplars shimmering on the banks, heading for where the current is. The sharp sun hits her in the chest and throat. She's an Indian in a jungle: deep water and the yell of birds over-head. She's young again, a child. When, as an adult woman, a mother, can you simply paddle your canoe straight upstream, in the path of the current, in the eye of the sun?

But no, he's right. She can't write another book about George Sand. There are too many already. He has a point there. She's wasting her time, she could be doing something else, something more worthwhile—but what? She's prob-ably writing about George Sand because she can't manage her own life. Paddle, paddle, farther upstream. No, she's on a trail, hot on a trail, she can do it, he's wrong, wrong. Burning in the mid-afternoon furnace, lulled in the heart of silence. She dips the paddle again and again into cool deep running water, brown as tea. Then she steps out where it's shallow, toes sinking in mud, pulls the canoe a little way up the bank. She ties it to a beached log with the frayed painter. Small trees grow close to the water's edge here, and hang over, the undersides of their trunks dappled with light. She thinks of the silver ripples drawn on the thighs of women aging; the frailty and beauty of flesh. Water and light caress the undersides of the willows continually. The canoe, its green paint blistered in the sun, lies slightly tipped on its side. She wades back into the cool water, swims against the push and pull of it, upstream, always upstream, because here you could be carried downstream so fast. Swimming upstream she stays in place, like being on an exercise bicycle, or on a conveyor belt. It takes an effort to stay in one place and not be swept away; she closes her eyes for a moment and feels the tug of the current, the water running like ropes between her legs. There's the sharp cry of a jay, a chatter of rooks, the plop of a fish a yard away. This sound, then that. The sun glittering through branches when she opens her eyes.

As she comes out of the river her limbs feel slow and heavy. Its taste and smell are on her, the dank secret river smell and metallic taste. She sits on the bank to dry. The voice of the man from Paris has faded. He wasn't even a literary critic, for God's sake, he didn't know what he was talking about; and anyway, he's far away now, an overweight man on a sofa, snoring probably, clutching a page from yesterday's paper, having forgotten all about it immediately after he dealt her his blow. He doesn't matter. Just as the Majorcan José María Cuadrado didn't matter, in the large scheme of things.

Somewhere behind poplars and walnut trees and fields of maize and sunflowers, a dog barks. Dragonflies flash their gas-flame blue close to the water that crawls like skin on milk. There are dancing white butterflies and big creeping black beetles, horseflies, probably snakes in the grass. Somewhere upstream, men are fishing, the long lines they play out taut over the water like threads of saliva. They plumb this river with their bright lines, their hooks, this river and the Vienne, deep under bridges, and the Indre, and the Cher, and the wide grey shining Loire in its gravelly bed. Fishermen, like literary critics, she thinks, waiting for the big one, throwing others back.

As she returns downstream, the sun claps her on the back, a departing guest. The canoe slides easily, she hardly has to paddle, but lifts the dripping double oar and skims the glassy surface, which holds the upside-down ballooning trees in the mirror version of the world. The sky in the water is silver. The real sky is a burnished afternoon blue. It may be later than she thinks. Shadows stretch on the water making places for hidden small animals to splash home. She treads sharp stones in warm shallow water and pulls the canoe up after her, ties it where it belongs with a good double half-hitch. She finds her bundle of clothes.

If she hadn't come back, they'd have found her clothes, her single footprints in mud, the canoe gone. What would they have thought then? But no, she's back, she walks back up the track, clothes sticking to damp flesh, past the loaded plum trees with their golden weights that drag their limbs down like tired dancers', past the vegetable garden, the orange pumpkins waiting under leaves, the marrows, the tomatoes ripening fast, the tall hollyhocks and gladioli, scarlet and pink and white among the green. She has mud streaked on her legs, and smells of the river. She crosses the blazing yard with its small corner of shade hunkered under the barn doors, goes up the stone steps and back into the cool kitchen, where there is nobody, but a bunch of wildflowers on the windowsill, a coffee pot on the table, crumbs, and silence. Her feet on the cool flags of the floor, leaving their damp prints, which quickly dry.

Maria and Marguerite plan to drive over to Nohant, to see George Sand's house that she inherited from her grandmother and the museum in the nearby village, La Châtre. From there they will go on to Gargilesse, also on the Creuse, where in later life George escaped to be with Manceau, her last lover, and write in peace.

Maria calls the museum. "Is it open every day, the Château de Nohant, or is there a day when it's closed?"

"Every day, Madame, it is open, from nine to twelve, and from two to six."

"And the museum?"

"Open every day."

"What is there to see in the museum?"

"Birds, Madame. And some other things."

"Birds?"

She runs to tell Marguerite. Birds? Maria tells her friend about birds in the early life of Aurore Dupin. Birds! Her mother's father was a bird-seller on the quais of the Seine. There were those pigeons she saw convulsing into death on a kitchen table in Spain, when she and her mother and sick brother were travelling to find her father in Napoleon's army. Four years old, with the Peninsular War raging around her. They hadn't killed her pet, the one with the breast like a small pillow, but they tore the others apart, wing from breast, leg from groin, the throats ruffled, beaks starkly open. She watched, an appalled child with her eyes wide open at table level, and never forgot.

Then there was the pied bird in a cage who struck his beak at the bars and yelled at her in Spanish. "*Muerta! Muerta!*" The skinny twelve-year-old boy at her side said, "*Muerta* means death. He says it because he wishes you were dead."

Birds? They fall about laughing at the coincidence.

On the quais of the Seine, larks, a golden linnet, a thrush, all caged. He was not a bad man, her grandfather, not cruel, but poor. He had to feed his daughter. And his daughter Sophie, who grew up in poverty, had to feed her daughter, Aurore.

———

"It's a matter of form," Marguerite says when Maria shows her the messy growing manuscript. "You haven't yet got the form. But it will come." She comes down from her morning writing stint in her high-up room, at midday. "It doesn't matter what people say about writers, really," she says. "Because their lives are like a river, a deep-running river, and all you can see is the surface, where dragonflies flit about. The rest can never quite be plumbed." She rolls her sleeves and plunges her hands into cold water, to wash the salad.

Her river, George Sand's river, the same stretch of water.

They have worked together so often on translation, she filling in for Marguerite the English idioms that so often do not move smoothly into French. She's read Marguerite's books, Marguerite read her thesis. Since those first days in Paris, when she was at the Sorbonne, and Marguerite newly married, living in the 5th arrondissement. From her own room on the rue de Broca to their flat near the Jardin des Plantes, running back and forth, sharing books, testing ideas. Now, here they are again, and Marguerite with her accurate French sense of form gives her parameters again. The river of their lives, the rhythm of days. Mid-life, midstream. Maria goes down to swim again as George did, and comes up each time, hair dripping, wet suit hanging from a finger, up through the vegetable gardens to tell Marguerite her latest idea. Marguerite gardens, and carries vegetables up to the house, carrots and potatoes, their roots dangling blobs of dry earth, and little lettuces, and a bag full of peas. She sits in her high room working over a sentence, a phrase. She looks up as Maria knocks.

"Ah, what have you found now? How is dear George today? You look like a dog that has dug up a bone."

The museum at La Châtre has one floor for George Sand memorabilia, copies of her books, the Nadar photograph, drawings of Nohant done by her son Maurice. But first there is the floor of stuffed birds. Eagles, buzzards, owls big and small, gulls in all species, the black-backed, the herring gulls, kittiwakes, cormorants, and swans, ducks, finches, kingfishers, larks, blackbirds, thrushes, robins, swallows, swifts, martins, penguins, stone-chats, curlews, herons both white and blue, pigeons, yes, and canaries, and linnets too.

The swans, the emu, the giant fighting cock with his black frills, the albatross borrowed by the Ancient Mariner, too big to be put behind glass. The emu is moulting and looks mad. The flamingo is brittle as sticks. The swans are dried out, grey with accumulated dust. There's a whole closet full of birds with tickets on them saying *Espèces Disparues*. The *canard du Labrador*, the *pic à bec d'Ivoire*, the *pigeon migrateur*. Extinct species. Then there are the tiny, ordinary birds that can flit in and out of rooms hardly noticed, like so much punctuation. Their bones like scraps of writing, marks of a thin long-ago pen, their flight a calligraphy that has been lost for good. Sparrows, house martins, wrens.

At Nohant, a few miles down the road, they go to look for George Sand and find—her things. In the salon, her aristocratic grandfather's filing cabinet, left over from his time as a lawyer. In the library at La Châtre there had been another one, with copies of all her correspondence. There are her clothes: the dresses with waists under the armpits and skirts so narrow that nobody could step across a ditch in them, the farm-boy's clothes that were Deschartres' idea for her when he took her hunting. There are the wide skirts of the 1820s, and behind them, making them unnecessary, the trousers, waistcoat, overcoat and long woollen scarf, the hat and stout boots of a Parisian student, made specially for a writer who needed to take to the street. At Gargilesse, there are the ruched brown cape, little flat straw hat and short boots of the 1860s and '70s, all displayed on the bed.

Maria and Marguerite look them over with alarm. Do they want their old clothes, or their friends' for that matter, laid out on view for tourists?

"We'll take them all to jumble sales before we die, right?" Maria takes her friend's arm. Marguerite is looking at the clothes that are laid on the bed, as if George herself were coming home in an hour to change. "There is something too personal. A person's clothes—no, it is too much."

Later, Maria thinks, something scared her, she was suddenly afraid.

Then there are locks of hair. One grey, cut off after her death, one nearly black, sent to Musset in her youth. It was an era that cut off and kept locks of hair. Chandeliers, not identical but similar, both sent from Venice, one by Musset, one by Pagello. Who had the idea first? Letters. It was a time of kept letters. Hardly objects; more like the flight of birds, the sound of wingbeats, the cry, footprints in dust.

"Nobody will know about us, not in that way. E-mails, hard-drives, everything will disappear. They won't know us, in a hundred years. We will have gone without a trace." This thought makes them both quiet.

"There will be your books," Maria says. But she wishes that they were not having this conversation, and again, doesn't know why.

Dolls. Cupboards full of dolls. The marionettes carved by her son Maurice and dressed by her. They are like the birds at La Châtre, they are all the characters in all the stories that anyone could ever want to use. The dragon, the crocodile, the mermaid, Napoleon's soldiers in the uniform of an extinct army. Chopin's idea, to have a puppet theatre. Maria thinks of long evenings and people making up plays for puppets. And here they hang, varnished and painted wood in their ragged silks, all this time after the people have gone.

———

They go outside and walk across the grass at Nohant. It's still wet from a heavy dew. Maria tells her friend the story of the pear tree, the one at the corner of the vegetable garden, beneath which lie the remains of George Sand's baby brother, born in Spain, to die here and be buried twice.

"And George only knew about it when her mother told her, decades later. But I suppose it can't be the original tree."

Marguerite, she can't help noticing, does not look well.

"Marguerite, are you all right?"

"Just a little tired. And I have a stomach pain from time to time, I don't know what it is. I'm fine, though, don't worry."

They find the pear tree at the corner of the vegetable garden, the one planted above the grave of the little brother who didn't survive, or its replacement. The trees say more, Maria thinks, about the woman who lived here than furniture does, or clothes. Life is lived in between the objects, in the spaces where something may grow. The ingredients are never quite the whole.

She begins to think about a book in which the spaces between objects say what can't be said. In which an empty room sings with an absence. In which trees move, and a few seeds fly from them, like the seeds from the lime tree at Jean-François' house, and lives are changed.

At Gargilesse, they arrive in a world of rain. Rain on the flagstones makes them gleam dark and wet. The chestnut tree drips at the door. They rush into George Sand's last house, to shelter. She didn't name it; in her memoirs it was always "my village."

Manceau understood, took the house in his name. Her last lover, he fed her need for peace and solitude. A butterfly hunter and naturalist, he went out all day, left her when she wanted to be left alone. Today, the steps up to the little house are slippery with rain. They go in through the low door. The rooms are intimate; it's like walking uninvited into an inhabited house.

In the front room there is a placard on the wall which says: GEORGE SAND, FÉMINISTE, RÉPUBLICAINE, PRÉCURSEUR. Precursor. Ancestor, forerunner. Of whom? Themselves? And there are those boots, in the bedroom, and her skirt, laid out on the bed . . .

They thank the young guide and run in the pouring rain up the street to the Hôtel des Artistes, which used to be Chez Malesset, where George ate her lunch, sometimes as early as ten thirty in the morning. ("Wonderful weather. Hot as summer. Perfect lunch. Shrimp omelette. *Pauvre Manceau, où es-tu?*")

On the piano today there's an immense apricot tart. All around is the sound of harp players in the rain, chirping and trilling from open windows, like a chorus of birds. The village of Gargilesse is hosting a harpists' reunion. Maria and Marguerite sit, wet-haired, umbrellas dripping at their sides; lulled by food, secure in the knowledge of their *précurseur*. Coffee and apricot tart and rain.

Maria hasn't yet told her friend about Edward, or Sean, or the changes in her life; it's here, in the restaurant at Gargilesse, that she tries to begin, because it's raining, because they are far from anywhere, because something signals her that now is the time for confidences and growing close, for having the kind of conversation you can only have with a woman friend of your own age, whether she has grown up in a different culture or not.

"I've broken up with Edward, or rather he has with me. I fell in love with someone else."

Silence. Then Marguerite says, "Sorry, excuse me, I have to find the toilet," and gets up as if she has not heard, and Maria is left wondering whether she has broken some unknown French rule, or if her friend is simply not interested in the events of her love life. She has always been slightly puritanical, Maria remembers.

Their first meeting, in the changing room of a swimming pool in the Midlands of England, all those years ago, when she had heard Marguerite speaking French to someone as she herself struggled out of her swimming costume and into her clothes; she had simply come out and addressed the unknown woman in French, and Marguerite, who stood there white and slim in a baggy black suit, her thin feet in a puddle of water, her long plait hanging soaked over her shoulder, wondering aloud if there was a hair dryer, had answered her. They left together, talking about translation, whether you should do it word for word or create a new whole. Twenty years ago, more. It was in the time of their lives when conversation could lead anywhere, and did, because there were really no agendas in life and nobody was waiting for them; only two future husbands, whom they had not yet met.

The sun comes out and dries the puddles and they pay their bill and go out into a gleaming drenched world. Marguerite drives her old Citroën, Maria sits beside her, noticing her blunt-fingered, veined gardener's hands on the wheel. She wonders if her friend simply did not hear what she said, or somehow failed to understand, and decides to let it go. They begin talking about George again, and the rooms at Gargilesse, and the notice about their *précurseur*. They find a hotel in the late afternoon, in which they will perhaps stay the night. It's at the end of a long drive, hidden behind trees like, she thinks, the house in *Le Grand Meaulnes*, but she doesn't say this to Marguerite, as there are so many houses like this in France. It's called the Hôtel de la Vallée Bleue, and they park and go in to ask about rooms. The rooms vary in price, the man at the desk tells them. There is the Gustave Flaubert, which is a few francs more than the Jules Sandeau, which is in turn a little more than the Alfred de Musset. The Frédéric Chopin is the most exorbitant, the Théophile Gautier quite a bargain. The handsome man in shirtsleeves looks down the register to see which rooms are free. Is this a game? Maria decides on the Gustave Flaubert.

Marguerite hesitates between the Musset and the Sandeau. The long forefinger of the man at the desk goes down the page. Unfortunately all the rooms are booked, unless, that is, they would consider the annex, where he has, ah, the Manceau and the Casimir Dudevant.

"I don't think so," says Marguerite.

They look at each other, stifling laughter. Who, in this deep rural silence, has booked all these rooms? Maria has a brief fantasy of foreign novelists, one in each room, writing away with the dedication of people locked up in writers' colonies. She'll tell Marguerite about it once they are in the car. But there is not a sound from inside, and nobody looks out of the high windows as they drive away.

"Imagine, in the Gustave Flaubert, lying awake or dreaming about bears and troubadours?"

"Yes, and listening to an old woman coughing, and being haunted by sentences that need to be rewritten seven times?" Marguerite, driving, her skirt hitched up and feet in old espadrilles on the pedals, joins in the game.

"Waking up to look at teeth blackened by mercury? Ugh. Or the Musset; there'd be Venetian chandeliers, a gondolier outside the window, the smell of Italian cakes when you woke up. Not bad. And then, there'd always be Dr. Pagello in the wings."

"And think of the Frédéric Chopin, you'd be lying awake worrying, listening to the rain on the roof, and that cough."

"Personally, I'd rather have Manceau. At least he knew how to fix a roof, and there was nothing wrong with him."

"We want different things as we age," Marguerite says, laughing, hands on the wheel. "A bit of solidity, wouldn't you say?"

But then she evidently remembers that Maria has no one solid to lean on, so she stops.

Maria thinks, if they were to hunt for it again, they probably wouldn't be able to find the Hôtel de la Vallée Bleue. Perhaps, like the shrimp omelette chez Malesset, it's not in the Michelin, at least not the one for this year. Did we dream that place? she wants to ask her. Was it real? But she remembers what Marguerite has said about wanting different things; and suddenly, she remembers her dream about the shed which grew to be a cottage, the man waiting for her there. It was Gargilesse. It was the small house of old age, the last home.

When they get back from Nohant, there are the pots of plum jam, in rows. For two days Jean-François has been making jam. He sits at the table with a sharp knife, slicing the yellow plums that are freckled sweetly with red. Juice drips from his fingers, the sliced plum-flesh falls into the bowl. Maria notices that his pans are exactly the same as the ones hanging on the kitchen wall at Nohant. The Reine Claudes from yesterday, labelled already, are in the cupboard. The mirabelles in the pan are sticky and turning brown. Jean-François sits on a high stool, legs crossed, peering over his glasses, stirring with a long wooden spoon.

"Well, did you find dear George at home?"

Soon all the pots will be cleaned, labelled and placed in the big cupboard, enough for a whole year, and the doors and windows of the house will be closed, and none of them will be here. The white cat out in the garden will wait for human voices in vain, and give up and go somewhere else to be fed. Winter will come, and spring, and another summer. And so on and on. The doors will open again, next year's plums will ripen on the trees, people will come together, the chairs will be set out on that patch of grass under the lime tree. This is how it has been every year in the Creuse Valley for the last two hundred years, in this house of Jean-François' family, and in the house at Nohant, since that revolution when property, history and literature changed hands. One day there is Madame George Sand in her kitchen making jam, and her friend the musician practising a phrase on the Pleyel. A small boy has jumped out of a window. The children are down by the river, building huts. The walls, the massive stone, the roofs and cellars are the same. Years later, only the trees will have grown.

Staying with Jean-François and Marguerite, she's lulled into their slow rhythm of days. They have breakfast together, tea made in the big old pewter teapot that Marguerite bought years ago when she was a student in

England, toast that Jean-François makes, slightly charred and laden with dollops of his own jam. The kitchen smells of toast when Maria comes in from the yard, walking diagonally across it from the Porcherie, where she sleeps and works. She has been translating George for the last few days. George on Nohant, George on the river, and at Gargilesse, writing while Manceau draws caterpillars and they play bezique in the evenings. The yard is a dazzle of white stone, with dark red, almost black hollyhocks growing against a wall. Inside the house, the floors are cool to bare feet—she kicks off her shoes at the door—and even the air is chilled, between the thick medieval walls. After breakfast, Jean-François does the dishes, as he does for every meal, brushing away offers of help, "But, my dear girl, you wouldn't know how! No, women don't do the dishes in this house." He's careful, thorough. His hands in the sink or placing stones back on walls or tenderly picking peas or feeling for the ripeness of a plum on a tree. Maria watches, and sees the solid framework within which her friend lives. But something is wrong, she sees this too. Marguerite is frailer than Maria has ever seen her, her long white legs unsteady as she walks, a tiredness around her eyes. There is something that no one is saying.

"Let me do it, you look exhausted." Maria says it one day, and Marguerite hands her a big heavy basket of vegetables to carry in from the kitchen garden.

"Yes, I haven't been feeling well lately. Jean-François

wants me to go for tests, when we go back to Paris. But, we're none of us getting younger. I don't think it's anything more than that."

"But you should probably have the tests."

"Yes. I know. But, Marie, what about you? I'm worried about you. You and Edward. What you told me. I'm sorry I didn't say anything at the time, I just couldn't take it in. Are you serious? And, do you mind me asking you, why? Why, after twenty years, more, isn't it? I can't imagine it somehow."

I know you can't imagine it, Maria thinks, because you have Jean-François, and he surrounds you with all the care and attention you need, so that you can grow, like the fragile rare plant that you are.

"I fell in love with this other man," Maria says. "We had an affair."

"And are you still with him? The man? Will you live with him?"

"No. He has ended it. He's married."

"Ah. I see." They sit at the big kitchen table now and begin to shell peas. The peas spring from their still-damp pods and into a glass bowl. Maria thinks, it's so long since I've even seen a fresh pea.

"I couldn't see the need to break up over it," Maria says. "But Edward couldn't take it. He was too jealous, too angry. He said I'd erased our marriage, more or less, by doing what I did."

Marguerite says, "He's still hurt. He'll get over it. If you don't see the man any more, what can upset him? So many people get over these things. I myself, for one."

"You?"

"Yes, Jean-François has been in love so many times with other women. But it never lasts. He always comes back to me."

"Jean-François? Really?"

"Oh, yes, really. All through our married life. But he's not going to leave me, any more than he will leave this house, or this garden. He's not the leaving kind of man. He just goes sometimes on—excursions. And comes back."

"And you don't mind?"

"I can't say I don't mind, but it doesn't destroy me, it happens, it stops, he's here, he's a good husband."

"He loves you."

"Yes, he loves me."

"I think Edward hates me, now."

"Hate is just an aspect of love. It's wounded love. Don't you think so, Marie?"

"I'd never thought about it that way. I ask myself, do I love him, and the answer's yes, but not in the way I loved the other man."

"Well, of course, you have been married to him for years, and the other man's new to you. Of course, it's different."

"And what I long for—this may sound stupid—is for someone to just be there. To love me whatever I do. You know?"

"Love like that is for babies," Marguerite says firmly. "You can't be loved whatever you do. You have to be someone good, to be loved. People can't just love you for existing."

"Hmm. Well, maybe. You don't believe in unconditional love?"

"Yes, I do, but it's for babies. You have to be worthy of love."

Their fingers work, stripping the pods till peas fill the glass bowl, small and green and tender, and Marguerite gets up to reach the potatoes waiting to be peeled. Jean-François comes in with a giant mushroom in each hand, as if he's doing a conjuring act.

"Look what I found."

"What about George Sand and Manceau?" Maria says. "He seems to have given her unconditional love."

"Ah, but then, she was George Sand. She was somebody."

"What are you women talking about? Unconditional love?" Jean-François dusts his hands clean of earth. "Always love, when two women get together."

"And when men get together?"

"Ah, we talk about our exploits. How we have made some woman crazy for us. It's usually all lies." He grins. Maria thinks of the cottage at Gargilesse, and Manceau who mended everything, fixed the roof, copied George's manuscripts, worked carefully at his own engravings, but was there to bring her a cup of coffee, to play bezique in the evenings. Did you have to be George Sand to have that kind of attention? There was Marguerite Duras, who had had a younger lover who did everything for her, Yann someone. But was it because of what they wrote, or who they were? Or was it being French? There was Colette and Maurice Goudeket, there were probably dozens of others, older women with men who adored them. But as Marguerite reminded her, these women were not just anyone.

She has just read what George wrote about Manceau, her last lover, whom she met at the age of forty-six: "I am happy, extremely happy. It's so good to be loved and to be able to love completely, that it would be stupid to imagine it ending. I'm forty-six, I have white hair, it doesn't matter. Old women are loved more than young ones, I know it now. It's not the person who has to last, but the love, and let God take care of that lasting because it is good."

Perhaps it's living in Scotland, Maria thinks. But then, are our feelings determined by our nationality? The country we find ourselves living in? No. But how we act on them or not, probably yes. Scots think it's wicked to have sex outwith marriage, the French don't. They probably suffer as much as one another, but if society says you should act on your suffering, then possibly you go on suffering longer, and more vociferously. You complain to all your friends, get a lawyer and start divorce proceedings. As Edward is doing now. Suddenly, she wonders if Edward, wherever he is, is suffering because of her. If he is, she is strangely moved by the thought. It will be the first time in their life together that she has ever allowed this to happen.

Maria's last birthday, in April, made her forty-two. She too will soon be forty-five, then fifty, and a long strand of her black hair has turned white, a look that reminds her, and she hopes others, of Susan Sontag, so that she hasn't bothered to dye it out. She doesn't, because this is the twenty-first century, think of herself as an old woman; but her lover being in his early thirties has made her wonder. She thinks with astonishment that this is the first time in twenty years that she has not put Edward's comfort first, worried about how he is feeling, given over a large part of her mind to him. The habit of loving him became so ingrained that she did not even notice when it stopped. Perhaps it did not stop; perhaps a part of her goes on loving him still, in the wings, off to one side; but the raw excitement, the unexpected beauty of Sean was surely another feeling altogether, like a new shoot, a new growth. And this part grows on in his absence, getting stronger even as the part that worries about Edward is shrinking. It isn't even about Sean himself, she notices now; it is about a part of herself that she allowed to lapse for a very long time.

On her last day, she borrows an old bike and takes off to explore the countryside she has hardly seen, having spent so many of her mornings indoors. She rides in shorts and a T-shirt to the next village, props the bike against a warm stone wall and goes in to a café for a drink. She sips Orangina through a straw, and then walks to the church, which is locked, perhaps to prevent vandalism. It's hot; the village street is divided into light and shade; nobody is about. She bicycles on, wobbling down the middle of the road, back into the forest. Travelling these roads, she thinks, would have been unthinkable once for a woman alone. Was this where Aurore saw her brigand woman, dangling from a tree? There are no lines of demarcation any more. This hill could well have been where the German army came to a halt, once in 1870, again in 1940. Nobody is going to stop her, search her or take her for a spy.

The woods grow denser, sunlight filtered from high up through the branches of chestnuts, oaks, beech trees. Suddenly she finds herself at a crossroads, a place where five, not four roads go off in different directions. Four other straight ways of going off into the forest from this place. Silence. Light plays its patterns on the forest floor. Maria thinks, I haven't for years been this much alone. There's a sign: PROPRIÉTÉ PRIVÉE. DÉFENSE DE PÉNÉTRER. Private property, no entry. She leans on her bicycle. The road she's on goes straight ahead for another ten kilometres or so, there's no reason to leave it, yet there are these other roads, straight wide pathways cut through forest, that must lead somewhere. There's this puzzling sense of choice, and yet immediate interdiction. She continues on the widest of the forest roads, leaving the notice behind, and freewheels downhill, knowing she can always turn around and go back the exact way she came, through the village, back down the road to the house; but somehow she doesn't want to. When she gets back, hours later, after bumping along miles of forest tracks guided by the position of the sun, she has a sense of exuberant accomplishment as she arrives, hot and sweaty, her hands grimy on the handlebars, back in the yard.

6

CONSOLATION

IT'S CURIOUS TO BE APPROACHING the bookshop again. It has its sign painted, LE PONT TRAVERSÉ, to link it with the one of the same name in Paris. Once she went in and asked for books by George Sand. And he came in, and they made it their place of rendezvous, being halfway between his workplace in the building where he did research into diseases of the immune system, and her own, where she taught would-be modern linguists about Duras and Modiano, Derrida and Gilles Deleuze. It snowed, she remembers. It was the winter. All through the spring and summer, and into the winter again. It seems a long time ago. Today, in a different season, the sky above the streets is blue and chased across with small harmless clouds, and there's no harshness in the air, nothing to take shelter from. Buildings are washed and gleaming, the streets dry. Down the street, some men are sandblasting the stone fronts of tenements, a program which has been going on all over the city for years now, to restore it to its original eighteenth-century cleanness before the soot of chimneys blackened it. First the public monuments, next the tenements.

There's a different display in the window and the place looks brighter somehow; perhaps the window glass has been cleaned, or the woodwork has been painted, she's not sure. Inside, there's more space between shelves and the arrangement is different; she pushes open the glass door and goes in. As soon as she's inside she knows it's a place she has been avoiding. There are these spots, on maps, in the geography of cities, that evoke too much. The ordinary street map never shows them, but we all know for ourselves, she thinks, where they are. It's as if there's a city within a city, its monuments made of moments in our lives. Yes, the whole place has changed, and it's a relief. Maybe the original woman who saw all their meetings is no longer here. But no, she comes out from the back of the store smiling, holding out a hand.

"How good to see you again. I've quite missed you. It's Maria, isn't it?"

"Yes. Hi. I'm sorry, I don't know—"

"My name? It's Catriona. I did see you pass, a few times. Sometimes I thought of calling out to you in the street, but you looked as if you were in a hurry. How's the book going?"

"Oh, quite well, I've been in France, researching it."

"In France? How wonderful. Did you get some holiday time too?"

"Oh, yes." She wants to go, but the woman—Katrina? Catriona?—she never knew her name before, never was interested, is still speaking to her.

"You know, maybe I shouldn't say it, but I've never forgotten those other times you came in. When we had all that snow. It may seem odd to you, that I should mention it, but you looked so happy. It did me a world of good."

"Really?" Maria looks away: at shelves of books, meaningless titles, all glossy, coloured, new. Particles of gold dust dance in the sunlight.

"Yes, it made quite an impression. To tell the truth, it changed my life. I felt I wanted to thank you."

"Thank me? What for?"

Maria thinks, I could tell her that I am not that happy, it was all an illusion, reality is not like that, it passes. She looks at the other woman—Katrina?—in the shafts of light that come in and make ordinary dust look golden, dancing in the air where nobody has dusted thoroughly enough. If you are unaware of the effect you're having on someone, can you be held responsible for their feelings, even thanked?

"You looked so happy, both of you, and it was kind of infectious."

Fine light-brown eyes, thin arched brows, greying hair combed back from a spacious forehead: a mouth full of feeling and humour. Maria thinks, I never even looked at her before, I was so busy feeling what I felt, waiting for him. What was it, during those days, that she saw in me? That I now feel the lack of, so acutely. Where has it gone?

"You see, the shop looks different, doesn't it? We've a good poetry section now, we didn't have that before. Some interesting new poets in translation, too."

"Yes, it all looks lighter, more spacious, I did notice. It's good." Sunlight, bronze chrysanthemums and the quiet welling of Bach's harpsichord in the background.

Someone saw them, someone remembered. They had an effect in the world, even if they have it no more.

The bookseller goes to the poetry section—"Wait a second"—and comes back with a book. "Do you know Adrienne Rich? Of course. Well, let me see if I can find it. There's a poem about walking to meet someone in an airport and suddenly realizing that all the feelings, the energy, the love, are yours. They aren't given or lent to you by the other person, they are your own. Do you know it?"

Maria says, "I never thought of that." She lays a finger on the sleek cover of a book that lies on the desk.

"Can I make you a cup of coffee? I usually have one around this time, and give one to anyone who comes in. I may even have some shortbread."

"Thanks. That would be great. Katrina?"

"Catriona."

"Catriona, sorry."

"You know, one day after you both came in here, I bought

myself a bottle of red wine on the way home, a good one, and I took one of the books, the George Sand, and I actually looked forward to getting back to my flat and spending my evening there."

The crescendos of Bach make Maria shiver. The coffee begins to percolate at the back of the shop. Catriona brings her a white cup and saucer with a gold rim. Sunlight dances between them, the air is thick with it where particles of dust, life, its residues are, and all the books are new and untouched and a small fire made of pressed logs leaps cleanly in a grate.

The shortbread fingers neatly in their tin. "No, thanks, just the coffee is fine."

"I'm looking forward to your book now," Catriona says. "You must tell me as soon as you know when it's coming out."

"Of course."

Something occurs to Maria, out of a memory of an evening when she found a snow-stained package laid on a table in the hall. "You know, the Flaubert letters? Was that you?"

"Well, you didn't come in to the shop, and the book had come, the one you ordered, so I just dropped it off when I was downtown one day."

The door to the street swings open and a young man in jeans and a sweatshirt with *Kabul* written on it comes in. He glances at them both, nods hello to Maria and makes for the shelf of new books. It's Ruaridh, from her Deleuze seminar.

Catriona calls out, "Those two shelves right in front of you! In alphabetical order, or it should be. And there's coffee when you're ready, if you want some."

He looks round, surprised, and smiles. Both women laugh, but don't seem to be excluding him, so he nods, thanks.

"Did you say coffee? Great. Oh, and shortbread." He takes two.

Catriona brings another cup. In his big cold hands it looks more delicate. He stirs in sugar and his cup rattles in its saucer.

"This is one of my students, Ruaridh. Do you two know each other?"

Ruaridh grins and says, "If you don't mind me saying so, Dr. Jameson, I still haven't a clue what yon man's on about."

"You're not alone there. Ruaridh's one of my best students, Catriona, he's great on difficult questions. You need to be a questioner when you're tangling with French philosophers."

Ruaridh, flattered, is like a chilled bird coming back to life. His shoulders drop and his gaze stops roaming. He drinks down his coffee in a couple of gulps and hands back the cup. "Thanks, hey, I'll be back."

When Maria turns to leave, he follows her and says, "Is it aye like that in there? It's so cozy. It's great."

"Yes, I think it's always like that."

"Amazing."

"Yes, isn't it?" And they wave each other away, turning

to go in different directions with the casual ease of people who know each other and will meet again.

"Have a great day, Dr. Jameson."

"You too! And don't take the structuralists too seriously, right?"

Maria is outside the shop, in the street, when she becomes aware of something she wants to do. It's an effort to go back inside, it makes her action not spontaneous but deliberate, not casual but willed. She goes back in and kisses Catriona on the cheek, gripping her thin upper arms as if to keep her in place.

"Thank you," she says.

Catriona flushes deeply, almost wriggles away; but she watches Maria go, a hand raised either to say goodbye or to mark the place in the air where this sudden unexpected thing has happened.

The autumn days are beautiful now in the way of Edinburgh Indian summers, when the tourists have gone, the Festival is over, summer is finished, but the sky blazes blue and cloudless, chrysanthemums give out their bitter flavour in borders, the trees in the Botanics cast long shadows still over the grass. At sunset the wardens of the gardens go round giving their long call, "Clo-o-osing time!" As the light fades slowly, leaves its gold afterglow. Through the tall thick hedges, the flickers of brightness. She hears them through the open windows of her house. "Clo-o-osing time!" There are stories about people being locked in behind the iron gates for the night.

Aidan and Emily have gone back to school, taller, browner, leggier than they were at the beginning of summer. They swing out of the house in the mornings and down the terrace whirling their school bags, all the way up the street to Inverleith Park and across it through the drifts of brown leaves to Broughton, where they both go to school. They are friends in a way they were not before, Maria sees. Aidan is less annoyed by his sister, and she is less prone to tears and rage. Something has happened, again. It has happened without her. Of the holiday in the Highlands, Aidan has said only, "It was okay. Dad was cool. Too many bugs, we got bitten all the time. But the fishing was great. Even Em got one, a big one, didn't you, Em?" They have accepted the way things are.

Edward came to the house to deliver them home. (How was France? Good. Great. When are you going to finish your book?) He too is tanned and dotted with mosquito bites. He dumps camping gear in her hall, and throws down boots, Aidan's fishing rod, the old tarpaulin they have had for years: no room for all this at his place, she can find a place to stash it, she doesn't mind? They may do it again. They climbed some of the lower slopes of the Cairngorms, they fished in lochs, they cooked on campfires, they met some cool people. There was an American family from Boston, who have invited them all to stay. They were way cool, says Emily, trying it out.

When their two children have gone to their rooms, he stands in the hall, looking at her across the heaps. Maria makes herself look back.

"So you're really okay?"

"Yes, really." If she hadn't just had that surprising moment in the bookshop, she might not have been so sure. But she faces him evenly, sees his blue gaze, flushed face, thinning blond hair; a pulse at his throat. Here they are again, in this house which they chose together. He gestures towards the street.

"I should move my car, I'm double-parked."

"Yes."

"I just wanted to tell you. I'm seeing someone."

"Oh." It's like a slap. She has half expected it, but not yet, not like this. She steps back from him, her hand at her mouth, her heart hammers, she feels sick. There's a silence; the front door still half-open, people going by on the street, his car with the door hanging open. Sun patterning the carpet in the hall.

"Who is she?"

"How did you know it's a woman?"

"Well, Edward, I assumed it wouldn't be a man, come on."

"Well, it is a woman, actually. She's tremendously perceptive. I told her everything. About us, about how I felt."

"Oh. Oh God, Edward, I don't think I can listen to this just now." The intense stab of jealousy, she supposes it is jealousy, makes her gasp again. And how can he be telling her this, so coolly, how can he have told another woman all about them, is nothing sacred, does he owe her no respect? This perceptive woman, God damn her eyes, who understands everything about him, who is told everything he feels?

"Why are you so upset? I don't get it. What I wanted to say was, she suggested you might see her too."

"I might? I might see some woman, some tremendously perceptive woman, some fucking bitch who understands you so bloody well, I might see her? Are you out of your mind?"

Edward raises his hands, palms up, an innocent man. Then he leans against the wall and starts to laugh. "Oh, I see! You thought I meant I was seeing someone as in *seeing* someone, dating someone, having a fling, right? Oh, I get it. No, I'm seeing a shrink. A lady shrink. She's helping me get some perspective on things, that's all."

Maria starts to cry, out of an unrecognizable emotion that shakes her, and then she starts to laugh, and soon they are both laughing hysterically, so that when the children come back downstairs, they are speechless, winded, amazed.

The dream is of a house full of mirrors and she's walking down a corridor to face herself in her mirrored reflection. It's her own house, but not one she has ever known. She lights candles as she goes, illuminating darkness, and listens to her own footfalls. She's exploring the house, and it's not frightening, not yet; the farther she walks, the more she feels a familiarity with the place, as if she lived here long ago. A voice is calling to her from one of the rooms, a man's voice, and she can't tell where it is coming from, but then she turns a corner and a deep anxiety strikes her, that she won't find her way out again. Urgently she strikes matches, one after the other, and they go out, fall to the floor as black wicks, and the candles begin to gutter, so she runs from one to another to try to keep them alight. The voice calls and she tries to answer, "I'm here!" and then in French, "*Je suis là!*"

Then she sees in the mirror the woman hanging, with long black hair. She catches her breath, screams (it comes out as a faint squeak), and is awake.

It's not long after the dream, a few days only, that she gets the letter from Jean-François. Before she even opens it, she has a feeling of dread. Why? Because it isn't an e-mail and because she has a hunch about what is in it. Because it is the first time he has written to her; it is always Marguerite who writes, and Maria hasn't heard from her since she was there. She sits down at the kitchen table, notices the stamp, which has a bird on it, some sort of bird of prey, and slits it open with a knife, the way no one opens letters any more, because she doesn't want to tear it. She recognizes his handwriting, but it's the little sticker on the back of the thin blue envelope that she's seen first. Her coffee cooling at her elbow, dust dancing in sunlight across her table, she reads his slant lines.

Marguerite has had liver cancer for some time. She knew about it in the summer, but did not want anyone to know—oh, the fatigue and the stomach pains, oh God. She has been having radiotherapy and chemo, but they don't hold out much hope. Liver cancer is a quick mover, and she's far too weak for a transplant. He is glad to say that the doctors know how to help her; that must mean drugs, probably morphine. Marguerite has asked, says Jean-François in the next paragraph, that Maria help him put her unpublished papers together, to be one of her literary executors. He hopes she will accept this task, out of friendship, but also because she is the writer Marguerite wants for the job. He hopes that her own work is going well, that George Sand is on her way to publication, and that she will get in touch with him soon.

Maria picks up the phone as soon as she has read the letter through twice, to be sure that she has deciphered his handwriting and got his meaning straight, and dials his number in Paris. A machine replies, asking her in French to leave a message and he will return her call. She imagines, remembers, the room in which she first met them together, the rather formal furniture, the big gilt-framed mirrors echoing the sky back into the room from beyond the rooftops opposite, the books everywhere, the coffee pot set down between them on a low table, coffee made always by Jean-François after lunch, poured carefully, rough lumps of brown sugar handed round. The way the sky came in, and the windows were opened, and the books in their soft yellow covers filled the wall, and how they overflowed on to the available surfaces, the floor. She hesitates a moment, then leaves her message.

"Jean-François. It's Maria. I've got your letter. Shall I come?"

While waiting for him to call back, she goes online to find a flight to Paris. She arranges it all without telling anyone, then calls Cathy to see if Aidan and Emily can stay with Justin and Kirsty that weekend.

"Marie," he calls back an hour later, he sounds suddenly older, his voice cracking, and everything she wants to say, I'm so sorry, oh, how awful for you, is lost before the sound of his voice, its weariness, its sheer sadness. "Do you really want to come?"

"Yes, I do. I'll be there—is Friday all right? I'll make my own way."

He agrees so easily that she knows this is what he wanted. If Marguerite wants her to work on her papers with him, they can talk about making a start; it's a good enough reason. But she's moved and surprised at how simply grateful he sounds.

"I will expect you on Friday. But the whole of England is between you and me, remember, so take care." His small joke tries to remind her that he is still able to be ironic, that she need not worry about him.

"Jean-François, is she there? Can I talk to her?"

"She's in the hospital."

"Oh, it's unbelievable, it was so quick!"

"It was far advanced already," he says. "She just didn't say."

"Do you mean, you didn't know?"

"No. No one knew. I suspected. But Marie, you know, she is such a private person, and I had to respect that." It takes her breath away, what love can do; and what it can deny.

On Friday, early, she drives her car out to the airport to get the first commuter flight to Paris, leaves the little Renault in the car park to await her return. As she walks into the airport, her thoughts turn and turn in her head, about Marguerite, about friendship, and the impossible fact that while you are totally involved in reading old books, a close friend can get cancer, and be about to die. She thinks of Jean-François, knowing but not asking; giving his wife one last uninterrupted summer in their loved place. Eating a snack lunch over northern France, she looks down, on a patchwork of fields, autumn mist hovering above them like a layer of thin sheep's wool caught on a fence. Then they are landing, the earth coming up like a shock, the plane bouncing slightly. She is here. She is back in France.

She walks down corridors, waits to collect her bag, is carried along moving conveyor belts and up and down escalators and finds herself outside the airport suddenly in the chill metallic-smelling October late afternoon. She feels at once sick with fatigue and extraordinarily alive. She takes the RER into central Paris and again sits, her hands folded upon her lap, watching the people, a man with a guitar, a North African woman with three small children; commuters, foreigners, travellers like herself, a man with a briefcase who sits down beside her and immediately opens it and begins work on a sudoku puzzle. All of them here, now, close to her and never to be seen again. She feels slight, transparent, not solid enough; she got up too early, she needs a proper meal, a shower, her armpits smell; she needs to speak to someone she knows, now, in order to feel real again. What will she do? Arrive on Jean-François' doorstep full of need, a ghostly visitor waiting to be revived, or go to a hotel? She decides on the hotel, one just round the corner from where he lives, and a good cup of coffee in a café, and a shower and change of clothes. Then she'll walk round and ring his doorbell and appear before him like someone who might be of some use.

She gets out of the huge train at Saint-Michel and takes the métro, her bag weighing more than she would have thought possible from the few things she has thrown into it, and then from her hotel near the Panthéon walks downhill to the familiar street; familiar from long ago, when she first knew them and she and Marguerite went to the Mosque together for mint tea and cakes, sat in the hammam being scrubbed under showers of hot water, walked around the Jardin des Plantes talking about love, talking about children, but above all, talking about It, the central thing, the thing that drew them on, heads close, serious under the trees: the meaning of life. Marguerite was a novelist, who had also written plays. Maria wrote poetry, in those days, and read everything in French that she could lay her hands on.

A student at the Sorbonne for the year after she'd finished her degree, she went to find the friend she had met that day at the swimming pool, and they began again. They loved Marguerite Duras before anyone else did, they heard her rehearsing one day at the theatre at the Gare d'Orsay, they went together to the Bouffes du Nord and saw plays directed by Ariane Mnouchkine, they watched Bernard Pivot on *Apostrophes* telling them what to read, they went to the cinema, the three of them, Jean-François in the middle, and saw films by Jean Renoir and René Clair, all the Fellini films, Truffaut and Godard, old war films with Jean Gabin, romantic films with Gérard Philipe, they walked back late at night to drink tea and whisky that she had brought, at the kitchen table, eat her shortbread and talk, talk till late, until Jean-François said, children, it's time for bed. When she told them she was going to marry Edward, the blond Englishman they had never met, they were gentle and disbelieving. Yes, but you will come back often, often! You will bring your husband. But for some reason to do with the history of their friendship and the language they had in common, she never did.

She'd met Edward in Cambridge—walking across Parker's Piece, where she dropped her purse, of all things, and he picked it up; and then immediately, again, at that party in Caius, Cambridge, where he taught then, and where she'd gone to finish her PhD, and that had been that. Another life had begun.

As soon as she arrives, she's amazed at the rightness of having come. Sometimes this is what you have to do. A certainty exists that has not been there before. It has propelled her here, all the way from Edinburgh and through Paris to Jean-François' door, on the top floor of that building where he has lived now for decades; up the street, through the door—once the code numbers have been punched in right—past the dustbins and the backyard and up five flights she has come, like a homing pigeon, he says, like an arrow; and he opens his door to her where she stands gasping for breath on the threshold, and simply hugs her to him, without a word. It is only later that she connects this whole unerring movement of hers with George Sand, and what she wrote to Flaubert, and what Flaubert, for all his brilliance, did not understand.

"You haven't yet got the form," was one of the last things that Marguerite said to her. "But it will come." Standing in Marguerite's study, she thinks, I still haven't got it. Not all of it. And perhaps that is impossible, perhaps I never will. But at least it will exist, and be read; and this is what she wants more than anything to tell Marguerite, before it is too late. It doesn't really matter what people say about writers, Marguerite said, because their lives are—what was it?—like a river, running deep, and you can never plumb their depths.

Here are Marguerite's books, her own and others, the ones she translated, John Berger, Julian Barnes, Virginia Woolf; and here is a book Maria gave her, of American women writers; and here are all the Woolf diaries, and the letters, and Marguerite's play, which was performed in a tiny theatre on rue Mouffetard—she and Marguerite, hurrying to the theatre, a shared umbrella, a sudden downpour of rain—and here are her pens and her computer and paper clips in a little bowl, rubber bands, a jar of dried lavender; surely she's here, will come down those ladder-like stairs in a moment or call, I've made tea! It's too much. Maria understands that Jean-François has been able to do nothing, touch nothing, that each time he has come into this room he has stood here just as he does now, stunned.

"Jean-François, is she going to be allowed home again?"

"I doubt it. They wanted to move her to a clinic, as they don't have long-term beds, but the doctor who's been seeing her wanted another try at the drug they've been using, and to monitor the results. It was supposed to replace the chemo, as that was making her so ill. Now, they think she is too weak. Do you really want to see her? She's very far off now, Marie."

"You mean, the way she is now? You mean, she doesn't want me to see her dying? But we're friends! I can't imagine she wouldn't want to see me! Are you sure?"

"I know she would like you to take some of the books," he says after a long moment of silence. "And please, take anything else you would like."

But once they start to move things, she will have gone for good. Once they start opening drawers, looking at papers. This is what you can't do when a person is alive, and doing it, daring the first move even, makes them dead.

"I can't possibly. She's alive! I can't take her things."

He won't be able to do it, once she's gone. So at last she fingers the little blue pottery bowl with the paper clips in it. The things which the French—she smiles—call *trombones*. "I'd like to have this, eventually. And maybe the Virginia Woolf, and some of the other books. If you're sure. But I can't think of her this way, she isn't dead yet, who knows, maybe there is still hope? But, we can talk about what to do with her unpublished stuff?"

He says, "Of course. Why don't I leave you here for a bit? I'll go and make some tea."

Does he feel criticized, Maria wonders, is there some privacy between the two of them that I have violated? How hard it is to know. She bends, shaking, to pick papers off the floor where they have been dropped. A sheet has Marguerite's strong sloping hand running across it, a sentence or a line of a poem, she can't tell. You are here, you are writing, you are real, and then quite suddenly you are removed from the world, you stop mid-sentence, halfway down a page, your words run out, your breath stops—and you are gone.

Maria sits down at the narrow desk beside the window, where Marguerite has worked for years. She breathes in, out. She waits. She hears her friend's voice, surely she is still here, her quiet voice, slightly singsong. *Marie, you haven't yet got the form.* Then she knows. The form is simply this back-and-forth, this to-and-fro, this conversation; between herself and Marguerite, herself and George Sand, herself and whoever is there, giving back to her, letting her in. It is the journey across these spaces: from Edinburgh to Paris, from Paris to Nohant, from France to Majorca, from Majorca back to Edinburgh. It is the shortest distance between all these lives which touch each other and go on touching, even after some of the voices are dead. She reaches out a hand to finger the spines of Marguerite's books.

"I'll have it," she says at last. "Because now, thanks to you, I know what it is."

When she begins to look at what Marguerite is leaving behind her, she realizes that here is another great expanse of work. There are stories, a whole play, a novel that she was working on before she got too ill to focus. There are letters. There are all the letters that she, Maria, has sent during her lifetime, held by a thick rubber band. Another packet, thinner, letters from Jean-François from years ago when he was in North Africa. She puts them to one side, for him.

He comes back in. "I don't know what to do with it all. Some of it should be published. Have you any ideas? What does she want? Did she tell you?"

They go to sit in the little kitchen, one on each side of the narrow table, drinking their tea from thick china cups. Tea, a homage to Marguerite, who since her days in England was always a tea drinker. The big pewter teapot, the smell of Darjeeling, as if they are deliberately evoking her. The walnuts in baskets on the floor, last year's, from the country. A cupboard full of labelled jars of plum jam.

He says, "I'll have to go down there sometime and get this year's nuts."

She sees the effort of beginning, after a lifetime of companionship, the unfamiliarity of life alone. But he has his house, his trees, his harvests; he still has all his inheritance, he's like a man with an extra limb, she thinks, that roots him in the earth. This is what it means to have a house for two hundred years. This is what George had. And Jean-François also has a certain strange detachment about him, an archaic aloofness, she thinks, that marks him as a landowner, an aristocrat, even though his family received the property as it was taken from murdered aristocrats at the Revolution. He is old France, rural France, he has the attitude to life, death and continuity that George herself might well have had. It shocks her, a modern woman; but Maria makes an effort.

"I thought, perhaps while I'm here, I could sort them into things for you to deal with, that can go to her publishers here, and the ones I can do something about. Would that be all right? But I was thinking—in the end—a biography. She's—she is—an important writer. All the stuff she did with Les Éditions des Femmes, it was groundbreaking. What do you think?"

He smiles at her, the first time since she arrived. "Another biography? Will you have another twenty years to spare, after you've finished with dear George?"

"Touché. But it's not going to take me twenty years. In fact, it will soon be done."

She is sitting in Marguerite's study, just breathing it in, the scent of her, faint yet present, and the slight dustiness of the books, when he comes back in. "Marie, do you want to go to the hospital? We can go if you want. It's quite near."

What has happened? Has he changed his mind? He has a mobile phone in his hand, as if he's going somewhere, and he's checking messages. Someone has called.

"If you are going, I would very much like to see her. I can't believe she wouldn't want me to, Jean-François, however she's looking. Our friendship goes deeper than that."

"We can go on the bus. Will you be ready in five minutes?"

"Yes."

There's a photograph of Virginia Woolf pinned to the wall, the one of her looking quizzical in middle age. Virginia Woolf, who was slightly older than Marguerite is now when she died. What would these women have written, if only they had had more time? There's a photograph too of Marguerite and Jean-François, young, the way she remembers them when she first came here and met them as a couple.

Marguerite with her long dark plait, her swallow's-wing eyebrows, her thin mouth that rises at the corners as if to prevent herself from laughing, her deep dark eyes. Jean-François with dark hair and no white in it, his long handsome face, the lines even then carved around his mouth. Photographs too of Jean-François' twins from his first marriage to a sculptor who reputedly went mad. Two little boys. Maria wonders where they are now. And there's the house in the Creuse Valley, the house the same age as Nohant, with its trees around it, its air of secrecy, shutters closed against summer sun.

Maria goes to the tiny bathroom, the size of a boat's, sits to pee looking at a poster of a Giorgio Morandi painting on the back of the door, and washes her hands. Against the iron railing outside the window, a potted geranium in starved earth; she pours a glassful of water over it. Marguerite would have made sure it had water. The inner courtyard is in shadow, and one by one, in the wall opposite, the lights go on and other, unknown people move about, beginning on their evening occupations.

Jean-François is waiting for her as she comes out and he locks the door behind them and lets her go ahead of him down the steep stairs that twist to the ground floor. The worn banister under her hands. How many times she has struggled up these stairs, out of breath from hurrying here, and sauntered carefully down. The staircase like so many Parisian staircases, secretive doors leading off it, a concierge at the bottom staring at everyone who comes and goes. Only now the old concierge is gone, and the smell of cat pee has gone, and there's a code to punch from the outside, to let you in. She and Jean-François walk unfamiliarly down the street together, two where there have always been three, to get the bus.

Their nearest hospital is the Pitié-Salpêtrière, and the bus stops at the corner of the Jardin des Plantes, where the buses turn and park. Of course; but it isn't what Maria has expected. The hospital where Louise Colet ended up, and Joséphine Baker and Princess Diana, the old poorhouse designed to keep the indigent off the streets of Paris. She would like to take his arm, but doesn't quite dare. Into another world, the world of the hospital, of nights in a blazingly lit place where people are awaiting death.

They go in from the boulevard de l'Hôpital, pass ACCUEIL and cross the inner courtyards, where once women were chained in straw, lunatics, losers, the debris of Parisian society. Where prostitutes and the mentally ill and the homeless were all flung together, in a century that only wanted them made invisible. If you think of that scene, everything since has to be an improvement. They walk on, into a newly transformed wing. The doctor from Lebanon who is treating Marguerite, Jean-François says, has tried everything to shrink the tumour, including this new drug, and now it is her heart which is weak. Jean-François walks like a man who knows his way blindfolded, with the unhesitating tread of a regular visitor. His head forward, his whole self somehow pathetic in this environment, as if he has shrunk. Maria has hardly been in hospitals at all, except when she had her children; she has visited her mother once, in the Royal Infirmary for something minor. She can't imagine ending her life in such a place, with the lights on, and knowing nobody, except the ghosts of history, the lost and the infamous, the ones society could do without. Marguerite is probably past caring that she's in the same place as Joséphine Baker, now.

She is in a side ward, they come upon her quite suddenly. She is motionless and maybe asleep. Maria sees a head upon a white pillow that she can't recognize, because it is wearing a chestnut wig made of very glossy hair, cut short. The face, turned towards her with eyes closed, is a waxwork of Marguerite's, yellowish, shiny. She lies there like a doll, surrounded by machines, linked by tubes. Maria lets Jean-François go ahead of her, to allow him his moment of privacy, this very private man, with his wife who is only just still here. He sits at the bedside on a chair, his back rounded, as he bends forward. Perhaps he is taking her hands. Perhaps he kisses her. Perhaps he is saying something that she can still hear. Then he turns and beckons Maria forward, and makes room for her by getting up and moving to one side.

Maria sits down where he was. Marguerite's face is carved, motionless. She says, "Marguerite, it's me, Maria," in French, and takes a hand that seems made of wire and wax. She's touched that Marguerite wears her wig even in bed, alone. Did she know they were coming to see her? Does Jean-François come at this time every evening?

There is nothing terrible here. Maria breathes out, and the hand moves just slightly under hers and Marguerite opens her eyes and looks at her and gives her the smallest sketch of a smile. A smile with the eyes only; a smile from far down. Saying, here I am, and here are you, and we have this connection. Maria squeezes the hand; a pulse between them, a slight sign. Thank you, she says. The signs of life and love are slight, when you come down to it, they are like leaves moving in a breeze to show you that the breeze exists.

Then Marguerite closes her eyes again and Maria draws back, looking at Jean-François, and he raises his eyebrows and smiles, and says to her, "It's good that you came."

That's it, the last gesture of a long friendship lived over distance and time, without frequent meetings, between two languages; a friendship built over books, plays, poems, the written word. As Maria walks with Jean-François towards the door and down the corridor beyond and out into the October dusk, she knows that it won't be long.

Jean-François says as they walk back down the boulevard de l'Hôpital to Saint-Marcel, "Thank God they are kind to her. Or she would be in a lot of pain. It's cruel, cancer of the liver."

Kind, she understands, is morphine. The kindness of doctors, never to be made explicit. The wooing of death on behalf of another, the easing of her passage. She nods, and he holds the door open for her, and she wonders how many more times he will come here, before the kindness will have led Marguerite away forever from the cruelty of life.

The dark of the night sky above the roofs and chimney pots, the well of the internal courtyard, the kitchen windows open to it, and Jean-François, his hands trembling slightly, gets cold roast chicken and some little cheeses out of the fridge. He reaches for a bottle from the floor, pulls the cork on one of his own wines, pours them each a small glass. His glance up at her, sudden and warning, tells her he wants them to move on, to not talk about Marguerite.

"I was going to tell you, I've begun working on a screenplay about our heroine. Isabelle Huppert wants to play her. She got in touch. What about that?"

"George Sand? I think that's great." A brief jealous thought, but she's mine, goes through her and is dismissed. She can hardly lay claim to one of France's greatest writers. "I've been wondering about her optimism. Reading her letters to Flaubert, she's so upbeat, and he's such a pessimist. I can't help wondering which of them is right."

"I think that if you agreed with Flaubert, you wouldn't be here now. You would be at home, rewriting something seven times. You know, I think life makes us, without our realizing it. We become who we are, not overnight, or because we have read something, or made a sudden decision. You are who you have become. Who else do I know who would have dropped everything at a moment's notice and flown just to be here with me? I can't tell you how I appreciate your doing that. It's hard to tell you, because I've become an old curmudgeon who finds it difficult to express emotion. Because for years I've lived with someone who knows me so well that it's never really been necessary. But, Marie, thank you. And forgive me if I tell you that you are far more like George Sand than Flaubert."

"You know, I dream about her. I sometimes think I'm dreaming her dreams. Writing about someone is a very odd thing."

He says, "Isabelle Huppert told me she had a dream about her, too. So, you are in excellent company."

"I thought I was going slightly crazy."

"No, it's completely normal, I assure you." He's smiling at her, his old irony in place; a man who is regaining his balance. "If you are becoming George Sand, it's probably all for the best, and you know, we incorporate the people we admire, and then move on. They become part of us. Also, the people we love."

"So, you think I was doing all that work simply in order to become George Sand?"

"Why do we do the work we do? Writing, I mean. I know why I have to prune my trees and mend my walls. But to immerse oneself in a work, especially when it concerns the life of another person—well, who knows. There is a reason, Marie, but I can't tell you what it is. Perhaps we just want to be in the stream of history, to be included."

She thinks: so, all the time I thought I had put life on hold, in order to read and write, I was living? Because one never stops living, not until it's all over, and then one puts down a pen in the middle of a sentence, or types half a sheet of paper, and takes to a hospital bed, to await death; only then is it all over.

George stood in the street outside number 6, rue Poissonnière, her mother's house. The house was soon to be demolished to make way for an iron bridge, but she didn't know that. She'd had the message and hurried here, leaving her children with friends as you had to when you were both mother and father in one; always these makeshift arrangements, rushed journeys.

She stood in the street, in the working-class Parisian neighbourhood, and looked up. An old woman came down the street with a handcart, and old clothes to sell. A boy went by, whistling, dragging a stick across railings. It was a July day, the sky high and clear above the rooftops, a freshness on the street from the water-cart that had just passed. Streams ran in the gutters. A heap of soaked cloths lay near a drain. Horse dung, washed into a brown stream, running into drains, the smell of country places. All this, the city that her mother loved, that she would never leave. Her own Paris was elsewhere, in the theatres and cafés close to the Seine. The old woman paused with her cart and sang out on a strange harsh note, "*Rags and bones, rags and bones!*"

The door was an iron grille that opened on to a stairway. The old man who sold fountains from his little shop and was also a kind of concierge usually stuck his head round the door and shouted out, "Go in! She's in, go on up!" She would cross the little courtyard, rough cobbles, light bisected by shade, a canary in a cage singing from high up, a speck of yellow in the gloom under the roof; to go up more steps and along a corridor and then up a further three floors. It was like a puzzle, a maze with her mother at the centre. It was in her dreams. Each time, it gave her time to brace herself. What would she be like today? Loving and generous, or mean and cantankerous? Criticizing her from her hat to her shoes, or praising her latest book, as if she had read it, to the skies? Or simply too close to death to do either? "Ah, it's my Aurore!" or the harsh shout "Who's there?"

Who's there. It fell like a stone dropped on her chest. Stopped her breathing. She would go on up, pushing each time against an ancient terror. And arrive, in her mother's apartment, where the rooms faced south and the sun flooded in, and there were always flowers bought from the flower markets of Paris, marigolds, blue iris, the bright blooms

Sophie loved. Windows open in summer, open to the dust, noise, sun, everything that rose from the streets, smells, shouts, heat on stone.

The July heat was intensifying, by midday the streets would be burning hot. She clanged open the grille, went down the couple of steps, and was met by the man in the shop that sold fountains. Only this time he did not tell her, go on up.

"Mademoiselle Aurore, Madame Dupin is not here."

She stared. The open window, with no one inside.

"No, no, she's not dead. She wanted to go to a *maison de santé* so as to have less noise, and a garden."

Sophie as a young woman in the garden at Nohant. Gardening, a trowel in her hand. The day after the baby died. She is close to the pear tree. George herself, aged four, picking up apricots, bringing them to her mother.

"Where is she? Do you have an address?"

In the nursing home, lying on what looked like a pauper's bed. The sheet that covered her was stained, the pillow made of striped ticking, straw poking out. She was old, she was at least a hundred.

At her side, a dark-haired young woman with pink cheeks and a sweet mouth.

"Caroline?" It was years since they had met, she and her half-sister Caroline; they had grown up together, until the grandmother had also made Caroline leave, because she was one of the people, because her father was not Maurice Dupin. They embraced, throwing their arms around each other. Aurore, *ma chérie, ma soeur.*

"She chose this grim room herself," Caroline explained. "She wanted it because she thought she was surrounded by thieves, had a bag of silver under her pillow, and would not be robbed if she was in a room like this. Go along with her. It's the only way."

She and Caroline. Again, after all these years, the two of them, conspiring. (Two little girls on the floor of the house in the rue Grange-Batelière, before everything. What shall we play? War. When you're dead you can get up again after you count to five.)

"Dr. Gaubert says give her anything she wants. What she wants is to go to the Champs-Élysées."

"Then let's go!"

Together, they dressed her and got her a carriage. Bay horses fidgeted in the shafts, the coachman looked handsome in his livery, together they lifted their mother high, into the open carriage, and handed a parasol up after her. The deep blue sky, the horses' hoofs clattering on stone, the rush of trees overhead, sunlight filtering sharply through the heavy bunched leaves of summer.

"To the Champs-Élysées!" The driver flicked his whip and the horses were already moving, their rumps like fat women's, and the nursing home with its dried-up gardens was left behind; for an afternoon, for a couple of hours,

Sophie Delaborde would see the Paris she loved, as if she were an aristocrat too.

"Look!" cried Sophie. Napoleon's tomb at Les Invalides, his pointing needle brought back from Egypt, the rearing horses against the sky, horses of battle and conquest, France's glory, the long reign of the man who had brought all Europe to his feet. Their emperor. "Look, Aurore! How lovely it is, all the carriages, all the horses, all the women in their beautiful clothes, look, the sun, isn't it lovely, and all the golden dust! One can't die in the middle of all this! No, one can't die in Paris!"

George looked at Caroline. Caroline was crying. She had stayed close to her mother, she knew the truth. They came up to the Arc de Triomphe.

Sophie shouted, "No, I can't go any farther. I've had enough." The mother they had wanted was gone. "Take me back!" she said angrily, and then added more gently, as if to herself, "Another day we'll go to the Bois de Boulogne."

Back in her room, they piled around her all the ripe fruit and pâtisseries she had asked for.

Caroline said, "Really, I don't think . . ."

But they were to give her everything she wanted. The Champs-Élysées. Ripe strawberries, *pain au chocolat*, coeurs d'Alsace.

Sophie touched a pear and said, "Later. I'll eat it later." But never did.

George took her down to sit in the garden, and there, in the last of the sun, Sophie closed her eyes.

"Aurore, your sister is religious. I am not. I know I'm going to die. I don't want a priest. I don't want even the whisker of a priest, do you hear? When I go, I want everything to be cheerful around me. After all, why should I be afraid to face God? I've always loved him. He can tell me off for anything else he likes, but not for not having loved him."

George thought, I love you. Maybe I can be reproached for everything else, but not for not having loved you.

When she came back, there it was again, the open window. This time, she knew. A servant was shaking a sheet out of the window, a white flag, the flag of surrender.

Caroline told her, "When you'd gone, she asked me to do her hair. She said, I want to have my hair done. She looked in the mirror and smiled. Then she let the mirror drop. Her soul flew away."

Only a few months later, George set off, with Frédéric Chopin, Maurice who was still convalescent, and the wild child Solange, for Majorca.

Maria's mother calls, from the other side of town.

"Mum, are you all right?" Guilt at not having telephoned first, and the thought of the mother dying in Paris, sharpen her voice.

"Of course I'm fine. It was just that I haven't heard from you in so long. When did you get back from Paris? How are you? How are the children?"

Maria, who still jumps at the first ring of the phone, stands in the kitchen holding it to her ear. She's still hearing her own mother's voice as if from beyond the grave. "Mum! I'm so sorry. I was going to phone you. Why don't you come over this weekend, we could go out somewhere, the kids would love to see you."

"Are you really all right, darling?"

Her mother has not mentioned the separation; it's as if in her mind it can't happen, so it has not. The most she can say, in a hushed special voice, is, "Are you sure you are really all right?"

Really all right, Maria wants to say; no, I don't think I am, I think I may be going nuts, if you really want to know, I thought for a moment that you had died in a room outside Paris with an opened window, and that was how I knew you were dead, seeing that window from the outside. But you are alive and living in Morningside, and you did not ask me to take you on a last ride around the Champs-Élysées or buy you coeurs d'Alsace. She walks about with the telephone and listens to her mother telling her about her neighbours, about a new boutique that sells wonderful linens, about a man who cuts her hair. It's her mother's way of telling her that she's fine, that she doesn't need her daughter's help or attention, that she has a life.

"Did I tell you I'm going to Venice with Mary Anderson? We're going for a week. There's a special offer in *The Scotsman*, I wonder if you saw it."

"No, no, I didn't. But that's great. Great idea." Since she was widowed, Maria's father having died suddenly on the last day of the old century, his heart finding no strength to go on into the new one, she has been entirely focused, it seems, on clothes and travel. It's the new look of widowhood, Maria supposes; and really, much preferable to the old.

"You haven't told me about you. And how you found your friend?"

"Not good, I'm afraid. It's cancer. I did see her though, I was glad of that. Really, yes, I'm really fine." I'm fine, that's what they say to each other, mother and daughter, what they will probably go on saying until the very end. "I'm working. I'm working on my book."

"Ah, that'll take your mind off things, then. But yes, I'll come for my tea Saturday, if that's okay. I'm coming uptown to meet Marjorie for lunch at Jenners, they have a luggage sale on, I could come on to you afterwards." Uptown, for both of them, means Princes Street: the piper on the corner by the Scott memorial, the surging, shopping crowds. Poised between the old town and the new, the spine of consumerism at the centre of the city.

"Fine, Mum, that'd be lovely," Maria says.

Suddenly the mention of a book seems to her absurd. Taking her mind off things, perhaps that's all it is. Not so

much better than new luggage, really. What was she thinking of?

The death of a mother. Is this, after all, the original love
story, the one which leaves you inconsolable? George had
spent her life upon love. She loved passionately, indiscreetly,
wildly, in public, in spite of everything. And she was loved,
·by many men, women, her children, her grandchildren, her
friends. But the one person whose love she desired most of
all, Sophie Victorine Dupin née Delaborde, daughter of a
bird-seller, camp-follower and working woman, republican,
flirt, who was self-centred, possibly mad, could not give it.
There was something that had never been healed, and could
not be. This, thinks Maria reading of George's mother's
death, is the original. This one was the one she could not
have.

Then there were the bitter paths of Majorca. The trip
George went on immediately after her mother's death, without stopping to mourn or realize it. *Les âpres sentiers:* the bitter paths. It's become a summary, this phrase, of what
happens in marriage, in relationships, when suddenly the
ways part and the shocking otherness of the other person is
revealed at the same time as is the shocking vulnerability of
both. She thinks of her own journey to Majorca, during
which her marriage ended. She remembers standing in the
intense cold outside the cells at Valldemossa and the brutal

silence between her and Edward as they drove to the airport. Sometimes journeys mark the end of things; you have to undertake them to make the endings clear.

The bitter paths. When George trod them again in memory, writing about them, she must have recognized bitterness not only in the harshness of the place, but in herself. The bitterness had been laid down in her, and what else could she do with it but what writers do, what use did she have for her feelings except to transform them always into something else? She had hoped for the alchemy to work, for disappointment to become irony or wit, but it did not quite come off. Perhaps it never does, when you begin to write out of painful emotion. But, Maria thinks now, I have nowhere else come quite so close to her as here, because disappointment shows the magnitude of what was hoped for; unhealed hurt shows something which calm optimism does not. Maybe our lives are always about what we tried for, rather than what we achieved.

Stake a claim here. With the dream, not the accomplishment. With the lived life and the urge always for more of it. With looking out, rather than in. With the great heart and the active mind that saw and understood its century and hoped for humanity always more than it could achieve.

She has hardly been thinking about herself and Edward since their last, peculiar exchange, when they ended up laughing, incoherent with feeling, in the hall, looking at each other across the dirty trainers and flung-down ruck-sacks of their children. His strange statement, "I'm seeing someone." And the stab of pain it gave her, as if a part of her had asserted its aliveness, a limb coming back to life. She had never felt jealous of him before; was that feeling anything like the one that had driven him to such fury when he heard she was making love with another man? For a first time she thinks about what he might have felt, that time in Majorca when he questioned her so hard, then closed him-self off from her with such firmness. Could it have been simply that he was in great pain?

Last week, in Paris, she saw what pain had the ability to create in Jean-François: an almost fastidious refusal to express feeling. And because she was his friend, it did not occur to her to judge him; it was simply how he was. How generations of French men, perhaps, had been before him. With her husband, or more exactly without him, because she has not heard from him since her return, she wonders delicately for the first time: to what extent has he needed to hide his true feelings from her?

Maria piles up her printed pages and searches directories and the Internet for an agent who may be interested in her book. Since reading the sarcastic account by Robert Graves of her heroine's Majorca expedition (he sitting just up the road at Deya, judging her harshly), she knows what she has to do. Put the record straight, quite simply, put her book before the public; say, this is the injustice that was done. Put herself firmly on the side of George, of Aurore, of the girl whose mother had refused her love, the woman who stood in the street appalled outside her mother's apartment, who was at that deathbed in Paris, and only months later, picked herself up out of the wreckage of her life with Casimir to set off to Majorca with Frédéric Chopin. That flawed, fallible, entirely recognizable woman.

She thinks of the Parisian cousin and his scorn, "Ah, George Sand, she had all those lovers, Chopin died of it." She thinks of Marguerite in her hospital bed. Marguerite, "You haven't yet got the form, but it will come." Jean-François, nearly unable to take her to the hospital, nearly denying her that last connection. Flaubert, who wouldn't budge from his house in Normandy to go and visit George, who counted his own tears at her funeral. All the refusals, the denials, the small meannesses of history, the people who gave way to them, the way that no higher standard of behaviour was ever demanded. The history of her own time, in which venal men lied and cheated and nobody condemned them. All this—all this drives Maria back to her desk this autumn, working late into the night, forgetting her own situation, making the effort at last. She thinks with surprise, I love this woman, I have come to love her. That's why.

She's home mid-afternoon from work, puts her key in the lock and pushes the heavy front door open. There are voices in the house, and as she goes down the hall she realizes they are coming from Aidan's bedroom, where the door is shut. Young voices laughing loudly, then falling into quiet, nearly inaudible talk.

"Aidan? Are you home?" He is supposed to be at school, surely: there are tryouts for the football team, he wanted to be in it.

After a moment the door opens a crack and her son looks out, flushed, his hair on end.

"Oh, hi, Mum."

"Hi." She is going to ask, why are you home, but stops herself.

The door opens wider, and she sees a girl sitting on the bed. She has red hair sticking out sideways in two bunches and big grey-green eyes ringed in black and she is wearing a version of the Broughton school uniform, a dirty white blouse and tiny pleated skirt. There's a sweetish herbal smell, which she recognizes as marijuana.

"Mum, this is Saskia. Sass, my mother."

"Hello," they both say on the same cautious note.

"We're doing some revision," says Aidan.

"Oh, okay. I'm going to make tea. Come down if you want some?"

"Thanks, but we had some already." He gestures to two striped mugs on the floor.

The bed is covered with exercise books, and the two of them are shoeless, Saskia sitting backed by bunched pillows, her black-stockinged legs crossed comfortably, her toes curling.

"Okay, see you in a wee while then."

She goes downstairs to the kitchen, sets the heavy kettle on the AGA burner and reflects that she has given up any right to be a censorious parent, even if she should want to, and that Aidan is after all fifteen. The fact that he has given up football for girls should not surprise her. She remembers his deliberate use of the word "lover" months ago, and wonders what he has been reading; she will ask. As for the marijuana, she will have to think what to say about that.

Saskia becomes a frequent visitor to her house. And Maria stops thinking of it as her house, as her children spread throughout it, bringing home friends, projects, increasing amounts of equipment, mostly electronic, and unknown young people are often lounging at the kitchen table drinking tea and talking. The house smells of cheap perfume, sweat and, occasionally, pot. This is what it's like living with teenagers; suddenly she is here as the adjunct, the occasional visitor, the one who interrupts conversations and rap sessions and the intense little crowd all crunched up together on the floor in front of the TV, or poring over the computer screen. Feet thud up and down the stairs, the doorbell rings on a long loud note, someone runs to answer it, there are muttered confabulations in the hall, should they go out, should they stay in, where's so-and-so, should we wait for him? Who's got money, who's got the address? And then they are out, streaming down the front steps and down the terrace, a shout of laughter, a complaint, wait for me; their voices seem to become more emphatically Edinburgh-accented, they are the new inhabitants of a capital city, in a country becoming more sure of itself every day.

Maria thinks of her own teenage years, the bus to school and back, Mary Erskine girls with their seventies school bags, their white socks, their hats on the backs of their heads, the gossip and the favouritisms, the cliques and clubs. But there weren't boys, she remembers. Boys were a lurking enemy, an ambush, a patrol. Nobody would have dreamed of going to a boy's house to sit on his bed and laugh aloud when his mother came in; nobody would have brought her school books (and even her laptop, if they had existed) and simply moved into a boy's room. When they smoked, it was never in anyone's house, but down along the banks of the Water of Leith, in among bushes, behind trees.

In one season, Maria has become the mother of the next adult generation. What they think, believe, do, will matter in ways that she can't even guess at. In allowing them the free use of her house, she's giving them the space to discover who they will be. It's all about the future, suddenly. Whiskers sprout where there were none a month ago, people grow mysteriously in the night, hair changes colour, someone who was fat is slim and someone with a boyish soprano suddenly breaks into bass. She sees her own children and the children of others rush past her, as she sits in her study alone with her book, and she has no real idea where they are going, but that they are all together seems to make them safe, even invincible; the cafés and clubs they go to are not the ones of her youth; she feels as if that youth, like something preserved and cherished even, as memory tells us who we are, has become irrelevant.

Emily, who is not yet fourteen, is sometimes one of them, her eyes wide and eager to understand, to keep up. Sometimes, though, she lags behind, stays home, comes to Maria as if to ask her something, wanders off again. Later stands at her desk, twisting her hair into a long rope.

"When are you going to finish your book?"

"Soon, very soon."

"What are you going to do then?"

"I don't know yet. Why, Em?"

"I just wondered. Will you write another one?"

"I might. What about you, hen, how are you?"

"I'm fine. I'm just a bit sick of Aidan's friends, you know? They're here all the time now."

"D'you feel a wee bit out of it?"

"Hmm, sometimes. You know Saskia, she's here all the time."

"I think he's fond of her, don't you?"

"I think he's soft in the head."

Jealousy, thinks Maria, here it is again. She slides an arm around Emily, who stands so tall now beside her, slim, beautiful, angry, with her pout and frown.

"Don't worry, hen, it's just the way he is at present. Let's you and me do something together tomorrow, okay? Go uptown, it's Saturday, what d'you think?"

Then she gets another letter from Jean-François, in his strangely unformed handwriting; he was dyslexic, she remembers, as a child.

Maria lays down the letter on the kitchen table and sits down to read it. She knows, because it's a letter, not an e-mail. Jean-François has needed to spend the time moving his hand across paper, choosing his words, making them permanent in ink. You don't send e-mails, even now, to announce death. She opens it, reads the first lines then stops reading, puts her head down on the ridged scrubbed pine of the table and sobs. Marguerite has died, after several days of unconsciousness. It was peaceful.

She sobs, not because Marguerite has at last escaped from the hospital bed and the drips and injections and her own decaying body, but because of time passing, and the fragility of it all, of life.

Then she reads the rest of the letter. It's a plea, couched in elegant phrases and using several subjunctives, for her to come soon and begin work on Marguerite's papers. She knows it's his way of telling her he needs her company. And even though it is term time, and her house and life are full these days, and she still doesn't know what to do about the marijuana, she knows that she must go; that somehow, this will have to be arranged.

Each time Maria reads an account of the death of George—and there are several—she is gripped by a sort of terror. It is like the death of a mother; you live it over and over, you can't believe you are left alone, an orphan. How can you live life without her? But once her manuscript has been sent out, she will have to let go. It will be done, whatever it is that she's known how to do, and her life will go on. She reads of Solange, reconciled with her mother at the very end, the wild girl, homing to the bedside. George clasped her hand and bit her knuckle; they were that close, bone-close, knit so tight they could not bear each other.

She will fly back to Paris as soon as term ends, to continue work on Marguerite's papers. Jean-François has called her editor at Le Seuil, who is interested in Marguerite's last unfinished novel but will let him know. Somebody has contacted him about putting on her play. Les Éditions des Femmes, who dropped Marguerite after a few years for not being enough of a feminist, has begun trying to claim her back as a feminist author. But we were all feminists, thinks Maria, because we had to be, because there was nothing else. *Féministe, républicaine, précurseur.* Yes, she was our ancestor. But what now? George Sand is dead, and Marguerite Février is dead, and she, Maria Jameson, is alive. She has been living her life in the shadow of a dead writer, a woman of great power and influence, whose wing, during these days of her aloneness, has somehow sheltered her in a way she needed. But that woman died, in her room at Nohant, after a last glance out of a window at the green garden she loved. So did Marguerite, who was living only last year, pulling up vegetables in her garden in the country. We die, Maria thinks, and what has it all been for, if not to try to understand how to live?

"Yes, okay," Edward says, his voice on the phone sounding warmer, nearer, than it has lately. "When do you want to go? And what about all these kids you say are living in our house—I mean, your house?"

"Well, they aren't exactly living here, just coming and going a lot. Aidan has a girlfriend, she's here quite often. Emily's going through a difficult patch, not being sure quite where she belongs. You'll see. But I can't ask my mother any more, it's just got too complicated, she'd work herself into a state. So, really, it would be good to have you here. Maybe they'll take more notice of you as a man."

"Sounds great," Edward says, but his voice is still light. "Like living in the middle of the Cirque du Soleil. But why not? It'll be a change for me, after my bachelor existence."

He doesn't say, ah, now I can stay in your house after all, can I, because it's convenient? Neither does he say, I'm not just a man, I'm their father. And she doesn't say, you owe it to me, or, it's about time. She doesn't say that some of them are smoking what is still an illegal drug. There are things she and Edward are not saying, because what they want to say is perhaps new, and they don't want to jeopardize its frail existence. It's like walking along a tightrope towards another person, both of you balancing something nearly impossible on your heads, your hands outstretched to stay upright, refuse gravity, take the small steps needed. Or is this image in her mind only because he has mentioned the Cirque du Soleil?

She comes in late, one night in early December, from her Paris flight. She has spent a week with Jean-François, sorting, tidying, putting things into envelopes to be sent to various different people, publishing houses, obituary writers, societies. Marguerite's work finished in mid-sentence: there's an unfinished play in her desk drawer that neither of them knew about. Her novel, which she was working on that summer less than six months ago, is still on her computer. It ends, literally, with a break for lunch: a day perhaps when the stomach pains that were really her swollen liver overwhelmed her and she had to take painkillers and lie down. For Jean-François and for herself, Maria thinks, there is the relief of the work to be done, which takes the place of simple mourning: there is a future for these things, they do not simply, like her clothes and her photographs, belong to the past. When you are a writer, there is always a future, she says to Jean-François. Like this, they are her inheritors, active on her behalf, rather than simply her mourners.

He sees her off at the métro station; he is about to buy a paper, some bread wrapped in a thin square of paper under his arm. He kisses her on both cheeks, she grips his arm in its corduroy jacket, he looks at her from his height.

"Thank you, Marie, thank you for coming. Once again, dear George would be proud of you. You know, what she said to Flaubert, you go in for desolation, I have to go for consolation? Well, you have consoled me."

On the flight home, Maria reads a book she has brought with her, from Marguerite's shelf of favourite books. It's by a French woman poet. In it, she reads of the links between the small things and the great in life, the need for both, the forging of the lasting myths out of the particular. There is the whole world, the poet says, and there are the details of our lives. What matters is to live at the place where the heart connects with the world. Is that where Maria lives? She can't tell. The poet doesn't tell her how to get there. Then in so short a time the plane sinks and prepares for landing, coming down surrounded by the hills of the lowlands, dark as burial mounds, spotted with snow. Dark wintry Scotland, the place in which she belongs. The glint of the Firth, the dark blobs of islands. Out of all the possibilities, back to this one place. The lit strip, on which like a nesting gull on a clifftop they will land.

She drives the crowded roads from the airport, parks her car on the street outside her house in the residential parking place between two white lines. She pulls up the hatchback, gets her suitcase out. The air on the street is like a knife. She locks the car. She finds her door key, and simultaneously notices with pleasure the bright windows of the house, which mean someone, or everyone, is home. She goes up the stone steps, inserts her key, pushes the heavy door ajar and goes in. It's an action she has performed so many times before, it could well have become automatic; but this time she is conscious of it, as once long ago she was conscious, opening her house to her lover, letting him inside. These are the actions of her life, repeated over and over; coming in, going out, opening the door to others, closing it behind herself. This time, it feels different, as if she has come from farther away than she has. The house is warm and smells of cooking meat: perhaps a stew? She's hungry. She goes to the stairs down to the basement kitchen, the source of the smell. Lights are on in the rest of the house, it's like a lighthouse, as if to guide her home, and even if it's a waste of electricity, she's glad, because she needs it, has needed it for a long time, a lit house and a smell of cooking and something happening that is not her doing.

"Hello?" she calls out. "Hello?" The hall is as usual full of flung-down coats, boots, bags. The door behind her shuts the cold night out. "Hello?" She goes on downstairs. Unbuttoning her coat, pulling off her gloves. Home.

Edward comes out of the kitchen and he's wearing—the first time she's ever seen it—an apron, and a baseball cap. She starts to laugh, but stops, seeing the look in his eyes. The kitchen is a mess, with the remains of chopped vegetables on the counter, a heap of pots in the sink. Above her, she hears the thump of feet, of her children about to come down and greet her. But before they arrive, trailing their projects and questions, their obsessive lives, their warm absent-mindedness, she steps forward towards the extraordinary sight of Edward and his cooking. He's wiping his hands on a towel.

"What are you making? It smells wonderful."

"Stew. Or maybe it's *boeuf en daube*, even, since you're just back from France. I put a lot of wine in. I thought you might be hungry."

"Oh, I am," she says, "I am."

At dinner, there are Aidan and Saskia, sitting very close to each other and muttering remarks which can't be heard by the others, and Saskia giggles, and Emily scowls, but on the other side of Emily there is Hamish, who hasn't appeared before, and who eats with his face close to his plate, forking in his meat as though he were famished. Hamish is a thin boy from Muirhouse in a very long sweater and jeans several sizes too big falling off his hips, and huge trainers, and he wraps his feet around the table legs and settles down to eat with single-minded energy. Edward sits across the table from Maria, and every now and then they catch each other's eye. The *daube*—how do you spell that, asks Aidan, and why since we're in Scotland does it have to be in French?—is tender and succulent, its juices grainy and vinous. It is dark, sweet, tender, it is amazing. She wonders where and when Edward learned to cook.

"Have you never heard," he asks Aidan, "of the old alliance?"

"No, what's that?"

"Scotland and France against the English."

"Sounds okay to me. No offence to you, Dad."

People here are talking again about secession: if the Nationalists get in at the next election, if the country abandons Labour after the debacle in Iraq, Scotland may go independent; Aidan and his friends all think it should.

Later, when everyone has scrambled from the table, claiming homework to do, jobs to see to—a likely tale, says Edward, and Saskia sends him a dimpled smile, escaping, her brief skirt only just covering her thighs, the cuffs of her sweater pulled down over her hands. They are us, thinks Maria, they are who we were; and yet we hardly know them.

Exhausted, she turns to Edward and the plates he is stacking, and says to him, "Sit for a moment, won't you, you must have put a lot of time into that."

He leaves the plates where they are stacked, and sits down. He sighs, and smiles tentatively, and stretches his arms above his head. Upstairs they hear scampering feet, a door slammed.

Maria says, "You know they're smoking?"

"Yes. What should we do?" It's a relief she has not imagined, that "we."

"Well, tell them not to, I suppose. Not that that will

do any good. Tell them not to get caught, and not to do it here."

At least it isn't anything harder, as far as she knows, or Ecstasy, which has killed a girl in the city this year. She wants to say, it's easy for you, you don't live here.

Then he pours more wine into her glass, and asks her, "How was Paris?"

"Oh, we got a lot done, in a short time. Jean-François is having a hard time, but he doesn't say much."

"Oh, men," Edward says. "How we don't say much. How we leave it all to you, the ones who talk, who know what to do."

She looks at him. "That was a wonderful homecoming, thank you so much."

"The pleasure was mine."

"Edward, tell me—about this woman you've been seeing, this shrink?"

"Well, she's middle-aged and she lives in Morningside, not far from your mother, actually. She's good. Martin put me on to her."

A world opens in which men, her husband and his old friend, talk therapists to each other.

"Oh. But what does she say?"

"Well, it's me who does most of the talking. I talk about how bad I felt, when you told me about Sean. I talk about my mother, dumping me at boarding school when I was eight, and how we couldn't even talk to our parents on the telephone. I talk about jealousy, and pain, and loss. I talk about how I wanted to cut you out of my life. I talk about fear, and the terror of dying. What else? I talk about love, and how it hurts. That's about it."

She is silenced. She stretches out a hand to him, and he takes it, across the plates.

"I'm sorry."

"Yes, I know. Me too. But what she's showed me is that it wasn't you."

"What do you mean?"

"Long ago, way before you got together with Sean, I dreaded it happening. Somebody taking everything away. I was terrified of losing you. I got out as fast as I could, so that at least that was within my control."

"Oh, Edward." The hands slip apart, because it's too much of a stretch. "Come on, let's get rid of these things and go and sit upstairs." It's not so much familiarity she feels as newness. They are feeling their way, acrobats of the new era, the high wire under their groping feet.

Later she says, "Do you want to stay?"

"D'you think it's a good idea?"

"I don't know. Let's see."

"My shrink, the woman you asked me about. She's called Dr. Ferguson. She asked me what you did. I said you were writing a book about George Sand."

"What happened to the plant, in Majorca, with the Latin name?"

"What plant?"

"The one you told me about, that the goats ate. It was nearly extinct. Did you find it?"

"Oh. Oh, yes. *Ligusticum huteri*. They've got the goats more or less under control. It has a chance of coming back. Anyway, the seeds are being stored in the wildflower seed bank in Soller, and they'll be replanted. I never imagined you'd remember that."

"And what happened to George Sand and Chopin? We left off in the middle, somehow."

"She wrote a novel about them. They were in disguise, of course. A man who was jealous and a woman who tried to give him everything. She read it aloud to him in the evenings, and he never understood."

"How did it end?"

"Their relationship? The last time she saw him, it was years later, they met on a staircase of a friend's house in Paris and he told her that Solange, her daughter, had had a baby two days before. They were estranged, you see. She held out a hand to him when they met and asked him how he was, but he didn't answer."

"And that was that?"

"Yes, that was the end."

———

In the bedroom, where she has got rid of the old bed, bought a new one, one for herself alone, she feels him up against her, standing there, dressed, his body in its solidity, with its stocky density, so different from Sean's. She mustn't make comparisons. He peels off his sweater, his shirt, and she does likewise; but then stops. She doesn't want it too ordinary, too unemphatic.

"Go in the bathroom, come back in a minute, okay? I'll be in bed."

He does what she says. Coming back in, he is a shadow against the faint light from the opened door. He closes the door and comes to her, invisible. Naked in the cold bed, she is shivering and tense, and then he comes in and warms her, holding her against him, and her hands find his forearms, feel the hair on them that's standing up just slightly, she takes his hands, leads them to her, shows him the way. As if he's new to her and she to him, she leads him, and when she takes his penis in her hand, and he gasps slightly, it's as if she has never done this before, and he has never felt her in quite this way. She lies beneath him and he arches over her, and then he turns her so that she's above him, the duvet slipping off her, the night air on her back, the whole long length of her spine exposed, his hand moving up and down the vertebrae, soothing her, as if settling a horse. She lies upon him, kisses his chest, finds the raised nipples and licks them, rubs her face in his chest hair, kisses his lips. He sighs, a long sigh.

"What is it? What?"

"Nothing, nothing."

Then he's turning her sideways and kissing her breasts, the handfuls of them that fall into his hands, and he comes into her so easily, on a long slide, so that they can rock together, curled into each other, curved together like creatures without bones, intent on feeling each other; caught, here in the moment, like this, on and on, the gentle rocking that is forever, going on and on until suddenly he tips her over on her back and comes in deep, and she gasps, cries, comes, and then so does he.

In the dark, in which they can just see each other, outlines, silhouettes, and where they can feel each other, skin on skin. Her head above his heart. It skips a beat now and then, always has, she hears it, rocky, indecisive, in league with mortality. She listens to the mysterious inner workings of another person, that can never really be known. One day, it will stop, skid to a halt, refuse to beat one more time. As will hers. And they can have no clue about when this will be.

Maria feels tears slide down her face and she hiccups a sob. It's so easy. How did they forget it was so easy? It's on the tender inside of life, where everything begins again, and she is back there, with him soft inside her now, a mollusk, a creature sucked up on a beach in the beginning of time.

She rolls away from him and they lie together on their backs, the air cooling their sweat, and the dark of the

Edinburgh winter night pressing up against the tall windows, where they have not even closed the shutters. He feels for her hand, holds it. They hear thumps on the stairs as if a herd of animals ran up and down them, somebody calls out "Good night!" and the front door slams. The jingle of a mobile phone, a young male voice. Somebody says, "Shh!" They hide at the centre of their house, as the new generation hurtles by just outside the door, young people with their passions and secrets and plans. It's all right. It's easy. They laugh, stifling the sound, and then Edward gets up, feels for his trousers, opens the door a crack and peers outside.

"Stay," she says. "Won't you?"

"Of course. I'm just going for a pee, and to put the cat out. Back soon."

Maria pulls the duvet up to her chin and lies in the dark, listening to the sounds of her house, its creaks and ticks, its human noises. She thinks that she has come full circle; only no, it's not so much a circle as a spiral, opening and rising, never quite crossing the same point twice.

In the early morning, they wake to the pale rectangles of lighter sky beyond the unshuttered windows. The glow of a winter dawn, wind coming in from the sea.

"Go," she says to him. "Before anybody sees you. Then we won't have to explain."

He has become her secret. For how long, or what will come of it, she can't say. The present is what counts. She watches him dress, his solid body with its bright bushes of hair even though the hair on his head is fading, the white bulge of his biceps as he stretches to get into his sweater, the swell of his shoulders, a definite waist. He hops to put on socks, one after the other, in the way she remembers.

"Have you been exercising? You look good."

"One of the ways bachelors pass their time is going to the gym."

"Ah."

"You've changed too."

"Have I?"

"You're thinner. You look beautiful."

He's facing the mirror, so that she sees his reflection in the glass, looking back at her where she lies sprawled under the puff of the duvet.

"It's good, surprising each other." She thinks with sadness that they may never move each other so deeply again.

"I'll see you later? Then we can have a marijuana and contraceptives conference. I see that in my absence we've become the parents of teenagers." He bends to kiss her, his lips already cooler from the morning air, his cheek rough. "I'll shave at my flat."

"Thank you for coming."

"Well, thank you for having me, as my mother taught me to say."

———

Maria wants to ask him, is it the times we live in that make it necessary to stay together rather than let ourselves fly apart? Is it because our world is suffering, our protective layers are eroded, because what has hurt other people for decades, poor people, people in other parts of the world, is coming for us? Is it because we are no longer Napoleonic, we people of the West, with our notions of uniqueness and immunity fading, the revolution, not the one we imagined, but something rougher, harder, at our doors? Or is it our age, in the middle of our lives, that makes us afraid to be out on our own, forging what used to look like independent lives? Are independent lives, in this era of naked greed and solipsism, all that desirable as an idea? Are we not bonded already, interconnected, vulnerable, each a part of the strength and the fragility of the whole?

But he's gone, to get on with his day.

She gets up slowly, to discover who has spent the night here; to make coffee in the kitchen downstairs on this Sunday morning in December, to greet the sleepy, smelly, tousled, half-dressed denizens of the house as they wander in, in T-shirts and sweatpants, needing a shave, a shower, a hair-cut, a hug, whatever it is that young people need at this threshold of their lives, whatever it is she can provide. An adult presence, a cup of coffee, a hand to hold, acceptance, a place to go. And she herself? What is it she needs, at this point in her life? To touch another life, to have it touch hers. To create, to understand. To give back. To be a part of a whole.

7

THE OWL

It's pouring with rain, because the tourists are here in force and the Festival has another two weeks to run. It always rains for the Festival. People are out streaming through the streets, their umbrellas clashing like peculiar pronged weapons, their plastic waterproofs dripping, their feet soaked, strange hats on their heads, because this is Edinburgh, this is the place to be. A new capital city with an ancient history; a town of feuds and fallings-out, of witches burned and summary executions, a place where history has batted its meanings back and forth, forged its three languages, made them one. A city built on black volcanic rock with a cooled eruption, the memory of lava, at its centre. A wild place, tamed over the centuries—Hume, Adam Smith, the giants of the Enlightenment were here, as was wily narrow-chested Stevenson with his forked imagination, his longing to escape. Edinburgh has been all things to all people: a Scottish town, an English-dominated town—even the North British Hotel lasted here into the eighties of the last century. It has had its long mournful wait for a representative assembly, its centuries-long sulk of abandonment. It has built its monuments to English kings, which stand at the centres of its spacious Georgian squares, its Victorian extravaganzas. It's been made of soot-blacked tenements, stinking steep alleys, cliff-like walls with hardly a window to show; it's been redesigned with air and light and space in mind, the rational eighteenth century laying its calming hand; it's been drained of its swamp water, connected up by railway, and now it is a maze of new roads, American-style highways, ring roads, joining it to its shabby, worn-out suburbs. It has the Scott monument—cleaned now, but in Maria's childhood resembling a dirty bolted lettuce. It has its National Gallery, scrubbed up and sandblasted too and now on a par with European museums, and no longer free to go into. It has its terrible new buildings, flung up in the affluent eighties, office blocks which now nobody wants, which, along with the sixties high-rises on the outskirts, are ripe to be torn down. Part of its Old Town has, only recently, been burned down, centuries of its history destroyed. It's spread itself out across its seven hills, craggy as Rome, discreet as Athens, a northern city like no other. And it has its Festival, which every year drives residents who want to cross town to work or pick up children crazy with frustration, because the world comes here to be informed and entertained.

Maria loved the Festival when she was a child and could escape to watch street theatre, clowns, acrobats, rock bands and jugglers instead of going straight home from school (the Festival being, mysteriously, always in term-time for Scottish schools). She remembers a man on stilts toppling towards her, a laughing painted-on face. And jugglers, flinging fire into the air and swallowing it back. Everyday life becoming suddenly a playground, a feast of strangeness. Since she has lived here as an adult, she has tolerated it. Now, in this rainy August, six years into the new century, she is part of it, a small part, her act on the high wire to be glimpsed and then over.

She has on, rarely, a skirt and heels, and she is wearing makeup, and her black hair has been well cut, the white swath above her high forehead more than ever an echo of Susan Sontag. She wears a mac, because you have to, however old and shabby it will make you look. She walks out of the house and down the terrace, turns right where the old butcher used to be, where there is now an estate agent's with hugely expensive houses advertised in its windows, where the dead animals used to lie out, shamelessly slaughtered and gutted, to be bought. She walks down past the hairdresser and the café where you can get almond croissants, and the insurance building, and the jewellery shop which sells pins and brooches in the shapes of Celtic crosses, and Scottish animals made of silver, with tiny ruby eyes. She crosses the bridge over the Water of Leith, crosses

Dundas Street (named for another of Scotland's dubious heroes) and waits for the bus. The bus still stops in the old place, but because there are roadworks, she has to stand fifty yards higher up, where a group of well-dressed impatient people also waits. The 22 bus will deposit her on the corner of George Street, saving her the walk up the hill; she can then saunter (as far as her heels will let her) along George Street to Charlotte Square. There's been a break in the rain, and the street is shiny, slick and black, like the umbrellas, like the uniforms of the office workers, like their shoes. She has her umbrella tucked in her bag, in case it begins again, which it will. She has an advance copy of her book, in a plastic bag, with places marked where she will read. The book is dedicated to Marguerite, at whose abandoned desk she found its form.

The bus stops, lets them on, and the engine roars as it pulls uphill, and it costs a pound, not twenty pence as it always did, how has she not noticed, and it is full. Umbrellas leaking on to the floor, a driver who gets angry when asked for change by a harmless German visitor, a wet dog that stands and pants beside her, rivulets running off him, a woman who wants to tell the whole bus about her son, who is coming to stay from Hong Kong. It's only one among so many hundreds, even thousands of bus rides, but it's what she wants, Maria thinks, it's what you have to have, it's reality: this city, this street, this bus, these people. And the ridiculous ones crossing the street in evening dress, the woman in the strapless gown, her shoulders slick with rain, limping—are they coming from a party or going, what are they thinking of?—and the lone piper on the corner, blowing his guts out, impervious, and the tourists in cowboy hats, in tartan trousers, in bright yellow raincoats like lifeboat-men, and all the while the storm coming down the hill from that deep black cloud poised over Old Town, where the castle is gloomy enough on its rock, and now the whole scene has this Gothic nightmare air, and there's a crack of thunder, and here comes the rain. She will be soaked when she arrives at Charlotte Square; why didn't she take a cab? It's impossible these days to go anywhere by car. Aidan, who is learning to drive, could have dropped her. She will arrive soaked, with a sodden book, in time to stand and drip in a leaking tent, in front of a damp audience, most of whom will already have given up and gone home. But this is Edinburgh, this is summer, this is the Festival, and this is where she is.

She jumps down off the bus into the middle of an urgently pushing little crowd on the corner of George Street and begins her scuttle—damn these shoes—along towards Charlotte Square, where the off-white tents of the book fair sag under the dark green of the trees, and little walkways made of wood, or plastic maybe, have been set up between the different tents, to keep people out of the churned, soaked grass that is rapidly turning to mud. There's an expensive café to her right, across from the Assembly Rooms, and she totters in to collapse at the nearest table, and order coffee, since there is time. It's an excuse to sit here, to get out of the driving rain (her umbrella, like everyone else's, has immediately been blown inside out). She drags her hair back from her face, shakes her wet coat, slips her feet out of her soaked shoes just for a minute, and gets out her book. There, with George's Nadar portrait on the front, the one which makes her look jowly and portentous, but the one her publisher says everyone knows and recognizes, the book, the one she has in the end known how to write. In it, between its covers, a child builds her altars to a forest god, a woman waits outside her mother's apartment on a Paris street, a mother bites a daughter's knuckles as she dies; and thousands upon thousands of words are written, in the small hours of a thousand nights, while the world is asleep. An owl flies by in these early hours, drops a small parcel of digested bones and blood upon the doorstep. There are marionettes and the soldiers of Napoleon; there is a ship full of pigs; there is an Arab helmsman singing to keep himself awake. There are a hundred human connections, and the reflections of them in human habitations: the view from the window at Gargilesse, the mirrors of Nohant, the leaky roof of a rented house in Majorca, the stuffy room in a nursing home in Paris. There's the river, George's river, Marguerite's river, the river Creuse that is flowing still today (rain swelling its banks, a sudden flood?) and always will. There's cranky Flaubert stuffing his pipe, and aging George, with her little black cigars.

Maria sips her coffee and after checking the sky—slightly lighter, a gleam like pewter in the west—sets out again. The crowds are streaming now towards the book fair, as if the most important thing is to get there. Perhaps they want shelter, perhaps they want books—who can tell? Maria walks, tries her umbrella once again, and just as it is doing the wild bucking in a gust of wind that umbrellas do before they give up the ghost and turn inside out, runs into Sean.

"Hey, it's you! Well, now. Maria, how are you?"

"I'm trying to get to the book fair, I'm reading at ten thirty. What are you doing here?"

"I'm just walking the wrong way along George Street. Going against the tide, like I usually do. Actually, I'm going for an interview, for a job. Have you time for a coffee?"

"I've just had one."

"Well, no," he laughs at her. "Not an actual coffee, I mean, time to sit down somewhere and have a chat? My appointment isn't for another half-hour, so."

"I have to be there, Sean. Tell you what, come and listen. I'm reading from my new book!"

"The one you were writing, about what's her name, George Sand?"

"The very one. Look." She shows him the book, pulled from its plastic bag. The cover, with the two portraits, and the owl of night.

"Well, congratulations. That's great. Fair play to you, Maria. But if I do come, I'll be late."

"What's the interview?"

"Well, I've been head-hunted, would you believe it. It's a job in America, in Chicago. Pretty good deal. Look, even if we don't have time to talk now, I'll see you sometime after, will I? There's a lot to catch up on, wouldn't you say?"

"Yes," she says, looking ahead of her now to the entrance of the tented village that is the book fair, half yurts, half tents, part hastily pitched camp, part nomad settlement. But she feels him gone already. She has felt him gone for some time. It's odd, she thinks, to love someone so completely, and then watch him cross the street in the rain among a hundred other people, all going their different ways, and disappear. A flash of pale face, a grin, a lifted hand. Goodbye.

Then she walks into the circus-like tent where the writers from all over the world come to read and talk about their books, where she is awaited. There are little tables in side booths, there are red chairs, and gilt is splashed around here as if they were circus performers, about to balance upon ponies, or swing through the air. George's face looks back at her, coupled with her own; the opened book-jackets show them twinned, the placid middle-aged nineteenth-century woman and the anxious-looking one with the streak in her hair, from the new century, the twenty-first, which so short a time ago nobody could even imagine. Between them, joining them, the spread wings, a hunting owl. Maria steps forward to the dais, meets the other writers, a young Scottish poet who has written a new biography of Stevenson, a man from the Borders who has a memoir about being an orphan. All of us, she thinks, searching for our parents, both real and literary: and here, at last, they are. A vigorous young woman in a black leather jacket, from the radio station that is sponsoring them, introduces her. She is to be first, though she has offered this to the young poet, who is biting his nails. She opens the book and looks at her audience, their faces raw from the rain, their damp hair. There's Catriona, from the bookshop; there's Cath; there's Muriel from Extra-Mural, who calls herself extra-Muriel when she feels put-upon. There's Anne, from Modern Languages. There—surprising her—is Edward, at the back, still standing. He makes her a little sign, thumbs-up. Here are the people who know her, who have made the effort to come. All that matters is to be here. Slow down, Maria. Take your time. All that matters is to be alive, and able to do this, and part of it all: the Festival, the city, Scotland, the world, the universe, as she used to write in her school books a lifetime ago. She reads.

ACKNOWLEDGEMENTS

I would like to thank the following for their help and support as this novel was written and published: Marie-Claire Blais, Edith Sorel, Claude and Erik Eriksen, Delia Morris and Gillian Stern as tireless readers of the manuscript at various different stages; Vivienne Schuster, my agent at Curtis Brown; Margaret Atwood; my husband Allen Meece; Kathryn Kilgore for the Writers' and Artists' House in Key West. Thanks to many good biographies of George Sand, including Huguette Bouchardeau's *George Sand: La Lune et Les Sabots*, and to Julian Barnes for his essay "Consolation v. Desolation" in the collection *Something To Declare: Essays on France*. Thanks also to Michael Redhill for publishing an earlier version of part of the section "The House on the Creuse" in *Brick* magazine, Toronto. Lastly, I would like to appreciate Kristin Cochrane and the team at Doubleday for their enthusiasm and creativity in the production of this book.